TONY PREEDY

MUSTAFA'S LAST WELL

novum pro

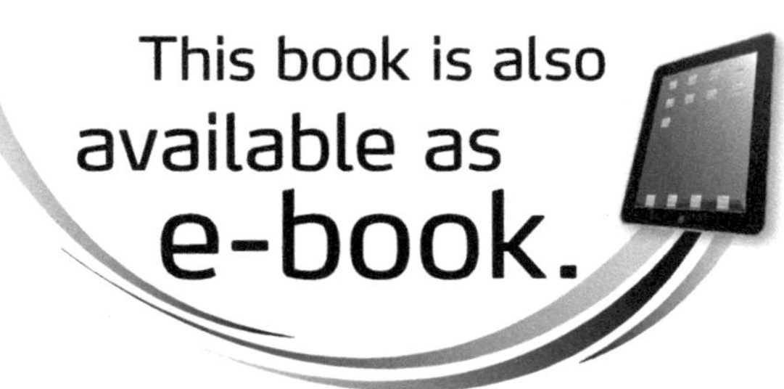

www.novum-publishing.co.uk

© 2021 novum publishing

ISBN 978-3-99107-637-7
Editing: Ashleigh Brassfield, DipEdit
Cover photos: Tom Wang, Jan Skwara, Wirestock, Wacomka | Dreamstime.com
Cover design, layout & typesetting: novum publishing

www.novum-publishing.co.uk

DISCLAIMER

The characters and events in this novel, as with the countries in which it takes place, are entirely fictitious and not intended to represent any real country or person alive or dead. Specifically, the tribal names of the characters are imaginary. The medieval practices described here are not necessarily in chronological context. The name of the country, Naamlah, in which most of the story is set was formed by combining the Arabic Naam, yes with lah, No.

ACKNOWLEDGEMENTS

I am grateful to my friends; The late Geoff Bagley for revealing his experimental work with torsion waves, Zuaina al-Busaiidi for inspiring the novel and Patricia Lake for encouraging me to finish it.

LIST OF CHARACTERS

Female

Asia bint Salem al-Wyly	Emir's 1st Married daughter
Fahtia bint Salim al-Wyly	Emir's 2nd Married daughter
Fatima bint Yacoob al-Wyly	Emir's young 3rd wife
Fousia bint Salem al-Wyly	Emir's 3rd daughter
Hooda al-Wyly	Moosa's wife and cousin
Layla al-Wyly	Emir's 1st wife
Mariam bint Talib (Mermaid)	Malaysian servant
Nahla bint Salim al-Wyly	Emir's 4th daughter
Rasha Farnham	Egyptian wife of Farnham
Shalma bint Hammed al-Wyly	Emir's sister

Middle Eastern Male

Abdul Bawani	Camel trader
Abdulazziz bin Hammed al-Wyly	Emir's 1st brother
Afghan	Emir's driver
Ahmed bin Talib	Malaysian Embassy secretary
Ali	Eunuch slave/servant
Big Sikh	Fousia's driver/bodyguard
Hammed bin Hammed al-Wyly	Emir's 2nd brother
Hassan	1st slave of Mustafa
Ibrahim	Malay yacht skipper
Idris bin Mubarak al Jaboo	Head of crime family
Iranian	Assassin and butcher

Issa	Son of an Imam
Joseph	Nubian slave
Juma bin Sidiqu al-Wyly	Son and heir of early Emir
Kareem	Haqum ruler's 1st son
Khaled bin Hammed al-Wyly	Son of Hammed
Malik	Lybian *Bedouin* boy
Mohammed	Haqum ruler's 2nd son
Moosa bin Salim al-Wyly	Emir Salim's 1st son
Mustafa al-Wyly	Water diviner
Nasser	Fousia's assistant
Sheikh al-Haqum	Later Haqum ruler
Old shepherd	Early Haqum ruler
Patel	Indian foundry manager
Ranjit	Bernhardt's servant
Rashiid	Lybian *Bedouin* boy
Saif bin Salim al-Wyly	Emir Salim's 2nd son
Saleh	Fousia's office boy
Salim (young)	2nd slave of Mustafa
Salim bin Hammed al-Wyly	Emir of Naamlah
Suliman	Son of Abdul Bawani
Tariq	Fousia's secretary
Young shepherd	Son of early Haqum ruler
Yacoob bin Sidiqu al-Wyly	Emir Salim's cousin

European male

Adams, Henry	Guard sergeant
Farnham, James	Adviser to Emir Salim
Graff	Swiss bank proprietor
Grobanov, Boris	Russian immigrant scientist
Grover, Bernhardt	German Panzer corporal
Harper, Samuel	Geologist
Kowalski, Mick	Russian immigrant Pilot
Lightfoot, Commander	Captain HMS Pegasus
Martan, Professor	Swiss urologist
Phillips, Commander	Royal Navy cartographer

CHAPTER 1

It is 1207 Hijri: AD 1776

The year in which America declares independence from Britain

Within seconds of the drum beat that proclaimed the start of the race, the small boy had fallen amongst the trampling feet of the pursuing camels. The child now lay whimpering motionless on the ground, surrounded by a cloud of dust. The camels that had been behind him had now passed by.

Mustafa al-Wyly, the 17-year-old son of a widowed date farmer, had accompanied his friend Issa, the crippled son of the local Imam, to the camel race. Mustafa's father supplemented their meagre income from the date farm by divining for water when a well was required. This was an activity that Mustafa had been encouraged to take over, as the old man was becoming infirm. He had proved to be particularly adept at finding water but was not so enthusiastic when it became necessary to follow this up by digging the wells.

Today, Mustafa and Issa had joined the men who came in from their desert camps, as the camel race was a good excuse to avoid such work. Minutes before, as the owners gave their final encouragement and instructions to the children who were strapped behind their camel's humps, a man of the al-Jaboo had removed a knife from his robe. Unseen in the excitement, he deftly wielded his knife to weaken the harness of the favourite's jockey, who now lay on the ground before Mustafa. Mustafa ran towards the child and, as he would with an injured animal, moved his hands over the boy's limbs. He detected only bruises; the soft broad footpads of the camels, and their natural instinct to avoid stepping on a living creature, had spared the child from broken bones. Unknown to Mustafa, the child had, like Issa, been lame since birth.

Mustafa and Issa had been friends since infancy, when Mustafa had first protected Issa from the taunts of older boys. Issa, had since birth, suffered from a weakness of his left leg which caused a conspicuous limp.

The child's stunted growth had attracted him to the camel's owner, who realised he could put the child to good use as a jockey because he was unlikely to put on weight as quickly as other small boys of his age.

Before the drumbeat, Mustafa and Issa had been arguing over which camel would win. Issa supported the light-coated favourite, imported from Somalia, from which the child had fallen, whilst Mustafa was loyal to the locally bred entry of his tribal leader. As his hands passed over the child's lame left leg, Mustafa experienced a feeling of weakness, as though energy was leaving his body. The child, however, felt himself gently relaxing into unconsciousness. Those men who had supported the favourite had now lost interest in the outcome of the race, and with childlike curiosity gathered around Mustafa and the boy. No women were present, as they were not permitted to attend public gatherings. In this year, just as in medieval times, men assured them that their place was in their tent, even as many women of their faith of later generations would, even two centuries hence, be confined to their homes.

This was the crucial instant when the boy was healed of his disability. Neither healer nor patient had any understanding of how it had transpired. Two centuries later there would be those who claimed that it was an unconscious application of torsion wave energy. They would explain how the child's DNA spiral became synchronised to the torsion wave field emanating from Mustafa's DNA. As Mustafa was weakened by the energy imparted to the torsion field, the defective gene responsible for the child's disability had been altered to replicate the corresponding gene in Mustafa's DNA.

After several minutes, during which Mustafa silently prayed for assurance from the Almighty that he had done the child no harm, the child regained consciousness and started to clamber first onto all fours, and then to his feet, where he stood as erect as an athlete. After a quick conspiratorial smile directed at his saviour, the boy ran, for the first time in his short life, towards his angry, disappointed master.

The spectators, some now muttering to each other their suspicions of sorcery, backed away in fear for their souls. Others, who did not know him, convinced themselves that Mustafa must be a Jinn in disguise, and in defiance of custom raised their dish-dashes above their knees and ran away from the scene. They left only Issa to support his exhausted friend. Issa, otherwise lost for words after witnessing the healing spectacle, told Mustafa that his choice had won the race by a head, just in front of the al-Jaboo animal.

When the crowd dispersed, Issa, who had with other spectators, been watching Mustafa's performance, asked, "What did you do to produce that cure?"

"Only Allah knows, for something went from my body that has made me feel weak," he replied.

Mustafa slowly regained his strength as the friends departed for the farm, where they expected to find Mustafa's elderly father waiting for news. The old man and his son lived there with no woman, for Mustafa's mother had died after giving a son to his father in her thirteenth year.

"If only you could do that to me," Issa lamented.

"I do not know, but there have been other times when I have felt that strange loss of my strength," replied Mustafa, as he was thinking; "I will try it."

When they reached the farm, they found no one there. Mustafa said, "Come and lie down here, and I will pretend you are the camel rider."

Issa obeyed; he had confidence in his friend. He lay on the wicker sleeping frame that sat beneath the palm covered veranda at the front of the house, grinning.

"He is not treating the occasion seriously," thought Mustafa, as he placed his hand on the lame leg and started to move it over the part that was weak. Immediately he felt the healing sensation start to build. "Do you feel anything yet?" Mustafa asked. Issa was about to say no, but then he felt a strange but pleasant sensation starting to strengthen in his leg. Issa relaxed. Mustafa held his hand steady, even though he continued to feel weakened as the energy transfer intensified. Issa started to become apprehensive, and would have stopped his friend, had he not suddenly lost consciousness. As he felt the healing sensation diminish, Mustafa watched his friend for a reaction, but had to wait several minutes before Issa opened his eyes.

Issa did not know where he was except that the sun was above and shining in his eyes. Then, in the shade of the palms, he saw the familiar beam of palm wood over the doorway to the farmhouse and remembered where he was. "How are you now?" asked Mustafa, concern in his voice.

"Let me get up, and we will see." Issa swung his legs to place his feet on the floor and started to raise himself from the bed, realising with the utmost pleasure that he had been cured.

Issa departed excitedly to show his father what had happened, and Mustafa entered the house to join his own father. Within the house there was no sign of the old man.

A search amongst the date palms revieled his father's body. He had died of a heart attack.

★

When Issa arrived home and met his father, the Imam, he showed him what Mustafa had done and told him how the young camel rider had also been healed. The Imam, shocked by these events, muttered a prayer, and told Issa to take him to Mustafa, but before they could set out, Mustafa came into their house to tell the Imam of his father's death.

After giving condolences to Mustafa and agreeing to arrange for the burial of his father, the Imam became serious. His reaction was ambivalent; gratitude on one hand, whilst on the other hand he was concerned that Mustafa had been blasphemous; had not Allah punished himself or his son for some evil in a past life? The Imam pressured Mustafa to refrain from future attempts to heal. He told of Jesus, the man whose followers claimed him to be the son of Allah, who came six centuries before Allah's messenger, the prophet Mohamed. Jesus possessed similar powers, for which he was crucified by the Romans who occupied the land. Later, he was worshipped by the Christians in Europe, the same tribes who sent crusaders to recapture the lands conquered by the followers of Mohamed, and burned alive, as witches, all those who emulated Jesus.

The Imam warned, "By continuing to defy the will of Allah, by healing those He had caused to suffer, Mustafa, unless you are the Mahdi, sent by Allah, and that is most unlikely, you risk death for blasphemy at the hands of religious zealots." Mustafa was visibly frightened by these words. "Promise me you will never attempt such healing again, or I will not be able to protect you from those who would have you killed." Mustafa agreed.

★

From that time Mustafa confined his use of torsion wave energy (not that he knew anything of this "science") to his other skill, locating underground sources of water. It was, he knew, only his ability to provide this vital service that had protected him from the Islamic extremists, who needed minimal justification to proclaim a fatwa for his death. To dispel any doubts, as soon as his father had been buried, he crudely engraved the beam above the entrance to his house with a sign declaring "water finding" to be his only business.

CHAPTER 2

It was the year 1234 Hijri: AD 1819

*Queen Victoria is born, along with British democracy, after
the massacre of the Peterloo protesters in Manchester*

Some who had known Mustafa al-Wyly since childhood called him a healer, after word spread of his performance at the camel race, and others called him a mystic, but the fear of fatwa made him reclusive from all men. The farm lay outside the coastal town that was the capital of the Emirate of Naamlah. Now suffering the ravages of sixty years, his back was bent, and the deterioration of his lungs, due to a fondness for the hookah, caused him difficulty breathing. His reputation came about when, as a boy, he demonstrated that he was blessed with an unnatural power; today this is believed to have been the ability to harness the energy of torsion waves, by which he was able to correct errors in the DNA of his patients – but in his country, at that time, it was considered sorcery.

Naamlah lay on the southern coast of the Persian Gulf, separated from its eastern neighbour, the small country of Haqum, by a natural geological fault known *as al wadi al kabier*, the great dry river. This stretched from the mountains, which lay several hundred miles inland, to the south, and out into the sea. Some claimed that occasionally, when storms occurred in the mountains, the *wadi* would carry water to the sea, but no one living could recall such an event. The Naamlahn side of the sea was shallow and famous for pearl-bearing oysters, which were relatively easy to harvest. On the eastern side, the waters of their neighbours were deep, and any oysters that lived there were beyond the range of divers. Naamlah prospered on trade whilst the neighbours, who were still mostly nomadic, subsisted only on their flocks of goats and sheep, which they exported to Persia through their small seaport. Later generations on both sides of the border would have hopes of oil being discovered in their land, as it would be in some other Gulf countries.

★

Mustafa never took a wife because he was only attracted to young men. His adult life was, therefore, one of frustration, because the Prophet gave no advice in such circumstances and such relationships were thus declared either as sodomy or non-existent by the religious men. He consulted the Imam, who said it was his duty to father children, but Mustafa found the prospect distasteful. When he had aged and become unfit to dig wells, nor pick dates, he decided to purchase two slaves. He found that the bids for physically fit specimens at the auction were beyond his means but when two young Somali brothers were displayed, a plan came to mind. They were both displaying signs of ill health; other potential slave owners had rejected Hassan because he had a withered arm, and Salim was considered defective because of a persistent cough. Mustafa, therefore, bought them both for a pittance and installed them at his farm. Ever since he had healed the lame jockey, he had yearned to attempt another healing. He saw the brothers as his opportunity to covertly experiment with his mystic power. In defiance of his promise as a boy to the now-dead Imam, he successfully used his healing technique to convert the slaves into healthy, strong workers. The boys therefore felt an uncharacteristic obligation of loyalty towards their owner, both for allowing them to stay together and for healing them.

★

Naamlah's traders, who travelled through the desert to sell their pearls via the port of Salalah in the Hadramat, had long needed a source of drinking water to sustain them, for they could barely survive the journey with the quantity that their camels could carry. Mustafa had been commissioned by a consortium of traders to provide a well on the Naamlahn side of the mountains, where the trail ran close to the *wadi*. A price had been agreed and half payment had been accepted, with the balance due on completion. Preparations were made for the task by the boys, Hassan and Salim. They had now been with Mustafa for twelve years, during which they had matured into strong young men as a consequence of their healing, working on the farm and digging wells. Hassan thought that he might be 19 years old, which would make his brother 17, as there were two years between them. Hassan was cultivating a beard, which gave him an imperious appearance, belying his slave status. Salim was clean shaven and was taller than his older brother. Either could have overpowered Mustafa and run from his service, but they had remained dependent on him as they had no funds to sustain them if they did succeed in escaping. Besides, they had come to accept their status because they were devout Muslims, and did not the Holy Book tell of their social status as slaves?

Three camels were burdened by himself, the slaves, their food, bundles of straw, a tent, tools, and a generous ration of water. To the annoyance of the boys, their master insisted on accommodation being found for his hookah. After traveling south for five days, which took its toll on Mustafa's health, their caravan had arrived at a depression in the *wadi* where gravel and rocks were visible among the sand and where, from his years of experience, Mustafa was confident of finding water. The boys were set to work erecting the tent in which their master would rest as soon as they had hobbled and unloaded the camels. By the time the camp was established, the sun was near the horizon. After ritual washing, as was dictated by their religion, using sand rather than precious water, it was time for all three to prostrate themselves towards Mecca in prayer before the sun disappeared. After their meal, the boys lay with the camels, whilst Mustafa retired to the tent, where he would attend to his journal and then relax smoking his hookah.

As dawn broke, after *fajr* prayers, Mustafa was summoned to eat with the boys, who had prepared milk from the camels and dates that they had harvested from Mustafa's farm. Whilst *cawah* was brewing on the fire they had made of camel dung within a ring of stones,

Mustafa collected his dousing equipment from the tent. He carried a bundle of short sisal rope ends over an arm and a Y-shaped dowsing stick in one hand. The dowsing stick was made from hazel, a wood imported from Europe and known for its favourable reaction to the "mystical" torsion waves/"dowsing fields." Before the sun was high, he marched, puffing and panting, back and forth with the stick held before him until a field was detected and transmitted to his arthritic fingers, causing the apex of the stick to dip. At this point, he dropped a piece of rope. He continued until another response was observed, and dropped another piece of rope. Eventually, when satisfied that he had formed a suitable line of rope pieces, he changed direction and repeated the process until he had two lines that crossed. The boys were ordered to dig at the intersection, even though whether they were in Naamlah or the adjacent land of Haqum would be debatable.

The boys shovelled sand all day, with breaks only for refreshment and prayer, whilst Mustafa rested and puffed in his tent. The routine continued on the second day, when the sand gave way to gravel, but no sign of water. Their working conditions improved as they descended into shade. That evening the gravel gave way to rock and progress slowed, as the boys picked and chiselled at the rock and carried the off cuts to the surface. At this point in their digging, Salim made a discovery that brought their work to a halt. He made sure that Mustafa was resting before showing to Hassan the *dahab* he had found. In his hand was a nugget, unmistakably of gold, which was the size and shape of a ripe fig, with three nodules on its surface. Spurred on by this discovery, the boys worked harder than ever.

"We must tell the master," said Salim.

"No; he would not share the gold with us. It must be our secret," replied Hassan, and that was what they agreed. As smaller pieces of gold continued to be liberated from the rock, they were hidden in the camel blanket in which they kept the dates. They knew Mustafa never looked in there. On the fourth day of excavation, they were past the gold-bearing rock, which had progressively been replaced by clay.

Mustafa was pleased with their progress and ordered them to make a separate pile for clay. As his mind was now deteriorating, he unnecessarily informed them because they had done it many times before: "Inshallah (if Allah wills it), the first water from the well will be added to clay to make bricks, reinforced with the straw we have brought on the camels." The boys were now working about four meters below the surface and progress was slow, as they had to form steps in the rock to enable them to bring up the clay. Slowly, the clay beneath them became damp, and water started to flow into the hole to cover their feet. Mustafa was summoned and showed his delight by giving thanks to Allah, but not to his slaves. Mustafa made the oldest slave, Hassan, taste the water. After no adverse reaction, he offered water to the camels, who drank it rapidly.

That night the boys plotted to abandon their master and try to return to their homeland. It was, therefore, with feelings of guilt that they made plans to desert the man to whom they owed so much.

Now that they had resources their loyalty to Mustafa was of secondary importance. Neither of them could remember much from before their abduction. They had been taken by armed men from their family's camp between Hargeisa and Berbera. After two days marching, whilst chained by their ankles, they arrived at the port of Berbera. From here they were taken by *dhow* to the Persian Gulf. They were not sure which direction to take, but they knew they must travel to the south. From what little he knew of geography, gained from listening to traders, Hassan said that they should aim for Al'Adan on the coast of Yemen and ask how to cross to Somaliland. Hassan added that he knew the dhows sailed from their old country to Al'Adan, and must return. Until now they had not had the means to escape, but now they were confident of buying passage by *dhow* across the Arabian Sea from Al'Adan to the port of Berbera in Somaliland. From there, they thought, it could only be a camel ride to Hargeisa, where they would search for their tribe.

The following day the boys were set to making bricks with which to reinforce the well above the rock level, and then to extend above the surface to enclose the well against drifting sand. As the bricks in the wall hardened in the sun, Mustafa prepared a map by which the traders, guided by stars, could find the new well. In his tent, whilst puffing contentedly on the hookah, Mustafa was anticipating breaking camp and starting the journey home that evening – tomorrow in the old Arabic calendar, in which the new day started at sunset – but the boys outside were already preparing to abandon him. Two of the camels were laden with food and well water, but the blanket that concealed their find was heavy and could only be placed on the camel whilst she was sitting. Getting her on to her feet took much effort from both boys, because her burden now was more than she was used to carrying. Whilst loading the camels in haste, Salim had dropped the large nugget in the sand, but before he could recover it one of the camels kicked it away into the distance. It was abandoned, because Hassan would not wait whilst Salim searched for it by moonlight.

★

When Mustafa awoke, he found only one camel and little food. He managed to get water for himself and the camel from his well. He cursed the boys as he set out for home, guided only by the oppressive sun on his back by day and the stars by night. The effort was too much for a man in poor health, and Mustafa did not survive. His camel returned to the farm. Its owner's body was never discovered, but a record of the activity at the well and a map of its location were found with his hookah in the blanket pocket of the camel. The traders held out for a month, hoping by then that no near relative would come forward to claim the balance of Mustafa's payment. They were disappointed when the Emir, who was of the same tribe as Mustafa, insisted the money, if not claimed, should be given to the Imam for charitable work. The Emir decreed that henceforth, in recognition of his sacrifice, the watering-place would be known as the Well of Mustafa.

★

Without knowledge of stellar navigation, the boys wandered across the desert in the general direction of Yemen by observing the direction of the sun at its zenith but failed to find a passage through the mountains. Their food and then water ran out, causing a slow death from the mixture of hunger, thirst, and exposure. One of their camels returned weeks later to the date farm, but the one carrying the gold could not keep up, for she was weighed down by her burden, and perished.

★

Two riders searching for grazing had been surprised the previous day to come across a newly built well at the near side of the great *wadi*, from which they eagerly drew water for their flock of sheep. They decided that it must have been built by their neighbours. The two, father and son, argued as to in whose territory it was situated.

The son said, "We should claim it to be on our land," but the older man, the Sheikh who ruled the country, replied:

"Son, it is not important where the border lies. No one has ever disputed this because the relationship with our neighbours has always been amicable, and besides, the *wadi* land is a worthless desert."

They found no vegetation and moved the flock back to what was undisputedly their territory, where they agreed that, after prayers, they would tell the rest of their tribal group to camp for the night.

The pair were wakened from their sleep beneath the stars by the sound of the wind rapidly strengthening from the South and burying them in sand. Hastily they loaded their camels, which were hobbled nearby, and started searching for their flock.

★

The traders, being keen to inspect the new well and have it blessed, organized a caravan headed by a brother of the Emir, which included the Imam and a youth, Juma, the eldest son and heir of the Emir. They were accompanied by three slaves from the Emir's household; two young men from Burundi, who had been sold to the Arabs of Dar-es-Salaam by the chief of their tribe to punish their father, with whom the chief had quarrelled – they had been taken to Zanzibar and held until the arrival of the monsoon that allowed their transport by *dhow* to the Gulf; the third was Joseph, an older man with thin, grey hair, who had served the Emir since his arrival from Nubia as a child. Joseph stood head and shoulders above the other two men. Their arrival, which coincided with the festival of *Eid al Fittah*, saw them setting up camp near the Well of Mustafa. The slaves were ordered to erect their tent quickly, as a strong wind had started to rise from the south, where dark clouds and lightning could be seen over the mountains. After the men had retired to the tent a herd of sheep gathered in its lee, joining the camels and slaves, where they sought shelter from sand carried on the wind.

CHAPTER 3

Her body swayed from side to side, oblivious to the raging storm. Her vision, protected by long lashes which, like the rest of her strange physiology, had evolved over millions of years to survive in these conditions. On her back, the youthful rider was confident of his mount being able to proceed at her usual reliable ambling pace in the teeth of the storm, not much faster than if he walked alone. The boy and his elderly father, the Sheikh, had set out from their camp to search for their flock of sheep that had strayed whilst their companions, all men of the Haqum tribe, had been celebrating *Eid*. Suddenly her hypnotic swaying stopped, as a sound like a breaking stick reached the ear of her young rider. She fell to her knees and he was thrown from her, landing among the stones and sand, without knowing the cause of his fall.

His companion, from whom he had become separated, was at that moment shouting *"huna, huna dahab,"* but his words were lost, carried away on the howling wind and obliterated by the agonized screams of the suffering camel.

The Sheikh, confused by the sandstorm and having lost sight of his son, had been searching for the footprints of the other camel, in sand and gravel which before his smarting eyes was being swept away by the desert wind. In all his days he had not seen a storm of such violence in their land. It was thus that his attention was taken by the lines of metallic yellow among the rock, exposed by the disappearing sand. He dismounted, took a large piece that was loose, and held it in his hand. There was no mistaking its texture and weight. The nugget had a distinctive shape; a near-spherical lump the size of a ripe fig with three small nodules on one side. The old man re-mounted, and it was then that he shouted the news to the boy, momentarily visible, kneeling by his camel in the distance. "Surely he has also found gold," thought the old man, until he detected the agonized cries of the boy's animal. One of her broad hooves had wedged in a fissure of the rock, exposed as the wind whipped away the covering of sand from the middle of the great *wadi*. It was plain that this was the cause of her broken leg, the source of her pain. The boy reacted quickly because he wanted to spare her suffering. He knew she was of no value now. From the pocket, within the blanket on her flank, he took an ancient flint-lock gun and, as his father hurried his mount towards the source of the animal's cries, loaded it. He fought both the elements and the tears that were welling in his eyes, causing sand to stick to his cheeks, placed the gun to his shoulder and then, with a single shot to her head, stopped the noise.

★

Not more than a hundred metres from the riders, in the bed of the *wadi* and invisible in the sandstorm, a tent had been pitched within which traders, members of the al-Wyly, were feasting. Inside their tent, where the sound of the storm was muffled by the thick lining of wool stuffed quilts, the al-Wyly men were relaxing and telling stories of past adventures over freshly brewed *cawah*. Earlier they had debated if it was right to feast on the sheep that they found sheltering among their camels; it was argued by their Imam that they had been a gift from Allah for this purpose, but the more realistic argument of their leader, that they were only a lost flock, prevailed. The party had to be content with rice, dates, and the fowl that they had carried in coops on their camels.

The bellowing of the camel had been unnoticed against the howling of the wind, but that same wind now carried the louder bark of the gun to the al-Wyly camp. Here the sheep had been found by the al-Wyly and held with their camels until whoever owned them came to claim them. One member of the tribe, Juma, son of their Emir, had left the tent where, as within their neighbour's camp, the feast of *Al-Fittah* was being celebrated. He had used the pretext of checking the ropes that were straining to hold their cover intact. The young man battled his way to the lee of the tent, where the camels and sheep were huddled together with the slaves sheltering between them, knelt with his back to Mecca, pulled his robe up to his thighs and relieved himself. Before he was done there came on the wind the unmistakable sound of gunfire. He rushed back inside and raised the alarm. The Naamlahn traders ran from the tent whilst binding their heads, leaving only slits for their eyes. Ancient guns in hand, they mounted their near buried kneeling camels and fought the wind, tearing at their clothes, each hastening to what he thought was the source of the sound that young Juma had reported. The impetuous and headstrong youth, who was first to have his gun prepared, raised the weapon intending to fire above the heads of the now visible intruders. Juma realised that his target was directly to windward of his position and therefore required no allowance for the wind to divert his shot to the side, but failed to allow for the headwind causing his shot to fall low and watched in disbelief as one of the intruders fell lifeless across their camel within seconds of him pulling the trigger. The old man died instantly as the shot penetrated his skull. The gold nugget dropped from his grasp before he could show it to his son and sank, lost in the sand. The other rider reached over the body of his father, grabbed the reins, and whipped the animal into a trot.

The Naamlahns started in pursuit, but their leader shouted above the wind to his nephew and the traders: "Leave the intruders, for they only search for their animals."

"But uncle, they were approaching our new well," replied young Juma, in a futile attempt to justify what he had done.

★

The young man, now owner of the missing sheep and from then the instant ruler of his *Bedouin* tribe, who for generations had roamed the land of Haqum east of the *wadi*, washed the body and prayed as he buried the Sheikh, his respected father, on that festive night. The new leader was oblivious to the wealth concealed within their land which might, but for a twist of fate, have liberated his people from poverty. In his anguish, he called on his sons as yet unborn, and their sons after them, to avenge the unprovoked murder of his father by the al-Wyly.

Before sunrise next morning, after the storm was spent, the Naamlahn leader had the sheep returned unseen to where they would be found, near the camp of their neighbours. Later that morning, as the sun was rising, he lay prostrate on his prayer mat desperately beseeching Allah to accept his generous act and thus prevent the inevitable retribution demanded for the death, even of a simple shepherd, by the hand of his nephew, as expected within their culture. Otherwise, it was written that a feud would exist for each of the four generations represented by the fingers on a hand, until only the thumb remained, and the metaphoric hand could no longer hold a dagger.

★

Later that day the Imam held a special ceremony to bless the new well, and the traders gave thanks to Allah in their prayers, whilst on the other side of the *wadi* the new leader gathered the men of his tribe to plan retribution for his father's murder. All who loved and respected their old leader were incensed and called for the blood of their new enemy to be spilled.

That night, whilst the traders slept, a party of *Bedouin* approached from across the *wadi*. They first encountered the three sleeping slaves, who they woke and threatened with death if they made a sound, saying they had no argument with them. Next, they set fire to the tent. The remnants of the wind soon fanned the flames such that many inside were suffocated by smoke before they were awake. Those that did wake found their enemies waiting at the only exit with their curved *khanjar*, daggers, drawn. As they staggered out, gasping for air, the *Bedouin* grabbed them and cut their throats in the *halal* manner, in which they were accustomed to killing sheep. Juma was the last out, having suffered from burning clothes which he had discarded, leaving him bare to the waist in only his scorched *izaar*. As he took in the carnage outside, he was about to protest and proclaim who he was when two *Bedu* took hold of his arms and a third brought his knife to Juma's throat.

Joseph, who had witnessed the slaughter, shouted at the top of his voice to the *Bedu*, "Stop, he is one of us!" The one with the knife looked as though he doubted this, but Joseph continued, "He is the plaything of his master and sleeps beside him." The *Bedu* gave Juma a look of disgust, turned him towards Joseph and gave Juma a kick that sent him spread-eagled at Joseph's feet. As Joseph lifted him by the shoulders, he whispered, "Stay quiet, young master, if you want to see your father again."

Juma was incapable of making a reply; he was in such a state of shock from seeing the carnage that he could not even think properly. The young leader of the *Bedu* then told his men to leave the slaves and let them tell their Emir of this day. He led his band back to their camp, leaving the slaves with six scorched corpses and six who had died slowly from loss of blood.

Realizing Juma's condition, Joseph assumed authority and instructed the other two slaves to start digging graves, after choosing a site on the Naamlahn side of the *wadi*. They found the tools that Mustafa's slaves had abandoned and set to work as daylight broke. Joseph meanwhile stripped the bodies and washed them with well water. Next, he cut shrouds from the remnants of the tent and bound the bodies. Juma watched as if in a trance, unable to grasp what had occurred. A few words of prayer were mumbled by one of the young slaves as each corpse was placed in its grave, with eyes towards Mecca and *khanjar* at its side. By the time each grave was filled the sun was high and the men were feeling hungry, but all of their food had been consumed in the fire. Joseph told them to kill and butcher one of the camels, of which they had fourteen, and gathered the remnants of ropes and tent poles for a fire. Throughout these activities, Juma remained in shock, watching in awe at Joseph's industry. As the steaks cooked, Joseph used the

last of the tent to make a cloak and took a headdress from one of
the dead for Juma, for his protection from the sun. Of the steaks,
some were for immediate consumption and others stowed on the
camels to sustain them on their homeward journey.

They drew water for the camels to drink and filled skins for
their own consumption, which they loaded onto the animals, together with the cooked meat. Joseph ordered the camels to be
tied together in line and put a man on each of the front four. Juma
had by now recovered and expressed gratitude to Joseph for saving him, but hoped that his reputation had not been ruined. The
party prayed before setting off to the north with their shadows
for guidance.

★

When they arrived back at the Emir's fort, Joseph had returned
to his subservient status, letting Juma lead the party to his father. He relayed the events to the Emir, but not how he had
been the cause, and told of how he owed his life to Joseph and
begged his father to reward the slaves by giving them freedom.
The Emir's thoughts were elsewhere. He told Juma that he was
surprised that their neighbours had taken such offense when they
discovered the new well in their territory and asked if there was
some other cause for their violent acts. Juma denied knowing
the real cause. The Emir decided that the well should not, in
future, be used by his subjects. Juma again raised the subject of
the slave's freedom. His father considered this for several minutes, before replying:

"It will be impossible for them to support themselves." He
paused, clearly in thought. "There is a farm that was the property of my distant cousin, Mustafa the water finder. No near relative
has been found who can claim it. They shall have it and make a
living as date farmers."

Juma reported this to Joseph, who broke into tears of gratitude, but Juma insisted it was he and the Emir who were in his
debt. Juma never mentioned that he was responsible for the death

of the other men, until on his deathbed, as Emir, he revealed the truth, for he feared that he would never experience the delights of heaven otherwise. Future descendent Emirs Sidiqu, Hammed and Salim would all suffer for Juma's misdeed at the Well of Mustafa. After the skirmish, no trader dared to approach the well, for they feared attack by their *Bedu* neighbours. The well was abandoned and the potential wealth that lay nearby in the *kabier wadi* was not to be re-discovered until several generations had passed, during which the intensity of the feud subsided.

CHAPTER 4

Libya, year 1361 Hijri: AD 1943

The European war meant little to the inhabitants of Naamlah, but in North Africa it was impossible to escape from its impact as Britain fought against Germany and its Italian ally.

Since arriving in Libya, after the sea journey from Italy to the little port of Surt, Bernhardt's panzer squadron of Rommel's Africa Corps had made rapid progress in their small part of the conquest of North Africa. Their panzer convoy of Tiger 3 tanks, headed by a type 233, eight-wheeled armoured reconnaissance vehicle, was proceeding towards their destination, the British Egyptian military base in Alexandria. Earlier, the convoy had included half-track trucks carrying fuel, as the panzer tanks needed a gallon for every mile, but this supply had been exhausted, and they now relied on the widely separated fuel dumps of their Italian allies.

Corporal Bernhardt Grover had in six months seen his budding career as an entomologist replaced by that of a tank commander. He was intrigued by the desert, which to his four companions in the Tiger 3 was just a barren wilderness of endless sand, populated by a few inhospitable *Bedouin* natives. To Bernhardt, the sparse vegetation and unaccustomed life that is supported in the Misratah and more recently the Damah regions held a fascination which he fought to resist, as it replaced the propaganda induced fervour with which he had departed the Fatherland. Given the opportunity, he would have abandoned the tank and its crew of indoctrinated youths and instead collected samples for future study. He had anticipated that at least he would be able to practice his Arabic, hastily taught whilst in Italy, but had underestimated both the sparseness of the population and the reluctance of the few people he encountered to talk to a German invader.

Battle-hardened by increasing British opposition, successful in several skirmishes, they had added captured supplies of Allied forces to those dwindling in the depleted half-tracks that they had previously been following. Now, having entered the range of RAF daytime reconnaissance operating out of an Egyptian base, they had adopted a tactic of maintaining radio silence between the lead panzer and the 233 car, and restricted movements to night-time. Each morning, before the rising sun had time to transform the steel armour of the panzer into an inferno, they camped under camouflage nets and rested. The previous night two panzers had succumbed to the abrading sand, which weakened the joints in their steel tracks as though they were wood. When undertaken as a planned operation it was relatively straightforward – just a matter of releasing a pin, dropping the track onto the sand and driving the machine off her old track and onto the replacement. The crew had all practiced the operation many times in ideal conditions, but when it happened as now, unexpectedly, in the dark, on only one side of the vehicle and uneven ground, it could be a difficult, sometimes dangerous, and time-consuming operation involving other vehicles and extra men. Inevitably it took more time than they would have liked. The convoy, now approaching Al Jaghbub, near the border with Egypt, was not, therefore, capable of moving until dawn, when it would be unsafe. They had therefore been unable to choose their daily hiding place with customary care.

The Germans were otherwise complacent in the knowledge that their efforts at camouflage would avoid detection from the air, because a few extra humps among those left by centuries of erosion in the desert would not be detected unless recent aerial photographs existed for comparison. Given the other failures, Bernhardt inspected the tracks of his panzer and decided he could not afford to miss the opportunity to fit replacements. The new track was unloaded and laid out in the sand ahead of the vehicle. The old one was released and joined to the new to form a straight steel road on which the panzer would move forward without drive sprockets ever disengaging.

In the crucial moment when the camouflage had been thrown clear to allow the panzer to move, they heard the whine of an aeroplane engine, and Bernhardt's heart sank as he watched the aircraft alter course and swoop towards them before the netting could be reinstated. The convoy leader ordered all of the gunners to open fire with their anti-aircraft machine guns in a desperate attempt to prevent their presence being announced by the pilot. Hampered by the nets, they were not successful, and they watched in disappointment as the plane departed. The order was given for the convoy to move, because it was now anticipated that the British Army would soon know their position. Bernhardt's panzer was the only one incapable of moving on and was now to complete the operation of track replacement and then try to catch up with the others.

★

The RAF observer relayed the German convoy's position to the staff at his base at Alexandria, who in turn informed the Army, who alerted the nearest British tank patrol, who were at that moment only a few miles to the south of Bur at Tarfawi. From a captured British type 19 radio set within the panzer, with its click dials still set to the frequency on which they found it tuned, Bernhardt heard the strong, brief, coded radio signal which the Germans guessed was the acknowledgement from a nearby British patrol. Bernhardt was now even more eager to be away and urged his men into action. He chose to go under the belly to make the vital connection which would complete the loop of track as the panzer moved slowly forward. So intent were they to complete the job quickly that no one noticed the rumble, muffled by intervening dunes, of approaching tanks until it was too late. The gun loader shouted as he first sensed the cooling effect of a shadow on his bare back. The shadow was caused by the muzzle of a gun. The Sherman tank to which it was attached appeared, its menacing shadow cast by the morning sun over the scene of frantic activity. Over a dune it climbed, as the loader continued to shout his warning to his commander. His cries were cut short by machine-gun fire as he and two others died. The driver, head projecting from the panzer's hatch, involuntarily stopped progress at track replacement, old track half off and new track still flat on the sand, when his skull was shattered by the machine gun of the Sherman. Meanwhile, the turret of the Sherman was turned, and its barrel aimed. The inevitable shell, as it exploded, lifted the panzer off both of her tracks, and she settled with wheels burying themselves in the sand. Bernhardt's mind went blank.

★

The British, finding no prisoners or any justification to further disable the panzer, departed to the east to join their comrades in pursuit of the German convoy.

The day passed without Bernhardt regaining consciousness. As darkness fell and the heat faded from the sand, the jackals emerged from their daytime slumber and soon found the scent of the bodies of Bernhardt's companions. They smelt him later, but made no effort to dig into his cover because, apart from one, they had by then already satiated their hunger. The last to depart was about to taste his outstretched hand as Bernhardt regained consciousness, his ears still ringing. The animal departed when the fingers began to move unexpectedly. Slowly, he recalled what had happened to put him in this situation; trapped beneath the hot steel belly. Whilst he had been unconscious grains of sand beneath him had moved to accommodate his body, such that the pressure of the smooth armoured underbody of his panzer was evenly distributed along his vertebrae. He tried to wriggle free but found that he could only move his head, in which the sound of the exploding shell still reverberated, plus the fingers of the extended left hand that had frightened the jackal. By moving his chin, he formed a pocket in the sand beneath his mouth and with his tongue, he cleared the sand that adhered to his lips and teeth. He was at least able to get air into his lungs via his throat, he realised. He exhaled in a futile and painful call for help that went unanswered. The depression by his mouth slowly filled with hot oil as it leaked from the damaged engine and trickled down his cheeks. He felt a different kind of depression as he became afraid that he would die a slow death. In a panic, he wet himself. Again, he lost consciousness.

When he next regained his senses, the earth had circled the sun and it was again approaching its zenith, turning the mass of steel above him into a furnace. Something brushed past his fingers, causing him to attempt to shout, but whatever it was, perhaps a snake or scorpion, he thought, scampered away. The oil had dispersed into the sand, but its acrid smell remained, and its liquidity taunted him. He needed to drink and knew that soon he would not even have moisture in his body for perspiration. His trousers dampened and became sticky when excrement filled the space between his buttocks and the panzer. He thought of his past and then what he would miss if he died. He wished he had collected those specimens when he had the opportunity. He cursed the Führer. He prayed. His only sense of time came from the cooling and heating of the panzer, as his watch was on his left wrist beyond vision.

Darkness fell again and he heard more animal activity, but it was the screech of birds fighting over the remains of his companions, he decided. Whilst it was cool, he slept a little but was awakened by cramp in his right leg, resulting he assumed from loss of salt to perspiration. Nothing he could do would relieve this new pain that compounded that from his chest, and again he lost consciousness. He came around when it was again hot, craving food and water. The oil that still felt wet but now cool on his cheeks still tempted him. A new sensation alerted him. The sand beneath was vibrating infinitesimally and he realised a panzer, no, several panzers, were responsible. His hopes were raised in the belief that his squadron was returning for him after defeating the British. Soon he could hear the engines, but they were not familiar and with dismay he realised it was the most likely victorious British avoiding mines by navigating in the tracks of his convoy. The sound grew louder as he resolved that they must find him. Rather their prisoner of war than a dehydrated flattened corpse, he thought. As he fought the pain, he filled his lungs with oily air, as far as the panzer above and sand below would allow. He waited, knowing that his shout would have to be audible above the din of machinery. Alas, that was as close as they came for the sound now diminished. Though it pained his ribs, he shouted as loud as he could but knew it was futile and he realised then that some ribs were broken.

Twice more the sun rose and set, and he went through the agony of daily roasting and nightly freezing, always fighting the temptation to lick the oil that surrounded his parched lips. He was losing body mass and realised that as he starved to death, he had the compensation of being able to move parts of his body, if only a few millimetres. With his free left hand, he started to scratch the sand until he was able to move his wrist. Then he could scoop sand with his hand. He found it tiring and painful but concentrated on the task to the exclusion of all else.

The boys found the tank after they first saw the birds hovering above and as they drew near, they were directed by the smell of the half-eaten corpses. They dismounted their camels, frightening the desert birds from their meal, and scurried down the dunes to the panzer and its corpses. With one hand they held their noses tight to reduce the offensive smell. With the other, they wafted away flies, cut away the wristwatches, identity tags, rings, purses and insignia of the Germans and placed their booty in the pockets of their robes. The boys took boots and hats and placed them in a camel blanket. One climbed onto the panzer and robbed the corpse of the driver, of a gold ring, by cutting off a bony finger that still gripped the throttle control.

Bernhardt felt the jolt as the boy descended inside. He stopped digging and listened, assuming it was a large animal. Then he felt a hand trying to remove his watch. Thinking he was in contact with something edible, he tried to grab it with his remaining strength, causing the boy to drop his knife. The boy reacted in shock, praying quietly to Allah, and then called in Arabic for his companion, who was now divesting the panzer of its stock of food and water. Bernhardt recalled the Arabic he had been taught before departing for Africa and beseeched the owner of the hand for help. His strength failed and the hand escaped. The other boy joined the "hand" and talked excitedly about "the live soldier," as far as Bernhardt understood. He realised from their conversation that they were reluctant to help because he could tell their father about their thefts. One wanted to leave him but the other, who Bernhardt gathered was called Rashiid, wanted to help. Bernhardt surprised them when he spoke in Arabic, trying to convince them that if they helped to dig him out, he would not tell on them. He was relieved when it was apparent that they understood his limited Arabic. His despondency returned when the other boy, named Malik, still insisted on leaving him to die and was sure no number of men could ever move the tank.

Rashiid said, "We could tell soldiers about him."

"We have not seen any for weeks," replied Malik.

Whilst they argued, Bernhardt remembered the shovels strapped to the deck and begged the boys to use these with what he now feared was his last breath. Malik argued that it was not manly to labour with shovels, but Rashiid disagreed and shamed his friend into helping. As the boys shifted sand from beneath him, Bernhardt was able to wriggle, but attempts to assist the boys only caused the panzer to sink further into the sand. The pain from extra pressure on his chest caused him to lose consciousness again. The boys then thought him dead, and Malik was for leaving him, but Rashiid would not give way. After more arguments and many rests, the boys were able to drag the stinking German out into the sun. They poured water onto his lips, which revived him, and wiped the oil from his face. Eventually, Bernhardt managed to drink, but could not stand unaided.

Bernhardt's Arabic improved rapidly when he realised the young Bedu understood no other language. He learned that he was now in British territory and that no Germans had been seen for a week. After feasting on the panzer's provisions, the boys helped him on to a camel and set off towards their camp, apparently near the Egyptian border.

★

At the camp, which consisted of a large tent surrounded by chickens, sheep, and a few camels, he was taken to meet the leader, who was also Rashiid's father. Bernhardt was welcomed and told that he would be able to stay and recuperate. The *Bedu* took his stinking, oil-soaked uniform and burned it. He was given an Arab robe and turban. Whilst he was still not fully conscious, the women of the camp used precious water and soap to wash him, marvelling at his fair skin, blue eyes and blonde hair. Thereafter he lived as they did, and took pleasure learning of their culture. He never forgot that he owed his life to the two boys, with whom he became great friends, and to Rashiid's sister, who nursed him. When his ribs had mended, and he was fit to walk and look after himself, the *Bedu* taught him all they could about the flora and creatures of the sand and survival. They made him earn his keep by tending first their hens and, as he became stronger, their sheep, a task that required only that he sit and watch in case they strayed out of sight. He took the opportunity to explore his surroundings and to become proficient in their language.

After two months, when he was fully recovered, the leader told him that he must now be handed over to the British because they were to move west in search of new grazing. Bernhardt was reluctant to leave, fearing that without a uniform he would be taken for a spy and possibly shot. However, he was accepted as a prisoner of war after the Bedu showed the British soldiers his tank and told them how he was found. On Bernhardt's insistence, the British agreed to formally bury the, now bleached bones of his crew.

The two boys had mixed feelings when their friend departed but they were at least grateful that he had not divulged their secret. They had feared that if he remained, he may one day use his knowledge against them. Rashiid's eldest sister was the most disappointed when her blue-eyed patient was taken from her. The German and his nurse, of whom he had seen no more than eyes, feet and henna decorated hands, were each conscious of the un-Islamic feelings that were developing between them. The would-be young lovers parted, each determined never to forget the other.

CHAPTER 5

Trucial Arabia, year 1367 Hijri: AD 1948

They had watched the grey ship approach their favourite spot on the sandy shore, washed by the blue waters of the Persian Gulf. It had passed many times over the past week. Today it had come close enough for her to see the men in their white uniforms standing on the deck. The ship, from which a small boat was being lowered into the sea, was now held by a chain. She knew every type of shell on that beach and had collected each in different sizes and with various coloured patterns to decorate the walls of her little room. Nahla, now seven years old, had been lonely ever since her two brothers had departed to schools in Europe a month ago. She missed her brother Saif, but not the older, teasing Moosa, who she loathed more than ever since he had killed her pet. Moosa habitually made the sound of a bee whenever he wanted to annoy Nahla, for that was what her name meant. Both boys were her stepbrothers, born to her father's first wife, Layla, who had earlier borne three daughters before Moosa, but the older pair had been given in marriage to their cousins soon after they started puberty, Layla said. Layla's third daughter, Fousia, who was many years older than Nahla, still lived in the harem, which Layla dominated. Layla was now beyond her menses and barren, she once confided to Nahla, but this meant nothing to her. Now Nahla's only male company, and that definition was questionable, was Ali the eunuch, who doted on her like a mother hen with a solitary chick.

Ali was, as usual, sleeping in what might have otherwise been the natural shade of a date palm while she gathered shells from the sand in front of the fort. It was winter, and the sun, hidden by cloud, did not now force them to spend their days sheltering in the harem. In there it was always dark, even by day, with shutters that blocked their world from men, closed behind the pierced teak screens that gave ventilation; screens through which the mosquitoes came, in search of blood, attracted by the scent of sleeping bodies; Screens through which she watched the stars and through which at night the cool breeze came, but not from the sea, for only the men slept on that side of the fort.

Behind her, where Ali now slept, two Indian servants were tending a fire that they had made in a pit. The Indians had three long-haired sheep, which they had brushed clean, tethered to the trunk of a palm, ready for slaughter. Ali had been with the al-Wyly family since, it was alleged, he was bought as a small child by Nahla's grandfather in the Christian year of 1922, she had been told. No one, not even Ali himself, knew his origin. Layla told her the story that Ali had been castrated by her uncles, whatever that meant, to maintain the honour of the al-Wyly family when they found that her mother, second wife of her father, had been showing an interest in the then slave, who carried the water.

Layla had said, "More likely they did it because she was not interested in them whilst their brother was away studying with the British."

Ali had been around to do her bidding for as long as Nahla could remember. She never knew her mother, who died very young at her birth. Ali said with great emotion once that her mother was the most beautiful woman he had ever seen. Her father had not taken another wife after her because he had been impotent, Layla told her, ever since she had given birth to her brother Saif, but she did not explain what impotent was, and neither would Ali when Nahla asked him.

As well as Nahla and Layla, two other women lived in the harem of the fort; Shalma, who was the sister of her father and had depression, whatever that was. She had never been married but had once, in an attempt to restore relations with their neighbours, been offered by Nahla's grandfather to, and subsequently fell in love with, someone of another tribe from the East. What Ali and the other women did not know was that Shalma, who was then only fourteen years old, had become pregnant. Salim was away in England, but the brothers who remained saw this as a terrible disgrace to their family and would have killed her, an act which would have been justified by such dishonour, but their father was compassionate. The traditional alternative story then used by families to justify a virgin birth was to claim impregnation by a *Jinn* whilst the girl was sleeping. In this case, the relationship was too obvious for this tactic to be acceptable. Her father, therefore, had Shalma confined to a cell in the basement of the fort to protect her from the brothers and ensure the secrecy of her condition. She gave birth to a boy, who was immediately taken from her and given to a woman of the neighbouring country who had lost her child. For the sake of honour, the brothers never mentioned this episode again, but if the question arose, they agreed to comply with the virgin birth mythology. When Salim returned, he insisted on Shalma's release. Only Salim's father knew that Ali was Shalma's son, and that knowledge was passed to Salim with his father's last breath and an oath of secrecy confirmed between them. The brothers ensured that the enmity between Naamlah and Haqum continued. Shalma now spent a lot of time in her room moping, and did not laugh with the other women. Then there was Fousia, a stepsister, born to Laylah after Shalma's disgrace, who was still not too old for marriage but was only interested in Mariam, the Malay girl who shared her age of sixteen. To the annoyance of the other women, they had become friends with no regard for their mistress–servant relationship. They started referring to her as the mermaid after Ali told them that in the language of the English, her name translated to a woman of the sea. All of the women, except Shalma, looked like older versions of Nahla, with black hair in a long plait, black eyes, and light brown flawless skin. Each was said to be very beautiful by Ali, who appeared to be a good judge of such things.

Shalma was less attractive, because during her imprisonment the brothers declined to provide adequate food for her. A diet of dates and water had caused her teeth to decay and now she had only two in her mouth. She also looked older than her years, but her depression gave her no incentive to make herself attractive like the other ladies.

The revival of the potency of Nahla's father was frequently a topic of conversation between the women, who had little else to spare them from an otherwise mundane and boring lifestyle, incarcerated in the hot south wing of the fort. Mariam, who had her Muslim upbringing diluted by a convent education in Johor Bahru, would read romantic books to them, whenever one could be found in the souk that was in Arabic with romantic content.

"Such books are very rare and came from Egypt, where the religious extremists had less influence," Ali said. He added, "Once, the Malay girl brought a European Vogue magazine which they all, even Shalma, poured over, envious of the freedom of the models in their fashionable Western clothes."

Ali was a mine of information and used to tell her of the old days when, as a child, he had been told of the tribes fighting each other over petty things like wells and grazing. Then the Persian built fort had been the stronghold of her grandfather, defended with cannons against the al-Jaboo and other tribes who wanted to replace the al-Wyly. The British had forced a truce, divided the countries at the West bank of the great wadi, and made the other tribes in Naamlah accept her grandfather as Emir. An incidental consequence was that the abandoned well of Mustafa now lay firmly in Haqum.

"A lot of gold was given to enforce the truce, but it failed to end the feud with the tribes of Haqum because of opposition by your uncles, who insisted custom required the feud to persist for another generation." The Arabs had a tradition, Ali said, of perpetuating a feud through each generation, as though they were counted on the fingers. As long as a finger and thumb remained to hold *a khanjar* the desire for revenge would continue. Ali was popular with the servants, Malays and Indians, without whom, he joked, the *Bedouin* could only exist in tents. It was beneath their dignity and, some thought, against their religion to maintain a home or do manual work, as the holy book told that this was the duty of slaves.

Nahla knew that the servants worked for a pittance and without holidays to make the Arabic ruling class comfortable.

Ali said, "Before the British came the foreigners would have been slaves, as I used to be."

Always eager to learn, Ali absorbed information on history and world affairs by maintaining friendship with the foreigners. He was very clever, she thought, because he had taught himself to read and write when he was a young man and had picked up the English speech from the Indians. Nahla had heard Ali and Mariam talking to each other in that strange language when they had secrets from the women they served. Ali once said six tribes had claimed the impoverished and inhospitable land of sand and rock over which her father now ruled. Since the British inspired truce, based on their gunboat diplomacy, many of the sons of the tribes had abandoned their tents and used their gold to build palaces in which they kept many wives and concubines, "or whatever they were," she thought. Some bought yachts and houses in more hospitable lands from which to gamble, dissipate and fornicate. Ali never explained what these words meant, but she thought they sounded wicked, and would rather not know.

"All hypocrites," he used to say, "but not your father. Emir Salim al-Wyly is a devout man who is worthy of his position as defender of Islamic faith and tradition." Ali did not say as much, but Salim could not do otherwise, or his status would have been untenable. Neither could he leave the country again, for fear of revolt, which would have his power usurped by the other tribes or worse, by the rising faction of religious fundamentalists. Many thought that only the British gunboats kept the fighting from re-starting.

Ali told her, "Some of the gold had not been wasted, because each tribe had nominated boys on whom it would be spent for their education. Some of the families had started businesses, usually trading in pearls or fishing because they knew no other honest way of making a living. Some were successful and had fortunes, which they banked overseas as Naamlah had no banks or even its own currency. When coins were required for trade, they used those of the Austro-Hungarian Empire, bearing the image of Marie-Louise of Austria. The Arabic students had been welcomed by American and European colleges, eager for a share of the gold." Nahla was proud that her father had been one of the first of his generation to receive a Western education. Almost all of Nahla's knowledge came from Ali, because no one else, including her father, had time for her questions and, as a girl, she could never expect to be educated. None of the other women with whom she lived, except the mermaid, had been. They knew only how to please men and bear their children. They could not even feed themselves without servants. If she had been a boy, life would have been different. The women would have worshipped her, met her every whim, and other men would have treated her with more respect even than that deserved by a fast camel, as was only right, she thought.

CHAPTER 6

The ladies had decided that what Salim needed to cure his impotency was a new young wife, to which end they had been making enquiries. They decided on Fatima.

Fatima was the younger of two daughters born to a cousin of Salim and Shalma, who owned and operated a fabric retail and importing business from their premises within the *souk* of Naamlah. The family lived behind the shop, where her two older brothers helped their father. As a child, she spent a lot of her time in the shop listening to the customers talking to her father and brothers. This had given her an unconventional interest and curiosity, for a girl, about the world outside the confines of her family and their home. Several customers were smitten by her beauty and high spirits, trying without success to reserve her for marriage to their sons or even themselves. When Fatima reached puberty, the time in her development when it was required that she cover her hair and limbs, wear the *hijab* and *abaya*, and generally dispose herself with modesty, she was now watched constantly by the men of her family. She was frustrated by no longer being allowed to meet or even be seen by strangers in the shop. She had always been inquisitive and resented the overnight change in attitude towards her by her family, who thought it unnatural and unnecessary for a girl to know anything beyond what her mother knew. They believed strongly that if she remained ignorant, she would be more pliable in the hands of her future husband. All men, they believed, preferred wives who were untainted by other men and who could be trained to be obedient, just like their camels. From their wedding night, many Arabic women of the past were taught the consequences of disobedience by their husbands. The ancient ritual of killing the cat was still preserved by some traditionalists.

Fatima refused to marry any of the four boys whose fathers had bid for her hand. Her father and brothers were beginning to despair and had decided that they would not allow her to refuse the next offer. As though in answer to her parent's prayers, Layla visited Fatima's mother and told her in confidence of Salim's problem. The two women agreed that a spirited girl like Fatima could be the solution, and so agreed that if Fatima approved the match she should be Salim's third wife. When told of this plan, the men agreed that they would not let her refuse this time. Fortunately, when she realised that she would be the wife of the Emir and live in the fort with servants to wait on her, Fatima did not hesitate.

★

After the wedding, Fatima and her newly acquired stepdaughter Nahla became friends immediately, and through Nahla she realised how useful Ali could be. Ali was not like the men of her family; he had no secrets and no fear of being belittled by a woman. He would happily gossip with them, keeping them informed about the world outside the fort.

★

On the day of the meeting between the tribes and the white men, after Nahla had left them, Fatima had Ali to herself, and asked him, "Who built the fort, Ali?"

"The Persians built it centuries ago to protect themselves from the Arabs. When they left, it fell to ruin, until the Turks came and rebuilt it," he replied.

"What happened to the Turks?" she asked.

"They were driven out by the Arabs under Lawrence, the English soldier. Then your husband's grandfather moved his family in for protection from the other tribes. The tribes started fighting each other after Lawrence lost support from his government, who reneged on their promise of Arab independence and with the French colonised Arabia and Mesopotamia, dividing it between Britain and France; but the al-Wyly tribe proved to be the stronger and became rulers of Naamlah with British backing," said Ali knowledgeably.

"When did you come here, Ali?"

"They say I came as a child to serve Salim's father. Salim was then a student." Ali replied, deflecting the focus of her interest from himself to her husband.

Fatima noticed that Ali looked uncomfortable, so she left that subject. "Did you ever see the cannon fired?" she asked.

"Yes; when I was very young they were used once against the al-Jaboo tribe when they threatened to depose the Emir. It was all that was necessary to prevent further attacks," replied Ali. Fatima was quiet for several minutes, and Ali wondered if she had finished this inquisition or if she was about to ask the inevitable question about how he lost his manhood.

Fatima asked, "Were the dungeons used recently?"

"The Turks had prisoners there before I came here, and the bones of some remained, I believe," was Ali's relieved response. "Salim's father used the cells a few times for holding criminals before their trial and punishment, but since he built a police station for that purpose, they have just been somewhere cool for storing dates and a place for children to play when it is hot," he continued. Ali reflected, "it is such a pity that she can't read. She could learn so much more than I can ever tell her."

CHAPTER 7

The courtyard of the fort was surrounded by buildings of mud bricks on two floors with battlements above. To the South, opposite the main gate, was the harem, occupying the first floor with stores and barracks below. The harem was accessible only by an enclosed brick staircase, at the top of which was a shaded porch where Ali slept. From the top of the stairs a wooden balcony enclosed by a teak latticed screen went all around the first-floor level. Ali's porch led to a communal room where the floor was carpeted and where along each wall there were cushions on which the ladies could relax. Exposed timber beams, heavily carved with Koranic verses, supported the roof. The doors of the women's bedrooms and that of a crude lavatory lead from here. Outside the lavatory, no more than a stinking unlit room with a hole in the floor, stood a row of high wooden platform shoes which protected the user from the mess that was by tradition, from the nomadic past, never cleaned from the floor except, as the religion dictated, by slaves, of which there were no more. Men slept in rooms on the north side, accessed via a separate staircase and a separate section of balcony. This was the shaded side, for Naamlah was north of the equator, where they received direct cooling breezes from the sea. Below was the big *majlis*, or reception area, which contained rows of cushions around the walls. On the east side were the kitchen, storerooms and servants' quarters. A windlass in the kitchen served to raise water from the basement. On the west side was the mosque, which included a court where Sharia law was enforced, Salim's office, the men's sitting room and the stables. A hole in the wall of the court had, before Salim's rule, received the arms of thieves, to divest them of their hands by an unseen operative. In the centre of the courtyard stood a brick construction with an iron gate that protected a staircase connecting to the basement. To this gate, criminals would be tied whilst they received their punishment lashes. In the basement, a spring rose which supplied water and which carried away waste to the sea. The remainder of the basement was divided into dungeon cells, each with iron doors, a guard's mess, strong room, and a torture room for confessions, as required by the court when there were no male witnesses, but now a store for dates, and an armoury. Above the main gate was a platform where cauldrons of fish oil could be heated on braziers to pour onto invaders and where spears could be aimed at unwelcome visitors. With one exception, the strong room, Nahla knew every corner of every room in the fort.

★

Today the courtyard was occupied by camels because the leaders of the tribes had arrived with escorts of fierce fighting men. Ali told her that the leaders were to meet the men from the grey ship in the *majlis*.

The little boat had reached the shore and was being held steady by sailors whilst white men, showing their big pink knees, which fascinated Nahla, were climbing out onto the sand. One carrying a white tube started approaching and waving to her. She covered her head and ignored him, because Ali had told her never to look into the eyes of a strange man, for he will interpret this as complicity. Nahla turned from the man and ran to Ali, where she punched his fat belly until he opened his eyes.

"What is wrong my child?" he asked.

"The men are coming from the grey ship, Ali, and one looked at me for complicity," said Nahla nervously, not knowing what the word implied.

"They will not harm you. Come, we will announce them at the fort," said Ali as he stood up, stretching away the last vestiges of his siesta, and brushed sand from his robe, where it adhered to his perspiration. The pair hurried ahead of the white men, towards the Indians who had their sheep cooking and were standing back from the heat of the fire, wiping their brows. They were ready with shovels to cover the carcasses once they were hot enough.

"That's for the visitors to eat," said Ali, as they passed the pit from which they could smell smoke and burning flesh. Ali shouted through a little hatch to the gatekeeper; "The foreigners have arrived." The old man, who was almost blind, strained and groaned as he lifted his arthritic bones from the cot where he spent his days and nights. He pulled back the great iron-studded wooden door, survivor of centuries of abuse, and wedged it open with a piece of driftwood.

A hive of activity was revealed inside the fort as the camels, abandoned by their riders, were being hobbled in one corner in front of the harem. Above them, Nahla could see reflections from the eyes of the women glinting as they admired the fighting men through the grilled shutters. Servants were sweeping away dung from the camels, saving it for fires, whilst the men from the tribes were arguing about positions in a line that they were forming — "An honour guard," Ali said knowledgeably.

By the time the white men had reached the gate the tribesmen were standing in line, belts of bullets across their chests, cherished ancient guns on their shoulders, "facing their front like English soldiers," Ali whispered. Nahla's father was standing at the near end of the line facing the gate, looking serious, she thought. She felt proud of him in his coloured turban and crisp white *dishdash*, fastened with a belt decorated with silver braid beneath his open black cloak, edged with gold thread. One hand rested on the silver covered horn handle of his *khanjar*, tucked into the front of his belt, and the other held a silver-tipped camel cane. She caught his eye, but as usual he appeared to be ignoring her, just as he ignored Ali.

Though outwardly Salim ignored them, they were both in his thoughts: How it gratified him to see Ali as he was today and not as he had been seven years earlier, when he had stolen the love of his favourite woman. Salim alone suspected that Ali had fathered Nahla, for he had himself suffered impotency from before the girl's conception. Now he was no more to a woman than the eunuch. Was this, as with her death at childbirth, his punishment from Allah for not saving the slave from his brothers? His thoughts were diverted as he became aware of the white men. "How undignified they look with their legs exposed. Why did no one tell them how to present themselves decently attired? I can accept this eccentricity, but hope the other guests do not take offence," he thought.

One by one the eyes of the tribesmen wavered from looking straight ahead and each managed to glimpse the bare pink knees. Some felt insulted, some an erotic sensation, and others were amused, but all resolved to not comment out of respect for their Emir. At the gate two of the white men held back to allow one, who had the decency to wear long trousers and a pith helmet, and who was their spokesman, to reach the front of their party. The man in front removed the helmet and clasped it to his chest. The other two followed his example by removing their white officer's caps.

As they came close to Salim the spokesman raised his right hand in a salute and Salim responded with the greeting, "*Salaam alaikum.*"

"*Wa alaikum asalaam,*" replied the one in trousers who, Salim was relieved to learn, could at least speak some Arabic. He knew it would offend the leaders if he used English to address the foreigners. The thought of speaking English reminded Salim of his return from England at the start of the War in Europe, when he had been filled with enthusiasm to follow the example of the European democracies and liberate his people from the backward feudal existence dictated by men who interpreted the words and writings of The Holy Prophet on behalf of those who embraced Islam. He would at least have caused his subjects to follow the example of the Turkish secular Muslim state, but whilst war persisted he could make no progress, and during this time his energy and enthusiasm waned, the country was driven by poverty further into the extreme Islamic camp, and he feared the task was now beyond him, unless the news that would be announced today altered the balance in favour of progress. His attention returned to the spokesman, who was introducing himself and his companions in Arabic. Salim, also in Arabic, invited the white men to inspect the guard. The spokesman, who was a representative of the British Colonial Office and named Farnham, translated for the Naval Officers. Clean shaven and with curled red hair, James Farnham would have felt more comfortable in the kilt of his native Scotland than in khaki flannels in the climate of the Gulf. With his two bearded Naval companions and the bearded Arabs, he felt completely out of place. All three visitors walked slowly past the row of armed men with Salim who, when they reached the end of the line, invited them to enter the *majlis* where the tribal leaders were waiting.

CHAPTER 8

They followed the example set by the pile of sandals at the entrance and abandoned their shoes. The English and Scots men found themselves in a scented, dark, and noisy room, around the walls of which ornate cushions had been arranged. Here sat the bare-footed leaders of the other influential tribes of the Emirate, who had all heard rumours about oil being discovered in their country and were expecting confirmation during this meeting.

As the eyes of the white men grew accustomed to the lack of direct sunlight, they saw that all were dressed like Salim. Farnham thought their beards made them look older and wiser than their years. He knew them to be simple men whose lives were ruled by Islamic tradition and, by his standards, a misplaced sense of family honour. At one end of the room was an empty seat, obviously the Emir's, he thought. At the opposite end was a table, hardly visible through the haze of burning frankincense rising from clay burners scattered about the floor. At the table two Indians in smart European dress were sitting, scribes, he decided. The beards stopped wagging as each of the leaders became aware of the stocking footed visitors.

The Arabs stood, then shuffled away from Salim's seat to make three spaces. Salim directed the visitors to one end of the incomplete circle that they had formed, where the first hand was offered. The visitors nervously shook it and received an enthusiastic but unrecognised greeting. Later, Farnham explained that they were asking after the state of their livestock and of the health of their relatives. The sailors mumbled *"zain"* in response, at what they thought might be appropriate breaks in the exchange, as Farnham had briefed them to do. His own response was more extensive, with greetings in Arabic, making appropriate enquiries of the Arabs and punctuating them with "*alhamdulillah.*" They moved to the next hand until all present had been likewise introduced by Salim. Salim then indicated for them to sit, before taking his seat. Farnham diplomatically ensured that the officers sat adjacent to Salim in order of seniority, with himself furthest away, indicating to the Arabs the sailor's seniority to himself.

Salim gave a blessing; "*Bismillah al-Rahman al-Rahim,*" and called for *cawah* to be brought. Servants went around the assembly in order of seniority, with bowls in which to wash hands, followed by little beaten silver cups into which they poured *cawah.* This was itself something of a ceremony, fascinating the sailors, because the servant demonstrated his skill by pouring from a jug held above the heads of the recipient into the tiny cup held at the height of the recipient's mouth without spilling a drop.

Salim started to address the meeting: "Honoured guests; as you know, I am sure, the Cornubia Company has confirmed that Allah has blessed our land with vast reserves of oil." The Arabs nodded, some even smiled, and some proclaimed "*Alhamdulillah,*" as they each thought of the wealth and security it would bring to their own families. Salim continued, "The Company forecasts that from known reserves our oil will last for 50 years before the cost of extraction from the ground exceeds half of one American Dollar per barrel. Today the crude oil of Bahrain, taken by the Americans, costs them three dollars per barrel."

Salim paused whilst the assembly savoured this good news, and gathered his courage to continue; "Cornubia have, unfortunately, more recently concluded that we would likely be dependent on the goodwill of our Eastern neighbour if we are to ship this oil out of our country to feed the worlds markets." The smiles faded from the bearded faces as Salim continued, "It is known to our fishermen and pearl divers that the waters of Naamlah are shallow and they tell us that no oil tanker could enter these waters." The expressions on the bearded faces now turned to anger, as they knew their neighbours would be jealous and awkward. Salim continued; "We understand that a Japanese company drilling there had concluded that the geology on their side of the great wadi was such that it could not offer any reserves of oil." They all suspected that the mutual distrust between the Naamlahns and their feuding Eastern neighbours would make it impossible, short of Allah's intervention, for an agreement to be reached which would allow their precious oil to be shipped via the deep waters of Haqum. In their culture, the *Bedu* attributed complicity in the news, particularly bad news, to the messenger. Thus, in this case, their anger was directed at Salim. As Farnham knew, because of this Europeans, when dealing with Arabs, frequently categorised their behaviour as untrustworthy when confronted with reluctance to convey unwelcome news or when failing to neither refuse or comply with a request. Often an unfavourable request would be met by agreement qualified by "*Inshallah*," Allah willing. The more experienced would interpret this as a polite refusal.

Salim paused whilst he sipped his cawah, then continued; "The British Navy were requested by their King's *wazir*, Churchill, to survey our waters and thereby confirm or disprove the words of our seafarers."

One of the Indian scribes stopped writing and approached Salim, bowing respectfully, and passed a paper to him. He dismissed the scribe and continued to address the gathering, but with a smile barely hidden; "Friends, our esteemed guests, Commander Phillips and Commander Lightfoot of His Majesty's ship Pegasus, have completed this survey of our waters and will report to you their findings."

Lightfoot stood up, regretting having risen quickly, as his legs were still cramped, and he had difficulty balancing. As he gained composure, he nervously started to speak in English which none of the Arabs understood. "Thank you, Your Highness; I shall rely on Mister Farnham of the Colonial Office to address the meeting on my behalf."

The Arabs were alarmed for they feared they were not to know the findings until a later translation was offered in their language when it would be too late to debate any problems that they anticipated. All present distrusted the spoken word unless it had been conveyed by the Holy Prophet. Some were already fearing financial ruin because their families had obtained loans on the strength of the rumoured findings by Cornubia. Several unconsciously moved their hands to the khanjar at their belts. Tension in the room subsided as Lightfoot stopped speaking and sat down, to be replaced by Farnham, who started to speak fluently in their language.

"Your Highness, Sheikhs, Gentlemen, Commander Lightfoot's crew have completed a survey, as you know, and charts based on his results have been drawn by Commander Phillips to be published by our Hydrographic Department of the Admiralty in Taunton of our country." He pointed to the white tube which Phillips had been nursing. "This copy will be left with his Highness and further copies will subsequently be available from Admiralty agents throughout the world. In the meantime, we confirm that the waters of Naamlah are not of sufficient depth to permit loading and shipment of oil from the shore." A gasp of dismay swept the room as Farnham was now cast as the messenger of bad news.

Farnham could understand that Arab secretiveness did not allow them to comprehend why a chart of their waters should be made available to foreign navigators. This did not go unnoticed by the Arabs present, but they were more concerned by Phillips's geographical revelation. Farnham sensed their anger and felt uneasy as he resumed; "However, the chart shows that there is a deep channel at the edge of the Eastern territorial limit where loading will be feasible either from lighters or from a floating pipe." The faces of the Arabs were now transformed, turning to smiles as they saw the messenger in a new light. The beards were animated once more as they postulated on their good fortune.

Salim relaxed, pleased with the outcome, internally thanking Allah for preventing the meeting from ending in acrimony with weapons drawn as was so often the case at such gatherings where tribal interests conflicted. Salim indicated to the Indians that the food should be brought, and to the gathering he said; "Let us prepare to eat."

The sailors, not knowing what was required of them, held back as the Arabs started raising themselves from their cushions, pulling themselves up by pressing on the tops of the canes that each carried. They started to leave the room, talking happily to each other.

Farnham whispered, "Don't worry; we are going outside to wash, as is their tradition." They found a servant waiting in the courtyard with a pitcher, from which he poured precious scented water over their hands. They watched the Arabs shaking off the water after wringing their hands. Some also wiped themselves on the *izaar*, which was all that they wore beneath their *dishdash*. The Englishmen settled for shaking, as Farnham explained; "Drying cloths are *haraam*, forbidden, by the Holy Prophet, because water to adequately cleanse them and thus prevent the passing of infection could not be spared in this part of the world."

When back inside they saw that an enormous silver plate, as big as a cartwheel, containing a mound of rice and pieces of cooked meat had been placed on a woollen rug where they had previously been sitting. Other similar plates and rugs had been placed in front of the other guests. Salim invited everyone to eat. The sailors followed his and Farnham's example, sitting with some difficulty and in an undignified manner on the rug because of their shorts, cross-legged around the plate. Farnham had warned them before leaving the ship that this would be expected of them, and if they found themselves in this situation, they should avoid presenting the soles of their feet to the view of the Arabs, who would otherwise be offended.

Salim selected the eyes and passed them to the sailors and broke off some tender shoulder meat for Farnham. The Arabs started to tuck in, but both sailors were wishing they could be elsewhere as they politely chewed the gelatinous lumps and felt the circulation failing in their legs. Now the Arabs were balling rice in their hands before skilfully tossing it into their mouths. The sailors tried to do the same but only succeeded in making a mess over their shorts and socks. Farnham mouthed something to Lightfoot which he missed but later learned was advice to be wary of the offal, particularly intestines, as they often did not get cooked sufficiently to kill inherent digestive bacteria. As they endured rather than enjoyed the meal the talk among the Arabs, in which Farnham participated, was about forming a government to administer the potential wealth of their country for the benefit of its citizens. What the leaders did not say, but were all thinking with varying degrees of selfishness was, "How may I manipulate the economy for the benefit of my family at the expense of the others?"

One such leader was Idris bin Mubarak al-Jaboo. Idris was the leader of a family whose ancestors had challenged the al-Wyly tribe for control of the country, but now they had become wealthy by operating fishing boats and exploiting pearl divers amongst other commercial, sometimes dubious, activities. He was, in appearance, with close-spaced sunken black eyes and thin hooked nose, the epitome of shifty-ness, thought Farnham. He attributed Idris' appearance to generations of inbreeding amongst first cousins.

Salim was impressed with Farnham's knowledge of the Arab culture and language and was curious to know his background; at the risk of being thought impertinent, he questioned him. Farnham explained, as they ate, that he had spent many years as a secretary at the British diplomatic mission in Mesopotamia and was later in Eritrea where he had met and married an Egyptian teacher of English.

CHAPTER 9

Seeing the gate, where her father had been standing, reminded Nahla of her oldest brother. Moosa's tendency toward sadistic cruelty had been present since her first memory of him. Ali had told her that he believed it started when he was a baby.

"Moosa was suckled by Layla as she sat with his aunts and your stepsisters, Asia and Fathia, behind the screen overlooking the courtyard. It was the highlight of their otherwise mundane week, to sit each Friday, after noon prayers, to watch the wretched criminals who had been condemned, to death by beheading or to receive lashes, by your grandfather's court. I suspect that Layla had felt vulnerable then because she had finally delivered a son who would ensure the line of the al-Wyly dynasty. She would have worried constantly how long it would be before your father chose another, younger wife," he said.

After the men had gone inside, Nahla and Ali waited to see what would happen next and resumed talking about Moosa. Ali said, "Sometimes the sisters would be moved to gasp when, with a single blow, the head of a murderer was separated from his trembling body by the executioner. They were easily aroused by the sight of the big Negro, stripped to his waist, who with rippling muscles wielded the broad sword or the lash and placed them with such precision; sword on the neck and lash on the back and legs of his victims. Your older sisters, just in their teens and ripe for marriage, would count the strokes, anticipating when the Negro would change his target area. They knew that many of the victims would be unconscious before their punishment ended and it could take days to receive all their strokes while conscious." After explaining the word 'conscious' to Nahla, Ali continued, "I assumed that as he received her milk, baby Moosa drank also the excitement of his mother. After he was weaned, Moosa still joined the ladies on Fridays, in his place at their feet, where he sat silently, enjoying the spectacle and subconsciously absorbing the crude insensitive comments and reactions of the women to the suffering of the victims."

★

That evening Salim was so elated with the apparent success of the meeting that he sent for Fatima, with whom he anticipated having one more attempt at the consummation of their union.

★

Back on-board Pegasus, as the two officers recovered from the under-cooked entrails of lamb, Farnham explained the origins of the country they were visiting. "The fort where they were entertained is about a mile from the town that gave the country its name, and this is where over several generations many tribal groups settled after abandoning the nomadic life. Some have become quite prosperous by dealing in commodities; fabrics, spices, slaves, and particularly pearls. The town Arabs were formidable traders with an inherent sense for spotting bargains and deriving the maximum profit. A successful man would be able to afford to support many wives, keeping them in equal style."

The next day the anchor was weighed, and the warship departed for Britain via the Gulf of Oman, the Red Sea, and the Suez Canal.

★

The two Indian clerks, who assisted Salim to administrate the hitherto poor country, were unable to cope with the burden that the discovery of oil now presented. The increasing numbers of foreigners were an embarrassment because there were no facilities in Naamlah, even to accommodate those who were to vis-

60

it Salim. It was soon obvious to the Indians that Salim needed more help, and it was they who had suggested that he seek this from the British protectors of Naamlah's sovereignty. It was thus that a request was made to the British Government that resulted in James Farnham's return as the resident adviser.

Farnham had been looking forward to a long leave with his wife and children, but no sooner than he set foot in England was he called to the Colonial Office and told that he and his wife were to return to Naamlah. The Minister said, "It appears that you made such a good impression on the Emir that he has requested the Prime Minister to make you his adviser." Farnham was not disappointed by the appointment because he was confident of being able to help Salim, with whom he had established a good working relationship, but he was not exactly convinced he had the necessary experience for such responsibility. Nevertheless, he responded, "I am delighted to oblige, Minister, providing arrangements can be made for my children's education."

"Do not worry on that score, they will be enrolled at a good school at the expense of the Government," the Minister assured him. "Arrangements have been made for the departure, on the Cunard ship, of you and your wife one week from today, so please put your affairs in order before then."

"Yes indeed, Minister," replied Farnham.

"That is all, you may return to your family." As Farnham made to go, the Minister added, "I am sorry, Farnham, that your leave has been cut short." Farnham did not comment as he could only have endorsed the Minister's statement, shook hands, and turned to depart. "Oh, I forgot to say that you will be promoted, and all of your living expenses will be met by the Naamlahn government, that is, after you have assisted in forming one," said the Minister, smiling.

★

A year had passed since the visit of the white men and Nahla and Ali were back on the beach, talking once more about Moosa and wondering what he was up to in Germany.

"Did you know your Uncle Hammed bought Moosa his whip when he was three, after he had been told how the boy had boasted that when he was a man, he would replace the Negro? With this new toy, Moosa would stand with feet apart, legs slightly bent, chest at right angles to the chair-back that received his blows," said Ali, clearly disgusted at the memory.

Nahla said, "I remember that when he was a boy, Moosa was always carrying his whip. He tried to use it on our brother, but Saif was too quick for him and easily avoided his fat brother."

"Yes, and he would have used it on you if your wet nurse had not protected you," he replied.

"But he was sometimes successful in finding a victim among our unsuspecting cousins, though more often he vented his aggression on defenceless animals," Nahla recalled.

Ali replied, "I remember after your grandfather had died, your father was still in Europe and the young uncles, Abdulaziz and Hammed, were in charge and providing more entertainment than that supplied by the court of your grandfather. In many of those cases, the victims had done no more than offend them by refusing an unreasonable demand." After explaining 'unreasonable,' Ali continued; "Moosa learned later that when he became a man his vocation would not be that of an executioner; he would be groomed to become Emir, a frightening thought for all who knew him. I think he looked forward to the power but not the responsibility. You know he started using the whip on me after I joined the harem."

"Poor Ali, you never deserved that," replied Nahla, remembering how Ali had apparently suffered as a young man.

"Oh, I used to get my revenge by hiding his whip," said Ali, laughing strangely in the way that she found so infectious.

"Do you remember the day before Moosa's departure for school in Germany, when he was so awful because he did not want to leave but could not disobey our father," said Nahla, looking sad at the memory. "I have hated him since then." Nahla had been given a puppy by the wife of Uncle Hammed, who was also to leave, with Cousin Khaled, on the same ship as Moosa. They were to join Uncle Hammed, who had been sent away, banished they said, for the offence against Ali, so she learned later. Moosa decided to work off his frustration on the animal by tying it to a palm and whipping it until it died. She never forgave him. Although Nahla did not know it, he had never previously found satisfaction like that, which then mingled with the pleasure of his adolescent early sexual arousal.

Nahla and Saif never attended the punishment exhibitions, which had no appeal to their sensitive natures. Saif was disgusted with his older brother's behaviour after he had rescued one of their second cousins, a little girl named Hooda, from Moosa and his whip. Nahla and Saif generally took the opportunity to play together without being annoyed by their brother. That particular afternoon, a Friday, the usual day when punishments would be offered as entertainment after noon prayers, Nahla did not want to play because she was in her room mourning the loss of her pet. Neither were the other women present to watch the spectacle in the courtyard. Layla was busy supervising the packing for her son's departure and the older sisters were both recently married and had left the fort. Fousia was consoling Shalma who was having one of her depressed days. Neither Nahla nor Ali knew that Moosa sat alone that afternoon, holding the whip in both hands, perspiration rising as he counted the lashes received first by a sailor convicted for drunkenness. The victim was cut down and dragged from the scene as a young woman, named Hafrida, was brought to replace him at the gate. Her husband, an aged relative of Idris al-Jaboo, had taken her to the court, accusing her of complicity, which she had denied, but was unable to produce male witnesses to support her case. A neighbouring man had made advances on her, which she had repelled, but in spite he had caused a rumour of her adultery. Without witnesses to support either side of the case the court had been lenient. Instead of stoning she was to have twelve lashes. Moosa was excited and impressed because she did not cower and appeal to the Negro as most had done before her, but she walked proudly, without any sign of fear. Hafrida was so confident of her innocence that she trusted Allah to protect her from pain. That morning she had insisted on wearing her best silk *abaya*, as she knew the ladies of the Emir were likely to be watching. The Negro bound her hands and ankles to the gate, pulled off her *hijab* and thrust a stick between her perfect teeth. Then he paced away to take up his usual stance that Moosa so desired to emulate. Hafrida strained to turn her head, trying in vain to see her tormentor. Moosa became more excited, first by the exposed honey-coloured skin of her face as she turned in his direction. He knew she could not see him sitting excitedly in the dark room behind the pierced screen. He was next entranced by her teeth, gripping the stick, perfect and white, contrasting with the big black eyes that glared defiantly until she received the first stroke. She winced then, but the defiant expression which so impressed the boy returned in anticipation of the second stroke. More strokes followed, causing her to suspect Allah had deserted her. The whip cut through the silk *abaya* until it fell from her shoulders, exposing to Moosa her perfectly formed breasts. The feelings Moosa had experienced after he had killed the dog now returned with greater force. By the final stroke, of which she had lost count, she was convinced Allah had ignored her. Moosa had dropped the whip and his hands were beneath his dishdash. When Hafrida was dragged away, he left to change into clean clothes before anyone came to join him. The face of the woman would haunt him that night on-board the ship and on many nights in the future when, as a man, he would try in vain to obtain the same degree of sexual excitement that witnessing her suffering had initiated.

CHAPTER 10

That night Nahla was still awake, peering at the familiar stars through the screen of her little room. She was thinking of Saif and how she missed him since he had departed to England for schooling. She knew it was wrong to think of her brother this way, but except for Ali and Saif, she felt loved by no one. She could not help picturing Saif and herself married one day and living together forever.

The moon was illuminating her shells and making chequered patterns on the net that hung from the posts of her cot. "The winter nights are so pleasant," she thought. Outside, Ali had been snoring sweetly, but now he had stopped, and she prayed he had not been wakened by his dream. Now she heard sobbing. Nahla's room, between those of her older stepsister Fousia and aunt Shalma, lacked sound insulation because, to aid circulation of air, the partition walls did not quite reach the ceiling. Often, she would hear Shalma crying as, presumably, she relived her suffering in the hands of her brothers, but this did not sound like Shalma.

Then she heard Ali speak to whoever it was, in a whisper, "Hello Fatima, what is the matter? Did he beat you, that you are so upset?" as though it was a common occurrence. Nahla strained to hear Fatima's reply because she did not like the thought of her father beating his women.

Fatima sounded amused now. "Silly Ali, you know he never does that." Nahla was reassured. "I am sure he blames me, though I do all that Layla says will arouse him, to no avail. He is so loving, and his touch excites me so, that I long for him to be successful. He became frustrated and then angrily made me leave him," she said, resuming her sobbing.

"Try to sleep, and tomorrow you will feel differently about him," reassured Ali.

Nahla heard the key in the lock and the squeak of the door as Fatima entered. The door soon closed and within minutes Ali was snoring. In the morning Nahla realised she must have fallen asleep soon after Ali, whilst still thinking of Saif and with Fatima's sobs still audible from the room next door.

★

No sooner had the meeting between the tribal leaders ended than the Indian clerks told the other servants from their own country what had been said. Ali soon knew the outcome of the visit of the white men and relayed the story to the women. It meant little to any of them, because they could not foresee how it would change their lives.

In the following months, the Emirate received numerous letters of congratulation from the leaders of foreign Governments, followed by requests for visas from businessmen all eager to have their companies represented by citizens of Naamlah. Foreigners next sought to establish diplomatic missions within the little country, for all wanted firms in their countries to participate in the inevitable distribution of wealth that would flow with the oil.

Since Salim had succeeded his father, the fort had become the centre of government. Here a man would apply for land on which to build a house. A man wishing to leave the country would call here for Salim's permission. Regular courts would be held at the mosque, where the religious men would order the severe punishments of mutilation, whipping, and beheading that maintained order and obedience to the sharia law. When a man died the court would ensure that his possessions were distributed among his relations according to the law. It was this part of the sharia that forced the arrangement of marriages between members of the same family, usually cousins, to avoid the break-up of tribal lands and fortunes. Here also matrimonial disputes would be settled, generally in favour of the husband, for only a foolish woman would attempt to seek satisfaction from the law which appeared to be biased against her gender.

★

In the few days before his departure, after an initial feeling of panic over what was now expected of him, Farnham set about learning as much as he could about how the other countries in the Gulf region were then being governed. From his previous job in Mesopotamia, he knew quite a lot about the cultural differences between his upbringing and that of the Arabs. Whereas his culture had developed progressively through generations of enlightenment, the Arabs development towards democracy was hindered by a code of behaviour dictated in the 7th century by the Holy Prophet Mohammed. Many zealous followers would consult religious men for guidance before embarking on any activity, choosing the interpretation that suited their own often medieval behaviour standards. Acceptance of the bicycle, for example, was at that time a debatable point amongst religious experts, although it was not considered important by the common man because it required more exertion than riding a donkey. The gun and the motorcar were accepted without debate because they were more effective than the sword or the camel, though neither existed at the time of Mohammed. There were no equivalent evolutionary concessions to women, who had no representation in the religious community and who now had less freedom than they had enjoyed in the 7th century.

He contacted colleagues in the Middle Eastern section of the Colonial Office who told him that, as in almost every other field of commerce, they had no law, other than that of *Sharia*, to govern activities. Although it is becoming less prevalent, he would find that loyalty to Tribe or family will override other considerations in business and government. For example, as local banks were established, they tended to look after the interests of the founding family rather than their depositors. A bank was seen by the family as a source of unsecured loans, using customer's cash, which when suitably invested reaped rewards previously unimagined. Only if the investment failed – and that was unlikely in the new expanding economy – would there be any embarrassment. International banks with stricter lending rules were allowed to establish branches only when a member of the ruling tribe, or one of his connections, was appointed to their boards and usually only then if they had some hold over their local manager. Such nepotism would not have been tolerated in Western countries, but it was often the normal method of defending family interests in Arab culture. They also told him of the Arab's expectation of a gratuity for facilitating the progress of a contract which, though essential for trade, would be difficult to justify to the shareholders of the business and would be seen as an illegal bribe by the British Government.

★

A house for James and Rasha Farnham was found in the town, at its southern extremity, where rent was paid for one year, during which a more appropriate residence would be built *inshallah*. The Farnhams' house was of typical mud-brick construction, a local building technique dating back thousands of years. The once rectangular bricks of dried mud, reinforced with straw, had lost their corners after decades of wind and occasional rain. At some time in their life, they had been painted to prevent them from eroding. The white paint had been reinstated for the new residents. The house belonged to one of the merchant families who had moved to a more palatial establishment nearer the coast. No one had lived there for two years before the Farnhams' arrival. The house formed the south side of a rectangular walled yard that was accessed from a street on the north side via an ancient teak gate that was liberally endowed with metal spikes, the object of which, in Africa, may have been to discourage elephants from relieving themselves of an itch; in Naamlah they served no purpose other than decoration. On the west side, the courtyard was formed by the wall of a bakery and on the east side by a mosque with the base of a minaret projecting into the yard. When they first visited the house, they were not impressed, but were told that nothing else was available because of the demand for staff accommodation by Ministries and businesses. As she saw him looking up to the top of the minaret, Rasha told her husband the men would ensure the privacy of their women by appointing a blind *muezzin* to call the faithful to prayers from the top of this tower.

"Not necessary for anyone to climb up there now my dear. Look at those Tannoy horns," said Farnham, pointing to the large metal loudspeaker cones near the top of the tower. Subsequently, they learned that the amplifier that drove the horns gave enough power to compete with other mosques near the centre of the town. Rasha said she would feel at home listening to the prayer calls, as they would remind her of her childhood in Cairo. She assured her husband that he would grow to appreciate it, but he doubted he would ever get a morning lie-in again.

The architectural style, late medieval, Farnham called it, resembled that of the al-Wyly fort but on a much-reduced scale. At some time the enclosed yard had been a garden, watered by its own, now salted, well. More recently it had become a miniature desert in which nothing grew except for a few cacti. The soil was now dust that took flight and whirled around in eddies set up by the slightest breeze, settling inevitably on the floors and furniture of the house. Once through the gate, which Farnham suspected was even older than the house and could date from the crusades, they approached the only entrance to the building, an equally old and ill-fitting teak door. Both the gate and door had many ancient holes, showing they had outlived numerous locks and bolts. The gate was secured now by a baulk of timber, pivoted on one side, that nestled in iron brackets set into posts that were attached to the wall. There were no openings for windows on the ground floor of the house except one into the yard, which had both loose-fitting glass panes and a wooden shutter. Inside, the ground-floors were of dirt, compressed by generations of occupants and swept by generations of slaves. They realised that the dust would once have been stabilised by woollen carpets.

After they settled in, the Farnhams obtained some linoleum from the captain of a two masted boum that had brought trade goods from Bombay. This made the ground floor more habitable, but they could not prevent the encroachment of dust from outside via the ill-fitting door and window, the latter designed to allow just enough sunlight to see and enough air for ventilation. Otherwise, the door and shutter were their only defence against dust, elements, smells, and visiting nocturnal creatures. There were two rooms on the ground floor, a sitting area and a cooking area, which shared light from the single window. In one corner of the yard was a crude toilet, colonised by cockroaches, which exuded a mass of flies. Exposed beams of coconut palm, the ends of which projected outside, supported the upper floor of the house, where there were two more rooms accessed via a ladder. In one the Farnhams slept, and the other was occupied by a married couple from the Philippines, who had been introduced as their servants. The upstairs rooms each had a shuttered window. Floorboards here, worn smooth by generations of barefooted occupants, were irregularly shaped pieces, possibly of driftwood of an obscure species renowned for resistance to the subterranean termites that permeated the fabric of the building. These insects ate their way in darkness through any material that could provide cellulose to sustain them and enable them to support their queen, safely protected deep within the ground. The only defence against termites and flies, another inconvenience, were the small resident lizards that patrolled the walls and ceilings. Mosquito nets, hung from bedposts, were their only protection against these nocturnal parasites. Rasha had added rugs, given to her by her parents when she married, to make the upper rooms more homely, and on the walls she had hung ethnically patterned handwoven woollen camel blankets. These she discovered to be available in the souk for a pittance, because the Toyota Land Cruiser was now replacing the camel as the Bedouin's preferred mode of transport. Their furniture was of the military type, Honduran mahogany, with brass-bound corners and recessed brass handles. It had been in Farnham's family since one of his ancestors had served with Wellington at Waterloo. Now the feet stood in pots, forming moats of oil as protection against termites and ants.

When Farnham was with the Emir, Rasha fought loneliness and depression, aggravated by the endless war against dust, by trying to convince herself that the setting of her new home had compensations: The red mahogany of the furniture blended beautifully with the newly oiled teak shutters and the dark polished wood of the upstairs floors. She loved the smells of oil and wax polish which blended with those from the cooking area that was almost a kitchen. Even after years of abandonment, she was convinced that the aromas of spices from ancient Eid feasts could still be detected. At night, which crept up on them so quickly at these tropical latitudes, they relied on oil lamps which announced their presence to the mosquitoes that whined around the nets of their beds.

Of their neighbours, the baker was friendly and had welcomed them with gifts of his produce. The men who visited the mosque and washed their feet and limbs in the street outside five times a day treated the foreigners with disdain, and their house as though it was a zoo, with its occupants placed there by Allah for their entertainment. How they found time to earn a living would be a mystery to most Europeans. Of course, as Rasha knew, they had others for whom prayer was not essential, women or servants to support them. On the opposite side of the street there lived an old man who was a cleric and something of an authority on Islam, they were told. Four women so young that they were almost children lived with him, but they rarely left the house. The old man frequently received visits from groups of men, but the Farnhams had never seen him leave his house.

Nearby was the souk, but Rasha soon gave up visiting it alone, because she was the only unaccompanied woman among the male or male-escorted female shoppers. The men, she knew, did not like their women to mingle with strangers who might give them 'ideas', but it was these same men who would intimately touch her as they jostled in the narrow lanes. She never caught the eye of her practised antagonists, who blended into the universally white-clothed crowd. "Oh, for something useful to occupy my time," she frequently said under her breath.

★

Salim saw Farnham and the advice that he offered as gifts from Allah. Like his fellow countrymen, he had difficulty accepting Farnham as anything but a servant. After all, he was not a Muslim. Farnham accepted his status and the unlimited drain on his time that the position required because he was well compensated financially. He did, however, worry about Rasha, who he knew was suffering from incarceration in their house for long periods without intelligent company, as the other expatriates were not accompanied by wives who could otherwise have provided such companionship.

Farnham could foresee many factors conspiring to inhibit the development of Naamlah as a self-governing nation:

» The absence of the work ethic amongst the Bedu population.
» A climate hostile to physical exertion.
» An exceptional differential between the affluent minority and the multitudinous poor.
» Religious devotion denigrating work by frequent prayer sessions, inhibiting productivity unless due to the effort of slaves in the past or servants now.
» A short concentration period stemming from a lack of mind-expanding education.

The culture, he summarised, was overly influenced by a religion based medieval legal system, and suffered from an affinity to paedophilia, near incestuous relationships, nepotism, and misogyny. It lagged the achievements of the Western nations in these respects by five or ten centuries. "Perhaps the work ethic will be revealed in future generations," he hoped.

He decided that he would be frank with Salim about his opinions, or they would not be able to work together. Salim was surprisingly receptive of Farnham's opinions, and though he admitted they were an impediment he felt constrained by the intransigence of the religious extremists who had considerable influence on his people. Farnham did not need to spell out to Salim that it was the accepted practice, in these developing circumstances in which a government was being formed, to ensure loyalty and maintain both wealth and power within the tribe by placing one's close relatives in positions of authority. Farnham knew that the culture placed great store on the belief that a man was given his wealth and status only by the will of Allah and it was only right that other men should respect Allah's will and maintain the chosen one in his elevated position. Should the chosen one desert that position, it was a different matter. Conversely, it was accepted that the beggar was such also by Allah's will, and should not have his status elevated by man in defiance of Allah.

Salim, unfortunately, did not have many close relatives, and those that he did have were hardly trustworthy. He had been notably unsuccessful with his seed, compared with his opponents. After discussing all of these factors at length, Farnham and Salim concluded that for all their other failings, his brothers had at least managed to make their livings without the privilege they had previously enjoyed in Naamlah. Salim therefore reluctantly agreed that emissaries should be sent to his brothers, offering amnesty, and requesting them to return, with offers of government positions. Salim prayed that they would show loyalty in gratitude for the opportunity to contribute to the development and hence share in the prosperity of their homeland.

CHAPTER 11

Although, so far, no oil had been extracted in Naamlah, there was plenty of speculation and anticipation of fortunes soon to be made. Those families, like that headed by Idris, who had for generations operated trading companies in Naamlah were already quarrelling over who should represent the major international organisations under the local "rental" practice. There was, they expected, a great fortune to be made, particularly from those companies concerned with infrastructure construction and oil extraction. In practice, the local agent did little except put his name to the documentation necessary to import the expatriate labour for which he receives a generous royalty on imports and a contribution to establishing local premises. The 'principals' provided all the necessary merchandise. Without the agent, with his inevitable family connections in government, it would be near impossible to circumvent what, to a Westerner, would be seen as bureaucracy and corruption, but which an Arab would have then seen as acceptable Allah-given privileges. It was not unknown for an official in government to refuse to deal with those foreigners, even if ahead of a queue, with whom he had appointments until members of his own family had been given priority. For its part, the foreign firm would often require that the agent had adequate funds to support the venture, for which a family-owned bank would be a secure source.

As facilities for their accommodation became available, there had followed a stream of government-sponsored advisers from developed countries who were experts on defence, media, medicine, telecommunications, transport, law, financial services, etc. Less reliable were the expatriate carpetbaggers who sought to gain a fortune by offering their dubious services. Although few of the appointed ministers in the neighbouring states had any formal education or relevant experience, they shared a natural sense of self-preservation, which had enabled them to rise within their families. Typically, they relied on a historical trading mentality and a layman's knowledge of *Sharia* law, gained from Koran reading. They had anticipated that expatriate civil servants would be necessary for the day-to-day working of their Ministries. This would enable them to devote time to involvement in the commercial activities of their families, where their position of power and influence would be invaluable. A typical example that Farnham later discovered in Naamlah was Yacoob al-Wyly, an older cousin of Salim and uncle to his wife, Fatima. Yacoob had at one time served in the British Indian Army, where he attained the rank of corporal. For want of anyone better qualified within the al-Wyly tribe, Yacoob was an early appointee by Salim to the post of Defence Minister. In his army days, Yacoob had saved his pay to acquire a coffee shop in the souk, not far from the fort. Here he sponsored three Indians to cook and serve the local dishes that were popular with sailors and fishermen. After his appointment, he saw himself joining his cousins in the upper class of society, where he could expect to pocket inducements from international arms manufacturers for choosing their equipment. Yacoob knew that typically a contingency of 5 % was included in contract prices just for this purpose, though officially called a sum to ease the inevitable bureaucratic delays of a developing country. Yacoob thereby obtained funds with which to expand his catering business, to which he still devoted most of his time and managed from his Ministry office whilst his expatriate advisers looked after Ministry business.

Farnham discovered that Salim had already been pressured by his family to make other ministerial appointments in their favour. Notably, the husbands of his two elder daughters were expecting to become Ministers of the Interior and Foreign Affairs, though neither of them had ever previously held down a job. Salim's brothers, Abdulazziz and Hammed, had resented the authority that their elder brother had inherited from their father after Salim's return from education in England. Until then they had shared the misplaced confidence of their father whilst he was losing mental capacity. With one exception they had a free hand in running the country. They had repaid their father's confidence by looking forward to his eventual meeting with Allah, when they would be free to exploit their position to gain access to the locked room in the basement of the fort, where it was rumoured the British gold was held. Abdulazziz did not know that their father felt guilty for denying his younger sons the advantage of an education because of lack of finance. To compensate he gave them, authority that they then exploited. Without education, the brothers retained traditional narrow mindedness when compared with Salim. They naturally opposed their father's attempt to make peace with their neighbour by offering their sister Shalma in marriage in an attempt to unite Naamlah and Haqum. They had previously opposed the mandate of protection after the efforts of the British Lawrence to unite the countries. They could not agree to Salim's leniency towards offenders of their tribe or the leniency shown to their sister Shalma when she subsequently brought dishonour by her affair with the son of the Sheikh of Haqum, the suitor chosen by their then dying father. For Salim, who was advised of his father's death and his elevation to Emir whilst in England, the final straw had been their attack on Ali the servant. It was then that he had banished them from the country.

★

On Farnham's advice, because he had himself been told by his Colonial Office colleagues that the government should consist of family members to ensure loyalty, Salim had invited his brothers to return. Salim wanted Abdulazziz to become *wazir*, minister, for immigration; ensuring that the control of essential foreign labour remained within the power of the family. Abdulazziz, who was a year younger than Salim, could have passed as Salim's father. He was short and obese, with an untrimmed beard stained with henna. He had a permanent stoop from a long-term attachment to a desk. Abdulazziz had managed to get himself educated and was then a clerk in the French Embassy of Syria, where he had resided for the past ten years. Now, with a reputation as an indolent man of dubious character, he supplemented his pay by accepting bribes from those seeking visas to enter Syria. He had been married twice to pubescent Syrian girls, but both had failed to bear him children and were subsequently divorced and returned to the houses of their respective fathers where, no doubt, as they were not virgins, they would stay unwed until they died. Abdulazziz would not admit that he was infertile and was, at the time he received Salim's request to return, about to take a third wife. He left Syria, taking with him the dowry of the girl before his fertility could be tested. Abdulazziz, grateful for the opportunity to return to Naamlah, considered himself adequately qualified. He delightedly looked forward to personally supervising the allocation of visas and the issuing of labour permits to foreign workers, as the uneducated Arabs were unlikely to be suitable employees because they expected women or, in the past, slaves to perform manual tasks. He anticipated adopting the 'rental' business practice, or taking baksheesh royalty payments, that was common in other developing Gulf States. Here a permit application required a resident citizen or local business, in exchange for a percentage of the employees' pay, to provide sponsorship. A local man with several such sponsorships need never do any work to support his family. To ensure compliance with the few local laws that were then written, and to prevent a foreign employee leaving behind a debt, the sponsor, often also the employer, held the passport of an employee and prevented him from transferring to another sponsor for better employment terms. This effectively restored the master-slave relationship of Islamic tradition, in which the employer always held the upper hand and was supported by the local *Sharia* court in any labour dispute, however unlikely. The absence of basic human rights was accepted by expatriate workers, along with the near-unlimited working hours and harsh living conditions, because they could earn many times what they would receive in their own countries, where in many cases human rights and employment conditions would be no better. Expatriate workers did not expect holidays in a land where there was no concept of entertainment other than racing camels mounted by children or taking one's wives to bed. Another attraction for the expatriate was that the democratic principle of no taxation without representation would apply in Naamlah. Abdulazziz expected to benefit from the contributions of many thousands of workers who would clamour to enter the country, for whom he would be sponsor, the remainder being sponsored by other government ministers, businesses, or households requiring domestic servants.

CHAPTER 12

The younger of Salim's brothers, Hammed, who along with Abdulazziz had been responsible for Ali's mutilation, had settled in Cairo after he left the ship that was taking Moosa to Europe. Hammed had found work in a bank where, by devious means, he had been elevated to the post of cashier without any formal education. Unlike his brother, Hammed was tall and slim, with a drooping moustache which he had a habit of stroking in an effort to get it to grow horizontally. His eyesight was poor, making him dependent on spectacles that had unusually thick lenses. Hammed initially left his wife and son Khaled behind in Naamlah until he could support them. They later joined him and Hammed enrolled Khaled at the school in Hamburg where Moosa was a student. How Hammed could afford this on the meagre salary of an Egyptian cashier could only be guessed. Salim was impressed, assuming that his brother was successful due to his efforts, and decided that he must have misjudged him and now thought him sufficiently qualified to be Finance Minister. Thus, he ensured family control of the Nation's wealth. Hammed immediately agreed to return, expressing gratitude and loyalty to Salim. Inside he still resented the treatment he had received from his brother and resolved to serve only his own interest from his new position, which he was sure would offer even greater potential for embezzlement than he had found at the Egyptian bank.

On his return from exile, Hammed had been invited to stay with Idris al-Jaboo until he could find a suitable house commensurate with his status as a minister of the government. Idris' motive was to have an influential contact within both the al-Wyly tribe and the government. Hammed had been impressed by the lifestyle and affluence acquired by his old friend during the decade of his exile in which he had struggled to make his way in Egypt. He was sufficiently sophisticated to realise that he would be expected, one day, to repay his host's generosity and saw nothing wrong in being placed under such an obligation.

Idris had established himself and his extended family in a secure location spread over several acres on a rocky peninsula overlooking the sea. Here he was in the process of gathering together the members of the al-Jaboo tribe in a complex of buildings which would ultimately be enclosed by a massive security wall, from where they could challenge the rule of the al-Wyly. Idris was optimistic that his prayers would result in ill fate befalling Salim and his tribe and that this would one day be the seat of the new ruler, Emir Idris. Hammed was offered a luxuriously appointed house awaiting occupation by one of Idris' family, who was currently living abroad. Idris impressed Hammed with plans for a palace and garden which would, one day dominate the tip of the peninsula, where it would be almost surrounded by sea. A private beach would be created by importing sand on a massive scale from the desert of the interior. A private security force was being established, virtually a small army and navy, which would protect the family from intrusion, consisting of armed men to patrol the parapet of the proposed wall and a flotilla of armed boats to patrol the coast around the peninsula. When Hammed showed interest in the plans, Idris went into more detail, saying that the complex would be self-sufficient, with water taken from the sea to cool diesel electricity generators. The heated water would be distilled and used as a supply of potable water. Treated effluent would be recovered and used for irrigation of lawns and gardens which were to be both decorative and a secure source of fresh vegetables and fruit. To Hammed, as to many other ordinary citizens who had been privileged to be shown the plans, it resembled their concept of heaven. The al-Jaboo tribe had built up their assets over generations as pirates and slave traders until the British and French Navies intervened after 1833. Then they diversified into monopolisation of the local pearl and fishing activities. During the two World

Wars they had invested in the American and European arms manufacturing industries, and were currently investing in European property.

Idris explained, "Unlike our country, which did not allow foreigners to hold property, in the West they gave financial assistance to foreigners who wanted to develop the land. It never ceases to amaze me how these governments, in their desperation to retain power, would give away their taxpayers money to foreigners to provide employment which would ensure their re-election."

"Seeing this consequence, it is little wonder that families like yours so vehemently oppose democratic reform," observed Hammed.

"We do indeed, but we use the West to educate our sons, who we were sending to European schools even before oil was discovered. If they survive the temptations of the decadent West, they will soon be returning with expectations of occupying influential positions in Naamlah's Government and private Businesses," replied Idris with a sly grin.

Hammed thought, "It is right that from these positions they would be expected to honour their family by ensuring its continued prosperity," as he intended to do by ensuring that Khaled would be placed in a position of authority following his education. It was during his stay with Idris that Hammed jealously aspired to match the wealth of his old friend and realised that his new appointment was to be the gateway to achieving this.

Hammed saw his first task as that of establishing a banking system and a currency.

★

Hammed explained to Salim when Farnham was present that Naamlah needed to have a currency and at least one bank, because it was not going to be practical to continue trading on the anticipated scale using the gold and silver coins issued by Austro-Hungary and other countries. Farnham agreed and recommended that they appoint an international banking expert to advise the Finance Ministry, as had the other Ministries in their respective fields.

Hammed quickly and forcefully responded, "No. That is not necessary. Unlike the others, I am already an expert in my field.

Why waste our resources paying the salary and expenses of such a person, who would probably rob our beloved country."

"You are probably right, brother," agreed Salim, and suggested that Hammed should, as soon as possible, visit Europe and establish an account there into which the oil revenues should be paid. Farnham, though suspicious of Hammed, thought it best not to argue against the united will of both brothers. Farnham was particularly concerned that Hammed's appointment as Finance Minister had inspired Idris al-Jaboo to re-establish their old boyhood friendship, as he had been warned in London about the criminal past of Idris and his tribe.

"I shall make my second task that of forming a National Bank of Naamlah, and then allow private sector banking," proclaimed Hammed.

"I agree, brother, but I understand that our currency would have to be tied to the US Dollar, because that is used by all of the oil producers," said Salim.

"It would be advisable not to call the new currency Dollars," added Farnham, showing alarm.

"Of course, Mister Farnham, let us use Rials like the neighbours," said Hammed, to which Salim nodded in agreement. "Do you also agree, brother, that I should seek designs for our currency whilst in Europe, and that I find a mint for our Rials?" asked Hammed. Salim confirmed this and ended the meeting.

After Hammed and Farnham had departed, Salim relaxed, thinking, "I am fortunate to have off-loaded another of my many burdens, and only hope that Hammed can be trusted."

★

Hammed had never visited Europe before, but he was aware that Switzerland was likely to provide the degree of banking secrecy necessary for his plan. Enquiries among his contacts in Egypt revealed the name of a bank known to be discreet when handling the dubious accounts of corrupt foreign politicians. After acquiring suitable European attire, he contacted the bank and arranged a meeting with its owner.

CHAPTER 13

Hammed, who was not accustomed to being seen in public with a naked head, was uncomfortable and felt that his movements were restricted by his expensive hand-made pin-striped suit, from the breast pocket of which sprouted a red spotted handkerchief. He was sitting in the panelled splendour of the proprietor's office at the small Banque Internationale de Zurich. He played nervously with his reluctant-to-straighten moustache. Although familiar with the interior of banks at their cash handling end, he had never before been received by the owner of one, particularly an owner such as Herr Graff, who occupied such a magnificent office in which hung a portrait of his monocled grandfather, founder of the establishment. The portrait immediately attracted Hammed's attention. He thought, "How like the portrait Graff looks." Of course, such conceit was haraam in Islamic culture, "but we have to deal with these infidels and must accept their strange ways when it suits our ends," he conceded. The "infidel" looked up from the papers Hammed had presented after their introductions.

"So, your Excellency, we are to accept all of the US Dollar funds incoming to the Treasury of Naamlah, and each month transfer it in your currency to your National Bank?"

Hammed had not yet become accustomed to his title and momentarily thought Graff was addressing someone else who had entered the office unannounced. He took the opportunity to relax until he realised Graff was staring at him and expecting a response. Hammed lost his composure and started to perspire, cursing the suit.

"Er, exactly, Herr Graff," he replied, using a pause to sip the coffee that had been provided by Graff's secretary to disguise his inattention. "Vile concoction," thought Hammed, picturing in his mind a urinating camel. He wiped his moustache on his sleeve and forced a smile as Graff continued.

"The monthly cash flow is, I believe, expected to be modest until your oil production is established, after which you anticipate an annual flow, if you will excuse my metaphor, near a hundred billion dollars." Hammed nodded nervously, momentarily unable to speak in his excitement at the realisation of how smoothly his plan was proceeding. "I realise that the payment of interest on the account balance is usually an embarrassment in your culture, Excellency."

"Not an embarrassment, but prohibited by Islam," replied Hammed.

"In this case, it will be a considerable sum. Does Naamlah have any requirements such as an alternative designation as profit for this money?" asked Graff. He had hopes of the simple Arab dismissing the requirement entirely and allowing the bank to make additional profit by disguising notional interest within charges for currency exchange.

"I, er … we shall require interest, or profit as we call it, to be credited to a separate deposit account. We shall use the proceeds for charitable work," replied Hammed hastily.

"Very commendable, Excellency," replied Graff, thinking, "The sly devil, next he will be asking to make himself the beneficiary, but that is not my business, as long as we have the account." "The accounts will be referred to only by number, I understand, Excellency?" asked Graff, anticipating Hammed's next move.

"Of course. For security, only I shall be given the numbers," replied Hammed. He maintained what he hoped to be a calm professional exterior appearance as he said this, but inside Hammed was tight as a bowstring. He decided to place the saucer on Graff's desk because he sensed his hand was about to reveal his anxiety by rattling his cup.

"I am afraid in the case of a national account like this we have to nominate a bank as beneficiary," replied Graff, thinking, "Perhaps that will persuade him to dismiss the requirement." Hammed's hand with the saucer jerked involuntarily as he feared his plan was to unravel and he nearly missed the desk. "In your case, I am sure there would never be a problem, but we have had, shall we say, embarrassments with some of the developing countries where their rulers treat the nations funds as their own, Excellency," grovelled Graff who was now as nervous as Hammed.

"I understand, Sir. Certainly, for the main account, but perhaps as I shall be the administrator and trustee of the interest or profit account it will not be necessary for that one," replied Hammed, his perspiration now starting to show. Hammed reached for the cup and took a long sip, replacing it on the saucer quickly, before his tendency to tremble was apparent to Graff.

"Of course, Excellency. You will understand that for the bank's protection we shall need your signature to a form of indemnity."

Hammed fought to maintain composure, gripping the arms of the chair so that his hands could not shake, as it became obvious that Graff realised his plan. "Excuse me. It is much warmer in Zurich than I expected," said Hammed, reluctantly releasing the chair to take the spotted handkerchief from his breast pocket. He wiped his forehead, returned the handkerchief, and re-attached himself to the chair.

Graff noticed Hammed's anxiety and added, "The document will not leave the bank, Excellency." Hammed could not conceal his relief and forced himself to finish the coffee. "More coffee, Excellency?" asked Graff.

"No, no thank you, Herr Graff."

"Then our business is complete. If tomorrow your Excellency can return for the official signing, the rest can be safely left to the bank," said Graff, rising to extend his hand. Hammed rose from the chair and grasped the hand firmly. Graff placed his arm around Hammed's shoulders and lead him towards the door, noticing with amusement how the heat of Hammed's perspiring body could be felt through the material of his suit. "I trust the personal arrangements at the hotel were to your liking, Excellency," asked Graff as they descended in the lift.

"Oh, indeed, Herr Graff, quite a change from the hospitality of our country." Hammed said, picturing the young blonde-haired companion with whom he had spent the previous night.

"You would like the same company this evening, Excellency?" whispered Graff.

"Indeed, yes," replied Hammed, impatiently anxious to be away before his composure was lost. Graff delivered Hammed to a waiting limousine and bade him a pleasant evening. Hammed relaxed in the car and expressed his gratitude to Allah in a silent prayer.

CHAPTER 14

One of the rooms in the dungeon of the fort, known as the strong room, had always been kept locked. Unlike the others, which had iron gates, this one had a heavy teak door, like a miniature version of the main gate of the fort. Fatima had asked Nahla about this room, but she said she had been unable to reveal its history. She said she knew only that the key was held by the Emir. The girls agreed that whoever of them next saw him she should ask Ali what secret it concealed. Ali and Nahla were walking along the shore when she remembered the mysterious room.

"Ali, what secret does my father keep in the cell with the wooden door?"

"That is the old treasury, child. Once I helped carry the English gold there," replied Ali proudly. "I suspect it has all been spent now," he added.

"Are there jewels in there?"

"I think there was Layla's wedding gold, and that of your mother. One day I expect some of it will be yours when you marry. There were some old weapons and Persian pots. Oh, and also some old rusting body armour, which I believe was also left by the Persians – they must have taken it from crusaders a long time ago." Nahla was not impressed and was soon distracted by a big red jellyfish, recently washed onto the beach. She gave no more thought to the strong room now that its mystery had been revealed.

★

When Ali had earlier passed on the disappointing news that Salim's brothers were to be re-instated, only he and Shalma reacted. She had a deep loathing of her brothers, for the treatment they had delivered to her when she was the girl who dishonoured the family. The other ladies could not mistake the deeper than usual depression that now dominated her pitiful life. Fousia, who was then a small child, had not been aware of the enmity between her uncles and her aunt, which was now explained by the other ladies. Ali, who had not seen the brothers since their exile, certainly had no desire to meet them again and was also upset. That night Nahla's starwatching, whilst thinking of Saif, was disturbed by aunt Shalma's weeping. She also noticed that night that Ali was not snoring. His mind was racing through the events that preceded the attack.

Then he was a headstrong and virile youth with a passionate desire for the young wife of the Emir. His passion had been reciprocated by the girl, who had been temporarily deserted by her husband. That night he had collected the water as usual and had placed a pitcher outside each of the lady's rooms, ready for their morning ablutions. Hers was the last one. He was wise enough not to take the water inside but left it outside so that the other ladies would not suspect anything untoward if they should visit the lavatory. The couple had always been quiet, though she longed to shout her gratitude at the climax, because both knew that the sound of their lovemaking would carry to the adjacent rooms, where on one side Layla and her little daughter Fousia slept, and the other where Shalma lay sulking.

Ali found the girl waiting impatiently in anticipation of their union. Silently and in haste she helped removed his turban and dishdash, throwing them to the floor, where Ali had already kicked his sandals, in her eagerness for him to embrace her nakedness. Ali joined her within the net that hung from the posts of her bed where the bliss of their nocturnal coupling was to be enjoyed.

Hammed had been suspicious of the water servant since he once had cause to return to the fort in the small hours of the morning, after an assignation with an obliging widow in the town. Then he had wondered, as he saw Ali leaving the harem; why was the servant about at this hour? He must be up again before prayers and has a day's work ahead of him. Hammed mentioned this event to his brother Abdulazziz and they decided to observe the activities of the servant the following night.

Hidden by the shadows beneath the stairs that lead to the gallery they saw that, after he had delivered water to the brother's rooms, he carried three pitchers to the harem and then returned to the kitchen windlass to draw one more. This time he did not return from the women's quarters. They guessed what was happening between Ali and the girl and it made them both jealous, as both of them coveted their elder brother's young wife. Neither had seen a girl so beautiful and desirable. They had both fantasised about her during the nights and longed to "comfort" her whilst Salim was in England. Salim was even then on the ship that carried him home through the Suez Canal at the end of his studies and his meeting with the English government in London. The brothers were both perplexed and asked themselves, "Why a servant, no better than a slave, when she could have chosen a man?"

"We shall render him unable to repeat this treachery," whispered Abdulazziz. They each drew their *khanjar* and crept up the stairs that lead to the gallery, where they found the door to the harem unlocked. Pushing open the door and by the moonlight that filtered through the screens, they could see four pitchers outside four doors but neither knew who slept in which room, as they had never previously entered this part of the fort. Abdulazziz signed for his brother to remain still whilst he listened in turn at each door that led from the main room. There was no mistaking the suppressed orgasmic sounds of delight that emanated from the room that was obviously hers. Abdulazziz beckoned Hammed to his side, and between them they forced open the locked door. They tore away the mosquito net, grabbed the naked, startled Ali and dragged him from the moaning girl. Her beauty was revealed by moonlight to excite their jealousy of the servant. She wanted to scream, but knew the price would be her death by stoning, if others learned of her adultery. Ali also stayed quiet for the same reason as he was dragged fighting from the harem and onto the stairs. He was held here with a *khanjar* to his throat by Hammed whilst Abdulazziz took Ali's manhood with his *khanjar*, throwing Ali's testes to the creatures of the night. For Ali, this nightmare continued year after sweating heart-pounding year as he lay in his bed.

★

Salim, now Emir, was distraught when he learned what had happened, but his love for her was so great that he showed compassion, insisted that her adultery be concealed and swore the brothers to secrecy. Out of respect for a promise made to his late father, Salim had Ali's wound treated and allowed him to remain at the fort. Salim's first night with the girl after his return was a disaster. He thought then that it was the knowledge of her infidelity, or possibly the burden suddenly placed on his shoulders by the death of his father, but on each subsequent meeting with his young wife, his impotence was still apparent. It was awareness of his impotence as much as his disgust of his brothers that made Salim angry enough to authorise their banishment. Salim reluctantly accepted the baby, Nahla, who ultimately arrived as his daughter, but he never again addressed or acknowledged Ali. Salim was distraught at the prospect of his enemies learning of his impotence and he pictured himself as being ridiculed for having weak knees, recalling the Arab saying: "A man with many sons must have strong knees."

CHAPTER 15

Though he had initially influenced Salim's policy of installing family members in government, Farnham now believed that, to avoid the problems he anticipated following his investigation of other countries that had passed through the initial phase of development, he should invite the other main families to nominate candidates to head at least some of the less critical ministries. The reaction was not as Salim and Farnham expected, as many arguments followed, but eventually Salim accepted nominees from the most important rival families who had educated their sons to serve as ministers and undersecretaries for the less critical sectors. Each tribal family was anticipating the employment of foreign experts to run their ministries, and for foreign workers to implement their policies. Although they anticipated retaining the workers, they expected the experts to leave as soon as younger members of the family returned to replace them following completion of their education abroad. These, usually the grandsons of tribal leaders, were often reluctant to return after enjoying life in the fleshpots of Europe and had to be induced with promises of ridiculously high salaries, impressive offices and, most importantly, a telephone with which they could run their businesses beyond the ministry.

As Farnham observed, the weakness in this philosophy was that one day, the countries that provided their labour force would themselves prosper and acquire a standard of living comparable with that to which the Naamlahns aspired. When that day came there would be no incentive for the expatriates to work away from their families in a hostile climate, supporting an alien economy that did not respect their human rights. At the same time, the Naamlahns would be enjoying such a high standard of living on the proceeds from oil trading that they would not be amenable to work for a living. He was consoled by the sure knowledge that he would not be around when that happened.

Thus, Naamlah, with its newly anticipated potential wealth, started to embrace the middle of the twentieth century. Coincident with this there was an upsurge of religious fundamentalism amongst those who wanted to maintain the old ways of the seventh century, when Islam was founded. Characteristically this manifested as opposition to democratic freedom, and, notably, the continued subjugation of women, in spite of the contrary practice established by the Holy Prophet in this respect.

CHAPTER 16

After Fatima's latest nuptial visit to Salim, the other ladies were eager to know if she had been successful in his bed. They jokingly questioned her in fine detail about the possible activity between Salim and herself. Fatima told Layla and Fousia of her disappointment and they agreed she had done all that could be expected and that they would have done the same if they had been given the opportunity. Layla, the self-appointed expert in these things, told her not to worry, she would think of something. Layla despaired because every herb with known or possible aphrodisiac properties had been tried, even, at great expense, rhinoceros horn, which had regularly been added to his food by the cooks, who were enthusiastically in on the conspiracy. She recalled for the amusement of the others the early days of her marriage to Salim when, in her ignorance, for she had only reached puberty a few months earlier, she had a mental picture of him as a ram amongst his ewes, with herself a ewe. After the marriage, she realised she had not been far wrong. Consequently, Layla found difficulty picturing her husband in his present condition. She continued to recount their early sexual experiences with enthusiasm to the others. Nahla was mystified by this conversation.

★

Farnham was called to the fort one day just as he and Rasha were about to set forth on a camping expedition into the cooler environment towards the mountains. Their house could be tolerably cool when there was a breeze off the sea, but it rarely penetrated as far inland as their location. They longed for the day the electricity supply would be connected, when they would be able to enjoy air conditioning. Until then, trips to the hills gave them their only sure release from the oppressive heat of summer. The Farnhams counted the days until their first leave, when they would be reunited with their sons at his parent's home in West Sussex. On this occasion, Rasha was invited to wait with the women of Salim's household whilst the men completed their business. Rasha was taken to them by a friendly and tubby man. He appeared to be on intimate terms with the ladies, who treated him like one of their own and covered neither their hair or their faces when he entered their sitting room. He introduced her to Layla. They were in a large room from which several doors led to sleeping rooms, she assumed. At the far end of this room was a curtain in front of which there was a row of high platform shoes. She guessed this was the lavatory. It reminded her that another of her ambitions was to have a flush toilet at the Farnham residence. The harem was less oppressive than her own house because of the pierced screens and proximity to the sea, she observed. She guessed that the men's quarters on the north side were even more comfortable. Rasha had been raised in a liberal family and had not suffered the segregation, or regime of herma, to inferior quarters which the Arab women accepted. She recalled attending an outdoor exhibition to celebrate a national festival in Naamlah, where the men and women spectators had been confined to opposite sides of the parade. If separation of a family in such circumstances was not bad enough, she was shocked to find that the men were sitting in the shade whilst the women had to endure glaring sunshine. The ladies, who she thought were all exceedingly attractive, although Layla's skin was showing her age, each had dark eyes, accentuated by kohl make-up and olive oil skin. They all wore plain loose cotton trousers which ended above their slippers, decorated with sequins and brightly coloured braids of silk. On top, they wore what she would have described as a caftan, with an embroidered front and neck openings. The caftan reached to their thighs. The young ones had gold head decorations, but the two older ladies had their hair in decorative combs. All four had plaits of jet-black hair that, without the combs, would have reached below their waists. Rasha felt out of place in her camping outfit of linen slacks and long-sleeved blouse. She removed her white scarf from her blonde hair when she realised that it was appropriate to do so. More even than their beauty, it was their jewels that fascinated Rasha. All of the ladies wore rows of bracelets of silver and gold with several expensive-looking jewelled rings on their fingers. They each wore heavy gold necklaces but the two young girls, as well as their head decorations, also had enormous silver ankle decorations, which were hollow and contained something that rattled musically as they moved gracefully about the room.

The ladies were all taken by Rasha's blonde hair, the colour of which neither of them had seen before, except in European magazines. They tried to avoid catching her eye as Layla welcomed Rasha in Arabic, which she was pleased to see that the visitor understood. She introduced Rasha to Fousia, Fatima and Nahla, who each bowed their heads and smiled. Rasha was invited to sit amongst them whilst the fat man they called Ali was sent to find the mermaid and ask her to bring tea. Rasha could not wait to see 'the mermaid'.

"I am sorry that you had to interrupt your journey with your husband, Mrs Farnham," said Layla politely.

"Oh, that is no problem, and please call me Rasha. If I had not been diverted, I would not have had the pleasure of meeting yourselves or seeing inside this beautiful room," replied Rasha, in what Layla decided was beautifully accented Arabic.

"You think our room is beautiful?" asked Fousia.

"Yes, particularly the carvings on the ceiling beams and all the fabrics on walls, and these wonderful cushions," enthused Rasha. She asked Layla, "Do you dress in such fine clothes and jewels all the time?"

"Oh, indeed we do, for there is no point in having these things unless we can make use of them, and otherwise our lives would be very dull."

"Would you like to see my shells?" asked the pretty youngest girl, called Nahla.

"Yes, please."

"Come. I will show you," said Nahla, rising gracefully and taking Rasha's hand.

Inside her little room, Nahla revealed her collection and explained how she had collected the shells since she first began to walk. Rasha was very impressed by her decorations and said, "Sometimes my husband and I picnic on the beach and I collect shells, but nothing on this scale."

Nahla looked puzzled and asked, "What is that word, 'picnic'?"

"I am sorry, it is a word we use in English for a meal away from home," Rasha replied.

"I have never had a meal away from the fort," said Nahla, sadly. "Do you have picnics in many places?"

"Yes. My favourite is near the mountains to the south, where we were going today, where it is so cool," said Rasha enthusiastically. They heard Fousia calling to tell them that the tea had arrived, so they joined the others and resumed their places on the cushions. Ali had brought the tea, so she assumed she was not going to see who or what was the 'mermaid,' unless that was what they called him. The thought amused her. Layla poured the tea into china bowls that she noticed were without handles. Nahla offered her halwa, which Ali carried in a bowl to each of the group as they daintily scooped out a small amount of the warm sticky toffee-like sweet with their fingers. He produced small cloths on which they wiped their hands.

"Layla, Rasha says that she and Mister Farnham take meals out to the beach and also to the mountains. Could we do that?" asked Nahla.

"I doubt if the Emir would allow us such freedom," replied Layla.

"You are fortunate to have visited our mountains. I went once when I was a little girl. It was so cool and fresh after being in the fort," said Fousia, thoughtfully.

"My brothers took me once, but it rained," said Fatima, speaking for the first time. She continued, "I expect you have been all over the world with your English husband?"

"Not quite, but I have seen a lot of Asia and Europe. Even before I met my husband in Eritrea, I had travelled a lot as a teacher," said Rasha.

"How exciting. You were working as a woman and unmarried?" asked Fousia.

"The men would never allow us to do that, would they Fatima?" asked Nahla.

"No. What did you teach?" asked Fatima.

"I taught the English language," replied Rasha.

"We have not even been taught our language, except for the Koran. At least, not to be able to write and read it," said Layla.

"Where did you learn to be a teacher?" asked Fousia.

"I attended a university in Cairo where I read, that is, studied English," replied Rasha.

"Oh. How fortunate you are."

At that moment one of the doors opened and a servant girl, who looked almost Chinese to Rasha, came out and smiled. Fousia smiled back conspicuously. The servant disappeared through the door by which Rasha had entered.

"She is our mermaid; that is what we call her. She is a Malay named Mariam," said Fousia.

Rasha was pleased that they did not call the fat man a mermaid. She wondered who else lived here. "Are there any more people here?" asked Rasha.

"Shalma, my elder aunt, is in her room. You are unlikely to meet her, I am afraid," said Fousia.

Rasha, whose first feelings were of envy for the ladies' comfortable lifestyle, now started to sympathise with the women of the fort as she discovered their ignorance and naivety and thought it especially sad that the young girls, Nahla and Fatima, should have to be brought up in such an environment.

★

When eventually they were enjoying the picnic, she spoke to her husband on the subject of educating at least the young girls.

"I can mention it to the Emir, but I fear he is not keen for the women to become too worldly because it would give ammunition to his fundamentalist critics. He certainly would not allow them to attend a class outside the fort."

"My dear, that would not be necessary; I have unlimited spare time and would welcome the opportunity to teach them, at least to read and write. It would get me out of our depressing house, and if I taught them English it would open their lives. The Arabic stories that the Malay girl reads to them are so puerile."

"You must be aware that Fousia has an unnatural relationship with the Malay servant, otherwise she would have been given in marriage years ago."

"I suspected that, and no doubt the young Nahla will soon be marriageable," replied Rasha.

"You must be careful not to compromise their marriage prospects by making them too wise, my dear."

★

Farnham approached Salim on behalf of his wife and asked if he would object if she gave lessons to the two princesses, Fousia and Nahla, and his wife Fatima. Salim reacted strangely and became serious, Farnham thought.

"Mister Farnham, I have no objection to the teaching, but I will not have the girls called princesses," Salim said sternly.

"Just as you wish, sir," replied Farnham.

"One day you may know why I have always discouraged the women from using that title."

★

When Rasha Farnham visited the harem again she found Nahla sitting in front of Fousia, who was kneeling to apply henna decorations to the feet of her young stepsister. Fousia stood to welcome Rasha, who asked about the treatment being received by Nahla.

"It is something that we do to each other to relieve our boredom," explained Fousia. Layla, who had heard them talking, came into the room and welcomed Rasha. The ladies were eager to know if the subject of tuition had been discussed by her husband with the Emir. Rasha confirmed that it had and told the women of her conversation with her husband and the news that Salim had subsequently agreed for her to visit daily to teach the girls to read and write in Arabic.

The two girls were full of enthusiasm, and Layla asked, "Dear Rasha, will you also be able to teach them English?"

"Well, your husband did not say I could not," she replied, smiling at the prospect.

"Oh, how wonderful!" said an excited Fatima, jumping up and down like a child promised a birthday party.

On Rasha's next visit she went prepared to teach the two young girls, but was surprised to find that Layla and her daughter Fousia wanted to join her class. After she realised how excited the others were becoming, in anticipation of Rasha's next visit, Shalma came out of her room and asked to join them. The others welcomed her, all thinking it could only be good for Shalma to have an interest outside herself.

CHAPTER 17

Salim's sons, unlike the female members of his family, had not been deprived of education. They were both in Europe learning the languages which would subsequently get them into University. Salim had been advised that Saif, designated to replace his uncle Hammed to control the finances of the Emirate, should read economics and accountancy whilst Moosa, who was his heir, should read politics and later enter a military academy. Saif had been enrolled in Salim's old school on the bank of the River Orwell in Suffolk, England. It had changed little since Salim had attended in the 1930s. Here he worked extra hard to divert his mind from a near depressed state, for he was homesick for the sea and sun of his country. He missed Nahla, who he then thought could never be replaced in his heart by another. Saif knew it was wicked to think of his sister the way he did, but he could not help his feelings, and as long as they were separated it could not do harm. At least he could maintain his interest in sailing. This was an interest shared by an older Arab boy who befriended him. Saif proved to be a model student and was soon sufficiently fluent in English to start further studies.

This was a language that Moosa should also have been studying in Germany, but he avoided classes in this subject because he saw it as irrelevant to his future as Emir and concentrated on German, as this was the language in which he would be taught other subjects. More importantly, to Moosa, German helped him to navigate the Hamburg night spots. As with many Muslim men, Moosa had no qualms about multiple sexual relationships, even when married, because Sharia law allows them when away from home, to take temporary *nykah mut'ah*, pleasure wives, who they should, in theory at least, divorce after the *fajr* morning prayer. Often this is interpreted loosely to allow casual sex with women other than Muslims, usually prostitutes, as Sharia does not have such a concession for Muslim women who must comply with the sex-only-in-marriage code, frequently on pain of death. Most nights Saif thought about Nahla, often wondering how she was managing without his company. He thought less frequently of how his elder brother Moosa was enjoying his schooling in Hamburg. Nahla, who was illiterate as far as Saif knew, had made Ali write to say that soon Naamlah would have telephones, and they would be able to communicate regularly. For Saif, that day could not come too soon. Saif's Arab friend, Kareem, came from Haqum. His father, the Sheikh who ruled that little impoverished country, had sent him to England to eventually learn about petroleum engineering. Kareem joked that his father, in spite of negative survey results, was ever optimistic of oil being discovered in their country and wanted to be prepared. Kareem said he had a younger brother, the same age as Saif, who was in America learning accountancy. Their father wanted Mohammed to read economics, with a view to having him look after the oil revenues for which he regularly prayed. The Sheikh had made great sacrifices to finance his sons' education and they were both therefore determined to repay him one day.

Kareem's home, like Saif's, was on the Persian Gulf Coast, where both boys had been keen sailors in their local craft, and they were surprised that they had not met whilst sailing. They needed no incentive to take advantage of the dingy sailing facilities at the school, but they wanted something bigger to enter in races. They found an old centre-board sloop for sale at Pin Mill, and between them they scraped together enough to buy her. Kareem was a particularly good sailor who, with Saif as crew, consistently did well in local races on the river in their small yacht. After one such event, the boys had returned the boat to her mooring, subsequently rowed to the school quay, and were now walking from the river to their dormitories.

"Your father would not allow our friendship if he knew of it, Saif," said Kareem.

"Why ever not?" asked Saif, wondering what had prompted this statement.

"Do you not know the history of our families?"

"I know there was a feud, but that was bought off by the British, I understood," replied Saif.

"Yes, in theory, but even after a hundred and fifty years the wound still festers in the heart of the older generation, particularly with your uncles, I believe. Besides, the gold has all gone now, and the reason it was given will soon be forgotten. I hope it does not destroy our friendship."

"We cannot disobey our fathers. I suppose if we do not tell them about it, they cannot tell us to end it," said Saif, thoughtfully.

Kareem laughed, "I have already told mine, and he did not object. That is why I raised the subject. I suspect your father is under greater influence from others in your family," said Kareem.

"I know you are right. He has always tried to be progressive, but he is watched by his rivals and by the clerics. They are not so ready to forget the past whilst the memory serves as a tool in their hands." The boys arrived at the dormitories and entered the showers.

★

Moosa was in his element at his school. He had met and befriended other boys older than himself, some from other Naamlah families, including his cousin Khaled, who had been brought up in Egypt, son of uncle Hammed. Moosa had first found no entertainment to replace the Friday punishment spectacles at the fort but after a few months in Hamburg, this soon changed. The two cousins became best friends, but decided not to let their families know because of the history of their fathers' quarrel over the eunuch. Only later, after Moosa learned of Hammed's recall to Naamlah to be Finance Minister, would the boys be free to admit their friendship with each other. Moosa was never short of friends, although it was not his personality that attracted them. He thought it was his spending power, or the fast sports car, but in reality it was the parents of his friends who insisted they stay close to the future Emir. The car, an MG, certainly impressed the German students, who were mostly from previously wealthy families, temporarily impoverished by the war. It was the Germans who took the Arab boys out of the school to reveal to them the pleasures of the town. The Arabs soon developed a taste for alcohol, forbidden to everyone in Naamlah. Having become bored with tobacco, which, although a drug and arguably *haraam*, was readily available, Moosa and Khaled tried more addictive substances, which were undoubtedly haraam. Unfortunately, Khaled, with less will power than Moosa, became addicted. Their circle frequented the red-light area, where they were regularly entertained by girls from bars who appreciated their generosity, but not Moosa's sadistic tendencies when they were alone with him. He was always expecting to see in the eyes of the prostitutes the defiant look that haunted him since he had witnessed the lashing of Hafrida in the courtyard of the fort. Even when he turned the whips, with which they excited their masochistic customers, on the girls, he only saw alarm and fear, never the black defiant eyes.

As he aged, Moosa decided this was the lifestyle he would like to continue. Only the thought of one day having power over his countrymen, when he became Emir, kept his interest in eventually returning home. Then he expected to continue his playboy role, accepting all the perks of leadership but not the attendant responsibilities. He decided that he would not worry himself about the country and its useless inhabitants like his pathetic overworked father was doing. In the meantime, he was determined to maximise his freedom whilst he was out of Naamlah. One aspect of his return he did find attractive, and that was the marriage that his father had arranged. He knew his wife would not be like the European women, who were all whores. She would, he knew, be untouched and brought up to obey the men of her family, as she would obey him whilst bearing his sons. A way of life to which he would ensure her continued compliance, not by mutual respect and love, for such concepts only existed between men in Moosa's distorted mind, but by violence and abuse. He regularly missed lessons, either because of drunkenness, drugs, or both, but always excelled when tested to assess his progress with the German language. He learned more German in the beds and bars of Hamburg than his fellow students ever learned in the classroom. The school authorities failed to report his behaviour to his father for fear they would lose the income derived from teaching Moosa and the other boys from his country, as they knew, in Arab culture, a bad report would reflect on the school, not on the students.

Salim's sons proceeded to university, where neither of them had been required to compete for a place, as diplomacy prevailed over academic achievement in the case of such high-status students. Saif found this embarrassing, but Moosa thought it only right that the sons of an Emir should be so respected. When it came to their eventual graduation, Saif insisted that he obtain his degree justly, and therefore successfully sat his exams, whilst Moosa accepted what the diplomats had arranged and Allah had provided without question.

In 1958 both of Salim's sons, now men, were looking forward to the end of their studies in Europe. Moosa was anticipating his marriage, if by then an acceptable cousin could be induced to accept him. Saif meanwhile could only think of seeing Nahla, wondering how the young woman, which she must now be, fitted her telephone voice.

★

For their first time, they were each able to fly directly to Naamlah, landing on the runway of the nearly completed airport. From here they were each, on separate occasions, to be conveyed by limousine via the new highway that took them to the fort. Ali was sent each time with the driver to handle their luggage. Saif, who was first to arrive, greeted Ali like an old friend, and cursorily acknowledged the stern-faced Afghan driver, who had not deigned to speak to the servant on the outward journey. The powerfully built Afghan was also a bodyguard who carried a visible firearm, which Saif thought to be quite unnecessary. Ali did not think that Saif, in spite of his height and trimmed beard, had changed from his old sensitive self, and he was pleased to see that Saif must have changed out of European clothes into dishdash and turban before leaving the plane. Ali mused. Gentle and honourable young Saif was to be Finance Minister of their country, whilst his despicable older brother, who had yet to return, was destined to be a soldier.

CHAPTER 18

Saif was surprised to find that the old, almost blind, gatekeeper had been replaced by foreign soldiers. Together with the armed driver, this only gave him a feeling of sadness that civilisation of the country should manifest in this way. He cheered up at the prospect of seeing both Nahla and his father. Before the Afghan could open his door, Saif climbed out and ran across the court-yard towards Salim, who shook his hand, kissed him and pulled him to his chest in a hug of affection. Saif sensed that Salim was worried and was not surprised when Salim soon excused him-self. Nahla had been watching the gate impatiently from behind the screen on the balcony, and as soon as Salim departed, she ran down the stairs to greet the strange, handsome young man who she could hardly believe was her brother. In her dreams he had always appeared just as he was when he left for Europe. Although his voice must have changed whilst they spoke together on the telephone, this had been gradual over many years, but now she could tell it was much deeper and more masculine. She embraced him in what was a particularly undignified manner for an Arab lady. Saif realised that there was indeed now a very desirable Arab lady behind her veil, and to preserve the honour of the family he suggested that they leave the courtyard. Nahla directed him to his old room, which she had insisted be made smart and tidy by Ali and Mariam. Saif suddenly realised from the presence of her veil that Nahla had past puberty. When they were inside and out of sight of the servants and guards, she removed the veil. Saif then saw how beautiful she had become and felt pride in her appearance. When he saw how her abaya hung from her prominent breasts he felt what he knew to be an unnatural longing to embrace the girl that he believed, in ignorance, to be his sister. Nahla, also ignorant of the fact that they shared neither parent, was surprised by how tall he had grown. She thought him very mature in the neatly trimmed beard and moustache that he had been cultivating at University. Suddenly she felt saddened, not because of the obvious fact that they both assumed they were siblings, but because she realised that they would never be able to share interests again. Their culture required that men and women live separate lives, with strict codes of behaviour, until they were wed. Then she shocked Saif by swapping from Arabic to English. This she had kept from him during all their conversations by telephone, because she wanted only to use the language when she was confident that he would not find amusement in her early attempts. She told him how for the past years Rasha Farnham, an Egyptian, had taught all of the ladies in both Arabic and English, and that they had the full support of Salim. Saif then asked her in English about the other family members, of whom Nahla quickly brought him up to date in what he realised was acceptable English. They talked for what was hours but seemed like minutes, swapping between the two languages whenever a word in one was easier to recall. She wanted to know all about England, university, his flying experience, and what he did in his spare time if he was not sailing with his friend Kareem. They talked about their childhood, when there had been no distinction between them on grounds of gender. Then, about when it was too hot to play outside and they had played in the dungeons of the fort. She reminded him of the time when he had rescued her after Moosa had once abandoned her terrified in darkness in one of the cells.

They then noticed the sudden silence as the cicadas switched off for the evening, and Nahla was reminded that it was prayer time. She assumed Saif would want to join the other men at the mosque. "If you are going to pray, I will leave you now," she said, sadly.

Saif was enjoying the company of the only girl he had ever really known and was determined to make the most of this opportunity. "No, I think on this occasion I would rather have your company," replied Saif. He took some matches from a draw in his dressing table, struck one and brought his old room to life with an oil lamp, which caused Nahla to laugh.

"We have electric lights, and Aunt Shalma even has wireless now."

"No doubt we do, but I wanted the atmosphere that I remember," replied Saif. Mention of his aunt reminded him of an earlier time. "Do you still have the doll that we found in one of the cells?" he asked as he moved the lamp to improve his view of her face. "She is stunning," he thought, "will I ever find someone like her whom I will be permitted to marry?" The glow of the lamp and the shadows that it cast refreshed his memory of the first time they had discovered the dungeons. "Do you remember, one of the cells still contained a filthy straw mattress, beneath which a doll had been hidden?"

"Oh, that was very sad. I kept it in my room for years until one day aunt Shalma saw it. She broke down and cried terribly. It belonged to her as a girl, apparently," said Nahla, looking unhappy for the first time since their meeting.

Outside it was dark now and they heard Ali humming as he crossed from the harem. Ali, in his wisdom, was aware of their unnatural attachment to each other and realised that they had been together for longer than was respectable. He realised also that in future he would need to chaperone their meetings more carefully. Nahla guessed that he had been impatiently waiting to come to take her back into his protection and was grateful that he had allowed her to stay with Saif as long as this.

"Do you still sleep at the door?" Saif asked Ali.

"Yes, young master, I still guard the ladies," he replied as he and Nahla started to leave.

"*Tisbah ala khair*," shouted Saif, as they disappeared up the stairs.

★

Saif slept better that night than he had on any night of the past two years. Less fortunate was Ali, who suffered the recurring dream where he was in the hands of Salim's brothers and, as he did frequently, woke in a state of distress, soaked in perspiration. Nahla slept soundly and, on this occasion, failed to notice that Ali's night had been disturbed.

★

When Moosa flew in, two days after Saif, he looked to Ali every bit the European, clean-shaven and in a double-breasted blazer, university tie and grey flannels. Ali thought he could only look more out of place if he still carried his whip. Moosa ignored Ali and ordered the driver to call at the house of his cousin Khaled, where he delivered a small parcel that he had brought from Hamburg and taken through airport security, claiming diplomatic immunity. The pasty-faced, fat Moosa was barely recognised by Ali, who tried to tell him that his father would be insulted by this diversion, but Moosa only cursed and humiliated the eunuch, to the amusement of the Afghan driver, by telling him to mind his own business. When they eventually arrived at the fort, Salim was still waiting to greet his eldest son, and in his enthusiasm to see Moosa he forgot his disappointment at Moosa's poor punctuality and made no comment on the matter. Salim was surprised by how his elder boy had filled out. He thought Moosa looked quite unhealthily obese, compared with his younger son. As they hugged and kissed Salim thought it must be the German diet. He will soon lose his fat when he starts military training.

The next time they met, Salim showed Moosa two photographs of girls, from which he was expected to choose a wife. One was named Hooda, a cousin of Fatima, Salim's recent wife. Since she had been five years old, Salim and Hooda's father had planned for Hooda to marry one of Salim's sons. The other girl was one of Moosa's many second cousins. Both girls, each fourteen years old, looked suitably attractive to Moosa. His eyes dwelt on the photograph of Hooda whilst he ignored the second photograph. Hooda was smiling and showed the perfect teeth and large dark eyes, matching those of the young wife, Hafrida, who he watched

109

being lashed and who haunted him. He tried to imagine Hooda's expression changed to one of defiance.

There was no hesitation in deciding which one he wanted to dominate, but Moosa said, "I would have them both."

Salim did not take him seriously and laughed, "Try one first son. Even she may be more than you can manage."

Moosa thought, "The old fool has not seen me in the whore houses of Hamburg, or he would not find it so funny. He thought he should humour the old man and said, "I will accept the girl Hooda," trying to sound appreciative, and thinking, "I can have more wives later."

"I shall tell her father that you are interested, and we will see if she will accept the future Emir of Naamlah," said Salim, jokingly.

Moosa, who had not given thought to the possibility that she might not find him acceptable, asked, "Would she, a mere girl, re-fuse me?"

"It is her future we must consider as well as yours, my son," re-plied Salim, surprised and disheartened by his son's attitude.

CHAPTER 19

When her father told Hooda that she had been accepted by the Emir's son to be his wife she thought only of Saif, the boy who had saved her from his older brother when she was a small child who Moosa had threatened with his whip. Ever since then she had admired Saif, and as she entered her teens, she had always thought of him as the man she would like to be the father of her children.

★

Salim's sons had been given a *sambuq* by their father when they were teenagers. This was a 20-metre traditional fishing boat, and one of the last remaining craft of its type, which Salim insisted on being built in a failed attempt to preserve the local boat building industry. The boat, with a single large lateen sail and large flat foredeck, had a Malay crew, who had been maintaining her to a high standard, under their skipper Ibrahim, whilst Saif and Moosa were away. Today the Malays were expected to work the boat as the boys and their friends relaxed. The Malays, who did not expect the Arabs to remain sober, resented having their routine disrupted. The young Arabs arrived at the mooring in their sports cars and were ferried to the *sambuq* via the small wooden boat normally carried on the raised aft deck, together with their food and alcohol, the latter hidden from prying eyes. The crew cast off, chanting in their language as they hoisted the lateen sail, taking the boat away to the north on a beam reach. The party relaxed on the extensive teak deck, savouring the cooling breeze of the boat's motion and drinking illicit beer. In Moosa's case, the drink was whisky. He found this mixed better with the harder stuff that he had earlier delivered to Khaled, and which the pair of them were soon sniffing. The other youths were taking turns at a hookah, in which tobacco had been replaced by hashish. All were determined to make the most of the seclusion provided by the boat whilst she was out of sight of land and their families. The Malays tacked the boat into the breeze as it veered to the north, until land could no longer be seen.

As the boat was to go about, after completing a tack to the north east, Ibrahim addressed Saif, who he observed was now the only one of the passengers sober enough to appreciate the sailing experience and who he knew to be a competent sailor: "Master Saif, there are enormous channel buoys ahead."

"Oh, yes Ibrahim, and why should that concern us?" replied Saif, nonchalantly.

"They are new, Master, and they are green. They will be showing the starboard hand approach of the deep water that leads to the little port of Haqum. Strange, that such a place of no importance to shipping should have such a properly marked entrance channel," replied the skipper.

Saif asked, "Where do you think will be the other side of this channel?" Ibrahim reached for binoculars, kept in a bracket on the aft deck where he and Saif stood near the helmsman. Ibrahim scanned the horizon beyond the buoys.

"There, Master. See, it is a very wide channel, must be they are expecting big ships, possibly tankers, I am thinking," he replied as he handed the glasses to Saif. This attracted the other Arabs, who all wanted to look, but most could not focus properly and lost interest.

Moosa was sufficiently conscious to comment, "Why should we be concerned? Haqum is not our country. Get back to handling the boat."

"Yes, Master Moosa," deferred Ibrahim. He then gave the order to go about and the crew eased the sheet, dipped the massive boom, heaved it to the opposite side of the stumpy mast and sheeted the sail on the new tack to head to the North West and away from the line of green buoys. They were now approaching a small uninhabited island, part of Naamlah, lying 20 miles north of the mainland. After rounding the island, the sail was eased for a fast run back to the mooring, as some of the passengers were now suffering sickness.

On arrival at the mooring in darkness, the crew made the sambuq fast and unloaded the drunken passengers into the small boat, which made several trips to deliver the Arabs to their cars. They dispersed noisily towards their respective homes. Saif drove Moosa back to the fort and delivered him to his room, where he flopped onto his bed and immediately started to snore. Saif also slept soundly that night, giving no more thought to the mysterious green buoys.

When Moosa regained consciousness in the morning his first thoughts were of the photographs. He looked at them, relishing the thought that soon he would legally hold the power of life and death over the girl, Hooda.

Because of their inevitable hangovers, the boys missed prayers before sunrise the following morning, Friday, but managed to attend at noon when they heard the *muezzin* calling. They joined Salim to wash before entering the mosque within the fort. Salim was pleased that they were with him because he wanted the congregation to see that his sons were devout and had not been corrupted by their time in Europe. They had not seen much of each other since their return because Salim, who, Saif realised, was still showing the signs of exhaustion that he had detected when they met on his arrival, had been burdened by affairs of government.

As they walked out of the mosque, Saif asked "Are you unwell, father?"

"I have many things to worry about, son. Who would be an Emir in these times?" he replied.

"I will be, one day," said Moosa, without sympathy for his father.

"How was your sail?" asked Salim, ignoring Moosa's remark.

"It was good to be in the warm waters of our country, but not eventful," replied Saif.

"Unless you can call finding a set of giant channel buoys eventful," said his brother, sarcastically.

"There are no buoys in our waters that I know of," said Salim.

"If you saw these you would think that Haqum was to be another Rotterdam," Saif joked.

Salim realised instantly the implication, and that he now had one more burden to contend with. "Excuse me. I must leave now," Salim said abruptly, as he hurried towards his office. As soon as he entered the office, he phoned his son-in-law, the Interior Minister, insisting that he immediately investigate the mysterious buoys.

Salim learned a few days later that the neighbouring country was enlarging their port, served by the deep channel, on which its meagre economy depended. The little country, it was now accepted, did not have oil. Its small population had for generations relied on the export by dhow of fruit and livestock to Persia to ensure their subsistence.

The report that Salim received, and which he and Farnham studied together revealed that Japan, now in the process of rebuilding its economy after the war against America, had been searching for a source of cheap oil. The Japanese, who had studied the Admiralty chart published following the survey of local waters, had realised the potential of Haqum as a deep-water port. They had secretly entered negotiation with the Sheikh to finance construction of an oil terminal, in his country, which was now well advanced. To Japan and Haqum this had been mutually attractive on three counts: first, the Japanese would meet the costs, and provide the necessary expertise and infrastructure. Second, Naamlah may eventually have no alternative to using the facility and would have to pay for the privilege. Third, although this had not subsequently materialised, if oil was found in Haqum, they would be ready for its export to Japan.

Farnham sought professional opinions from several maritime authorities, who all advised that, even if the buoys had not been in what was disputably the territory of Naamlah, it would be too dangerous for the proposed terminal for the oil pipe, on which Naamlah's future development hinged, to be established virtually within the entrance channel of a major port. No insurer would accept the risk.

CHAPTER 20

During her lessons, Rasha could not fail to hear of Salim's afflic-tion, because it was perpetually on the minds and lips of the older women. She told this to her husband when next they were togeth-er. Farnham was amused by this revelation and thought what fine ammunition it would hand to Salim's enemies if it became pub-lic knowledge. Nevertheless, he was sympathetic and offered to make discreet enquiries amongst his contacts at the new hospital.

The women of the fort were excited at the prospect of Moosa's marriage to Hooda. For many of the other women with whom they were acquainted, it would be the first time that their men had allowed them out of the house without a male guardian for many years. A wedding was one of a few social events in the lives of many Arab women. When Hooda had learned that it was Moosa, and not Saif, that she was to marry, she could not hide her disappoint-ment from her mother. Her mother was sympathetic, but told her it would bring dishonour on her father if she refused. "Perhaps he is not like he was as a small boy," she thought, decided not to protest, and was determined to make her father proud of her. Hooda left her father's house full of joy at the prospect of becoming the wife of the son of the Emir. She knew that her duty henceforth would be to obey and honour her husband, bear him many sons, and main-tain the modest disposition that would reflect honour on him. She hoped that in return he would treat her with respect and kindness.

Moosa was given, as a wedding present, a small house by Idris al-Jaboo, who as always was keen to ingratiate the future Emir. It had previously been occupied by one of his sons, who had recently moved to the al-Jaboo complex on the peninsula. It was here that the couple moved after their wedding. The pretty house was protected by a high, white-painted security wall against which bougainvillaea grew, overflowing from the garden inside into the street outside the enclosed compound. The only access gate was attended by two armed soldiers who occupied a small hut, within the compound, close to the gate. Two Muslim Indian servants, a young married couple, lived in a sun-scorched penthouse flat that sat on top of the house's flat roof.

Hooda, who had met Moosa when she was a child of five years and subsequently only briefly before the wedding, had then been impressed by his confidence and felt sure she could easily come to love the boy if he became her husband, even though she thought him quite fat and neither physically nor charismatically attractive. She knew that her family felt honoured that their daughter had been chosen as the first wife of the future Emir. She realised that her feelings towards Moosa were irrelevant and that she would have to honour the marriage regardless of these. On their wedding night, Moosa was determined to establish his dominant role in their relationship by resorting to an outdated and cruel tradition that he had once had described to him. He presented his bride with a white kitten, for which she thanked her husband profusely, cuddling it affectionately like the child she was. Hooda thought then that Moosa was perhaps a more sentimental person than she had previously envisaged. In the evening after the wedding, they retired to the bedroom. Moosa turned out the light beside their bed and asked her to undress. Hooda, having been told by her mother what to expect, obeyed and shyly climbed into the bed. She turned onto her back, taking hold of the kitten and holding it over her chest with one hand whilst with her other hand she pulled the sheet over her nakedness. She was trembling at the prospect of what was to happen next and praying that Moosa would be considerate of her state of anxiety. Whilst Moosa undressed, she affectionately cuddled her present as it lay on her bosom.

Moosa stood beside the bed displaying his manhood, in the light of the moon that illuminated the otherwise darkened room. He waited until she had stopped trembling and said, "Give me the cat."

"Are you taking back the first present you have given, dear husband?" asked Hooda who did not realise her first innocent mistake in questioning his order.

"If I ask you to do something, would you always question me?" asked Moosa, angrily.

"Of course not, dear husband. I am sorry," she replied, smiling because she was thinking only that he was teasing her.

"Then give me the animal that I may show you why a wife should not question her husband," replied Moosa, raising his voice in what Hooda thought to be mock anger. Above them the servants, who had been straining for sounds from the bedchamber, were shocked by this unexpected outburst. Hooda felt no fear and giggled childishly as she passed the little kitten to Moosa. He snatched it cruelly from her and shocked her by holding it by its tail, causing her to wince as the kitten screamed.

She lost her timidity and shouted, "Stupid Moosa! You are hurting the poor thing!"

Hooda no longer recognised Moosa, as his face distorted in anger and she realised he was not joking. He shouted back, "Never question me again for Allah has given me, a man, the power to treat you as I do this animal." He now held the kitten in both hands and twisted its neck, rendering Hooda speechless. When she regained control of her voice, she could only gasp between sobs.

Trembling more than ever she cried, "Forgive me for my impertinence, dearest Moosa." Her plea had no effect, and she stared in horror as the kitten's blood dripped onto the sheet. She realised that what could have been the happiest day of her life had become her worst nightmare. Moosa threw the lifeless carcass onto the floor. As she sobbed it became obvious that Moosa was not the boy she had expected to spend a happy life with. He had changed before her eyes from the honourable man who she had anticipated marrying and learning to love, as she did her father, to a man who she would always hate.

"Just to remind you of my authority. Disobey me, or tell tales to your family, and you will receive the same treatment as the cat," said Moosa, as he excitedly pulled the bloody sheet from her and joined her in their bed. The servants, who had overheard Moosa's louder side of the exchange, looked at each other in disbelief.

The following morning, the servants removed the blood-stained sheet from the matrimonial bed and sent it via one of the guards to Hooda's parents. They expected to see blood, because they were confident of their daughter's virginity, but they were too polite to comment on the unexpected quantity.

Hooda endured two nights of Moosa's physical and mental torture before he returned to Europe to start his military training. She knew now not to expect him to tell her of his plans and received this news from the servants. News that she received with great relief, for she knew that only without his presence would she be spared from a life crueller than death. Moosa left Naamlah disappointed; he had not been able to arouse in Hooda the look of defiance that would enable him to relive the excitement experienced whilst watching the punishment of the black-eyed Hafrida with perfect teeth. He tried to forget his wife by looking forward to resuming his liaisons with the prostitutes of Europe.

★

Layla had invited Hooda to stay at the fort until Moosa returned, but she had to decline because he had forbidden her to leave their house under any circumstances, not even to visit her family. Their servants, the guards and family members were to ensure that she complied with his orders. Moosa forbade her to send letters or use the telephone, which he had disconnected for the duration of his absence. Immediately after Moosa's departure, Hooda tried to leave their house and return to her father, because she was confident that if she explained to him how she was being treated by Moosa he would not let her return. The guards refused to let her pass and insisted that she stay in the house. Her next plan was to disguise herself as the servant, who frequently visited the souk, to get past the guards. She was sure the Indian girl would be sympathetic. Her sympathy did not extend this far, as she explained to Hooda that she and her husband would lose their comfortable positions if they frustrated Moosa's policy of restricting Hooda's movements. Hooda walked the grounds of the house, looking for a weakness in the wall of the enclosure built to protect the al-Jaboos from those they had tricked or robbed for generations, but saw none except the thick bougainvillaea that grew over the walls. She attempted one night to climb out of her prison by clinging to the plant but its thorns, that protected it from all but goats, cut into her skin and tore her clothes, making it impossible to climb. Once each week an Indian was admitted by the guards to tend the garden. Hooda tried to befriend him but he was too frightened to encourage her attempts at conversation. She tried to flirt with the guards, but they also were frightened by her advances, although they admitted sympathy for her plight. Frustrated after trying everything she could think of as a means of escape, she resolved that she would make the most of her imprisonment by directing the servants to maintain the house and garden to a high standard. At least she would make her prison a pleasant place in which to live, she decided.

*

Hooda discovered to her dismay that she was carrying Moosa's child. The thought of a smaller version of her husband at first filled her with horror, but as the creature, as she called it, grew inside her she began to accept the inevitable and started to prepare a room as a nursery.

CHAPTER 21

Rasha had expressed her concern to her husband about the unhealthy lifestyle of her students, who she said lived an unnaturally sedate existence in which they had no opportunity for exercise. After discussing the problem with Salim, it was decided that Moosa's now empty room at the fort should be converted to a gymnasium where the ladies could exercise in privacy.

★

Since his father's death, corresponding with the occasion when he had first noticed his erectile problem, Salim had been accustomed to having administrative problems solved by his Indian assistants, but now, even with Farnham's willing help, he was finding the burden overwhelming as each day seemed to present a new problem. Each minister had commenced construction of impressive buildings to house himself, his undersecretaries, department directors, advisers and civil servants. Not to mention that the oil installations, an assembly building, the airport, roads, hospital, schools, power station, military barracks, broadcasting station, mosques, resident and expatriate housing, and of course Salim's new palace were all draining the nation's finances. The fledgling country was going deeper into debt now that the remnants of gold from the dungeon had been exhausted, jewels that formed the future dowries of Fousia and Nahla had been mortgaged, and Graff's bank in Switzerland had refused any more credit. Their latest resort was a loan from the Bank of England. Such receipts as there were continued to be directed to the numbered account in Switzerland that Hammed had negotiated with Graff, from which regular monthly payments were transferred to Naamlah's National Bank. At the same time, any interest accruing during the month was diverted to Hammed's secret account, ostensibly for charitable purposes. The logical possibility of using this money to offset loan interest, as suggested by Graff, had been strongly discouraged by Hammed. As far as Salim knew, Hammed's arrangements, whereby a smooth cash flow was maintained, had been successful and accepted by the other ministers, as it facilitated the monthly payments of salaries and invoices for all the government departments without large quantities of cash either lying idle, or worse, from the Islamic viewpoint, earning interest. The loans that Hammed had achieved from abroad, together with investment by optimistic companies, had funded the construction of oil wells in the interior, of which several were now ready to go on stream. They only required the pipelines that would deliver oil to the recently completed storage tank farm on the coast. From here oil would be shipped to customers via the proposed deep-water floating terminal, which had yet to be delivered because of the unfortunate discovery that the deep-water had been annexed by their neighbouring country. This problem, for the time being, had been left to the will of Allah whilst progress was made on the construction of a refinery to meet the growing demands for motor fuel and electricity generation.

In response to lobbying by the important families, Hammed had not imposed any limit on the liquidity ratio of their banks, the proportion of funds to be kept in reserve. As each family had effective control of its bank, they had drawn heavily on reserves to meet their extravagance and to finance their particular interests in the private sector. Small depositors, mainly foreign workers, shopkeepers, subsistence farmers and fishermen were becoming aware of the unstable financial situation through their contacts with bank personnel. The expatriate workers were of late opting to take their salaries in cash or to remit it in gold, and this was causing rumours of imminent banking failure to spread amongst the population.

A fledgling stock market had been established to give ordinary citizens a stake in the potentially booming economy, but thus far confidence in Naamlah's businesses was low because of a natural distrust of the families behind them and of those who were also major stockholders. The families saw the local stock market as their private means of enhancing their fortunes and resented the common people, who dared to follow their examples, also benefiting. The best brains were employed by the families to flout rules intended to protect citizens from exploitation. One such citizen was Abdul Bawani, an enterprising but unsophisticated camel dealer who, when he realised roads were being constructed, decided that his business would be under threat from the motor car. Abdul sold everything necessary for the camel trade, including his breeding stock, to invest the resulting capital in war surplus vehicles. His thinking was that these would be suitable for both new roads and old desert trails. Abdul employed Indian mechanics, who had gained experience in the war and who enhanced his reputation for after-sales service. Soon he was receiving orders for Willis jeeps and Land Rovers from old camel customers from all parts of the country. The business thrived for a time, but as the desert trails were replaced by roads his customers were asking for less rugged but more comfortable transport. Abdul decided to expand into new auto sales, and knowing how popular one brand was in other Gulf countries, he went and bought three new air-conditioned saloons. These cost him every Rial that he could spare, but they sold immediately at a profit. His next move was to import vehicles directly from the German manufacturer. Even though they were impressed by his order book and after-sales reputation, to be their agent they needed him to invest in a showroom, parts warehouse and a more sophisticated workshop. Abdul called on the manager at the bank of the al-Jaboos and told him of his plans in expectation of obtaining a loan to finance the agency required by the auto manufacturer. The bank manager agreed that it was an attractive proposition, but was otherwise non-committal, and asked Abdul to wait until he could put the loan application before his directors.

Idris was informed of Abdul's loan request by the manager who was obliged to notify him of any propositions that looked like they would be successful. Idris realised that this was a proposal from which he could benefit and immediately contacted the German firm, offering one of his companies as an agent, with an assurance that he had ample funds, backed by his bank, to provide all of the facilities required from Abdul. This was accepted and Idris' company became sole agent for the German company in Naahmlah. Had they known that the bank was already overextended with Idris' other projects, they might have discovered that Abdul with his large customer base might have been a less risky partner. Attempts were made by Abdul to take legal action against the bank, but he was not successful because the family, which had members in both the legal profession and in the court, saw family honour as being more important than justice.

Abdul was left with only a small general garage, car hire, war surplus and second-hand auto business. He felt let down by the government when he saw that all the ministries were placing orders with Idris' company for their official cars. Other families followed Idris' example and set up agencies for foreign companies, such as American air-conditioner and refrigerator manufacturers. Representation had been made to Hammed at the Finance Ministry by other enterprising firms that had been let down by the banks in similar situations, but Hammed, who was beholden to Idris and the other big families, failed to support their complaints.

It was, to Saif, obvious that enterprise was being stifled unless it benefited at least one of the six big influential families. Saif, in his lowly position at the Finance Ministry, could not influence his uncle, but resolved to change the situation as soon as he had the power to do so.

CHAPTER 22

Moosa was nearing completion of his military officer training, and Saif was established working with his uncle Hammed at the Finance Ministry. Saif had decided that he should enter at the lowest level, working with the expatriate civil servants, to understand the workings of the Ministry by progressing through each department before taking over as Minister from his uncle.

Completion of a contract to provide the main pipe and intermediate pumping stations to bring oil from the interior to an as yet non-existent marine terminal was still outstanding, because the main contractor had been unable to procure the large diameter steel pipe. In those early years following the war, there was only one manufacturer of large steel pipes in the world, since Britain had nationalised and downsized its steel industry, resulting in closure of the facility at Bilston. The Japanese, now sole manufacturer, had procrastinated and avoided quoting for the vital pipe at the request of their compatriot contractor, who was equipping the port facilities of Haqum. A consequence was that the local company who was to provide Naamlah's pipes saw the value of its shares collapse. This would not go un-noticed by Shalma.

★

Farnham, to release Salim from his problem, had located a Swiss consultant urologist who specialised in cases like Salim's. Professor Martan was prepared to visit Salim for an appropriate fee. Farnham now had the task of persuading Salim to agree to examination by Martan without divulging how he knew what Salim's problem was, or even that he knew it existed. The consequences for the women of the fort would have been severe, and would probably have resulted in an end to their education. Over a protracted period, using every ounce of diplomatic tact that he could muster, Farnham tricked Salim into admitting that he was unwell, although, at first, he would not be specific about the symptoms of his illness. Subsequently, by showing sympathy, Farnham gained Salim's confidence and convinced him that their fates would be similar if Salim had a weakness that could give ammunition to his opponents. Farnham's tactic was to frighten Salim into thinking that whatever the problem was it may be early symptoms of some life-threatening decease. Salim admitted to himself that he feared it might be early symptoms of testicular cancer, and if it was it was just punishment by Allah for the abuse of Ali the servant. The outcome was that Farnham persuaded the Emir to allow Martan to attend him, on condition that the utmost secrecy would surround the visit.

★

One night, when no other arrivals or departures were scheduled for the airport, a chartered plane arrived from Zurich, and after touchdown its crew were instructed to taxi away from the terminal building to an unlit section of the airport where Salim's limousine, driven by the Afghan, was patiently waiting. A mysterious passenger was ushered into the car, driven out of the airport via a service gate, delivered to the fort, admitted by the guard, who had been suitably briefed, and shown to his accommodation in a spare room by the Afghan. The guest slept comfortably, recovering from his flight. In the morning he was served breakfast by Ali, who was not aware of the function of the visitor but assumed because of the attendant secrecy that he must be a man of some importance. Later, Ali was instructed to direct the guest to Salim's study.

Salim accepted the indignity of physical examination by the Professor in desperate hopes that his affliction would be cured. Salim was relieved to learn the initial confirmation that there were no signs of a tumour. When Salim raised the subject, they discussed the possibility of permanently adding erectile tissue, an operation which Salim had known to be possible. Martan told him that this could be an embarrassment to a man whose culture did not encourage constraint by underwear. Salim reacted in horror when he realised this would result in a permanent erection.

"There are other alternatives, such as injections of vasodilatory drugs, but I doubt they would be acceptable," said Martan, seeing Salim's expression. "Let me make a few more tests, Excellency." Salim then suffered a series of indignities which were causing his temper to rise. Eventually, Martan proclaimed, "Well, your Excellency, you are certainly not infertile, and there is nothing wrong with your physiology." Salim looked puzzled when told this. "In lay terms, there is no reason why you should not be able to function and father more children if suitably stimulated, Excellency."

"I have a young and beautiful wife who is embarrassingly eager to stimulate me. What more does a man need, sir?" replied Salim, indignantly holding his temper.

"I believe your problem lies in the mind, your Excellency."

"Are you saying I am mad?" asked Salim, becoming irritated but still holding his temper.

"No. Not at all, but please allow me to ask you some questions about your Excellency's lifestyle."

"Of course, go ahead," agreed Salim, sharply, as he was growing more irritated by the Professor.

The Professor started to ask Salim about his daily routine. From his answers Martan began to suspect that Salim was under unreasonable strain and on the verge of clinical depression, resulting from his failure to delegate responsibility for the day-to-day administration of the countries affairs.

"In normal circumstances, your Excellency, I would suggest that the patient takes a holiday with his wife to enable him to relax and allow nature to take its course. In parallel with this I would advise him to reduce his workload and to take up some recreational activity in the time that he has saved," said Martan. "Do you have any hobbies, Excellency?"

"Hobbies, what are they to a ruler?" asked a now fuming Emir.

"Does your Excellency do anything when he is not either working or sleeping?" asked the Professor.

"In my youth, I spent much time propagating, but now I have no ability, sir," replied Salim who was now losing his temper with the Professor.

"Ah, so you have a horticultural interest," exclaimed the Professor, who was seeing a new side to the Emir.

"You idiot, I mean that when I was not working or sleeping, I was trying to make my wives pregnant," shouted Salim.

"Ah, I understand, forgive me for intruding into your Excellency's personal preferences," replied the Professor, nervously.

Salim calmed down and said, "As for taking a holiday: that is out of the question. When I returned, I would find the fort occupied by my opponents."

"The choice is your Excellency's, but I do not believe you will obtain better advice and strongly recommend that you contrive to arrange a holiday, possibly in secret from your opponents," said the Professor.

The following night Professor Martan departed the same way he arrived, to the annoyance of Ali, who had failed to learn the purpose of his visit.

CHAPTER 23

Before the construction of the Emir's new palace could commence it had been necessary to build a road through the desert by which materials and plant could be transported. The new road was also the first phase of a connection through the mountains to the Red Sea port of Aden. The old camel trail, which had served for centuries, was considered unsuitable because of excessive gradients through the mountain section.

The new route, though deviating away from the wadi, was much easier to construct. When the British contractors had reached the proposed site of the palace, they came upon the bleached bones of a camel that had died many years ago. An Indian driver of an International Drott excavator was clearing away the bones when he noticed something shining in the gravel. He stopped the machine and climbed down to see what had been exposed. Where the bones had lain there were several pieces of gold, scattered amongst what he thought were old date stones and strands of ragged woollen cloth.

The man, who was working alone, excitedly gathered as much gold as he could stuff into his pockets before his English foreman appeared to question why he had stopped work. The attempt to hide the find did not go unseen by the foreman who was intrigued by the difficulty the Indian was having holding up his overalls. The Indian was forced to reveal what he was hiding in his pockets. The foreman immediately realized its importance. After an unsuccessful attempt at evasion by the Indian, the two men decided to share the gold between them and tell no one of the discovery. They spent the rest of that day recovering gold from the surrounding disturbed sand until they had as much as they could load into the bucket of the Drott. Within a week both had given notice of termination of their contracts, after which they departed Naamlah for a life of inexplicable affluence in their respective countries.

CHAPTER 24

While the boys had been receiving their education in Europe, the lessons in the harem proved to be the highlight of the lives of the residents, and with nothing to distract them from their studies, Rasha soon had them confidently reading Arabic. They had each benefited previously from some early religious education, from which they learned by heart some appropriately, for a woman, chosen passages from the Holy Koran, but now, for the first time, they could read the Holy book for themselves and interpret the ancient texts from a woman's point of view. This proved to be a revelation, whereby they saw that the sexist attitudes of their men could not be justified on religious grounds. Writing took longer to learn because it required a little more original input and dexterity, which the older ladies found difficult to provide. Fatima and Nahla, whose minds were less blinkered, and whose hands were more flexible when handling a pen, were soon ahead of the others. When Rasha had gone, leaving them homework, they were initially assisted by Ali. After three years their work was getting beyond him, and it was he who was learning from the two girls. Rasha started teaching English to the two young girls at that time, whilst the older ladies were still struggling with Arabic grammar and trying out their pronunciation on Ali. They could all now read the books that Mariam had previously read to them. This, together with the improvement to their health as a result of their activity in the gymnasium, had given them all a sense of achievement and a confidence boost. After four years Rasha started to teach only English, as she had decided that there was no more they could learn about

Arabic, and only Ali was benefiting in that language. As Fousia became more accomplished than Mariam, their friendship became less intense, which pleased the other ladies, who thought Fousia's attachment to the mermaid was unnatural.

Shalma, who for reading practice had been using Farnham's old copies of the Financial Times, had become fascinated by the world of finance. She followed international stock movements and was also following world news on her radio. Studying the local stock market had now become her main occupation. She had started an imaginary share portfolio which, she was pleased to discover, would have made her quite wealthy if it had been real. Holders of shares in the pipe company were less astute, and saw the value of their stock fall to the extent that they were in many cases facing financial ruin. They had borrowed money to finance what had been an apparently sound investment. When he learned of this, Salim saw it only as an event beyond his intervention and one more item to be added to his burden.

Just as her Aunt Shalma was fascinated by the world of business and finance, learned from Farnham's copies of the Financial Times and BBC radio broadcasts, so Fousia's attention was taken by natural history as portrayed in his copies of the National Geographic magazine. They each found these publications a great impetus to learning English, which helped them to catch up with the younger girls. Soon Fousia was obtaining books from England and America on natural history and diverted all her energy towards building a reference library on the subject.

Rasha, who was proud of Fousia's progress, thought that her student should have further studies in her chosen specialty that she could not provide. She suggested it to Fousia, who enthusiastically embraced the idea. Rasha researched the facilities in her own country, where she found a University in Cairo with a good reputation that offered a suitable course.

Through her husband, Rasha obtained Salim's agreement for Fousia to study abroad, after he was convinced that it would benefit the country. The Emir agreed to let Fousia travel to Cairo for an interview at the chosen university if another of the ladies would accompany her. All of the ladies volunteered, but Layla, being the senior, was allowed to be chaperone for her daughter. Once it became known that a woman was to be educated abroad like their sons, this ground-breaking event met with much disapproval from the religious establishment as no unmarried woman had previously been permitted to travel out of the country. The fact that the women would have no male escort from within their family was considered to be particularly *haraam*. Salim had to relent on this point because no such person was available. However, he insisted that Ali accompany the ladies to the airport, where no leaving ceremony, as would have been appropriate for a male relative, was to be held. Ali arranged for their luggage to be checked in and insisted on boarding the plane to see if their seating was appropriately separated from that of any male passengers.

Staff at the university had mixed feelings about the potential new student, because although they felt honoured to be receiving a princess, they had strong doubts about her abilities. They could not conceive how a woman could have received an education in Naamlah that would have been to a standard suitable for university entrance. Of particular concern was the fact that much of the course work relied on publications in the English language that they were sure she would not have learned.

★

On their arrival the ladies were met by staff from the university, who expressed their honour to be chosen as the seat of learning of the 'princess' from Naamlah. Fousia was embarrassed, because she had never thought of herself as a princess, and had never previously been addressed as such at home. Later, when they were alone, she mentioned it to her mother.

"I suppose you must be a Queen in the eyes of these Egyptians, who are used to being ruled by a King."

Laylah just laughed in response, and then said, "Until your sister Nahla was born your father always referred to you as a princess, but after her birth he forbade us from using that title and he would not say why, except that one day I will know."

The ladies had been escorted to a hotel, where arrangements had been made for them to stay for several days. Pending Fousia's interview, they were taken on tours of Cairo and Egypt's cultural attractions by a female member of the university, who had been instructed to learn as much as possible about Fousia's academic abilities. She was impressed by Fousia's scientific knowledge and pleasantly surprised to be able to converse with both ladies in their excellent English. When this was conveyed to members of the interview board their apprehensions were dispelled.

Layla accompanied her daughter to the University on the day of the interview where she made enquiries about *harem* facilities. She was assured that Fousia would have no contact with male students and that male tutors would be screened from the girls during lectures. From the information provided by the lady who had escorted the ladies on their sightseeing trip, the board had already decided to accept Fousia. The interview was, therefore, only a formality. However, the board were pleasantly surprised by both her English language ability and her scientific knowledge. They had no hesitation in unanimously accepting her. It was confirmed that Fousia should return for the next term to join a course that offered an appropriate degree.

Both Fousia and Layla had been excited by their visit to Egypt, where they had seen so much of civilized life, and were reluctant to return to their harem routines. Layla had been surprised to see schools where both boys and girls, though separated, were being taught from an early age, and started to make plans to persuade her husband to allow the introduction of a similar system in Naamlah.

★

When the time came for Fousia to depart for her studies, Salim's attitude had changed such that he was proud of his daughter, and this time a leaving ceremony was provided at the airport, to the annoyance of the religious establishment. Fousia, with little else to occupy her, became a model student, such that after two years she was awarded her degree in Environmental and Natural science.

★

Shalma, who had developed interests beyond her self-pity at her imprisonment and the loss of her child, was now out of her depression and was absorbed in world affairs and finance. She revelled in being able to obtain news that was not censored, or else propaganda circulated by religious extremists. Rasha, who had practically moved into the harem, as she decided anywhere was better than her depressing dusty and dark house (though Farnham had assured her they would soon be leaving for a new seaside villa), continued to bring newspapers. Shalma, whose English language studies had concentrated on Farnham's old copies of the Financial Times, continued to increase her knowledge of the world's stock markets, a subject that she studied by comparing share movements in old copies of the newspaper. She developed algorithms for predicting performance, which she had already tested on her fictitious share portfolio. Now she was confident and consulted a broker who reluctantly agreed to act on her behalf, as no woman had yet bought shares. She waited for an opportunity to put her knowledge into practice.

The ladies of the fort all shared an interest in clothes, on which they spent freely the allowances that Salim provided. These included Western styles that none would have dared to wear on their infrequent supervised outings within Naamlah.

Salim, as usual, had his worries, but he was pleased that his women were enjoying their liberated lives. He was in a quandary about the Professor's recommendation of taking Fatima on holiday. He was torn between the desire to overcome his affliction and risking accusations of abandoning the nation when it most needed leadership or ignoring the situation and risking loss of dignity and respect if his condition became common knowledge. Salim had only two sons, and if these were killed or died

134

naturally his line would end, and there would inevitably be large scale bloodshed as the other tribes fought each other to replace the al-Wyly. He decided, therefore, that in the interest of peace it was his duty to father more sons. With this in mind, he opted to proceed with the Professors advice. A further factor, and one that added to his burden, was his succession by Moosa, who by all reports was not of the best character and may not be the ideal choice to lead the nation.

Salim consulted Farnham about his decision to take Fatima for a holiday. Farnham guessed why this plan had suddenly materialised, but did not comment except to confirm that he thought it was well deserved. Farnham made no other response then, but later he came up with a plan which he put to Salim.

"Highness, your new palace is almost ready for occupation. Would it not be a good opportunity to take your holiday there?" Salim was puzzled. "During the move, no one will be surprised if you are not in the fort, because they can be lead to believe that you are at the palace, and conversely …"

Salim interrupted, "Yes. Yes, I see your point Farnham. Do you think we should risk being alone at the palace?"

"I anticipated that dilemma, Highness, and concluded that your wife would probably be more amenable if she thought that there was just two of you, and servants of course, as this would ensure no distraction on affairs of state for your Highness."

When it was announced that Fatima was to not only visit but take up residence in the new palace before themselves the other women were instantly jealous. They protested on Layla's behalf, that the Holy Book, they now knew, says that a man must treat all his wives equally. Only when they understood the object of the separation and the need for discretion did they agree to co-operate and withdraw their objection.

Layla herself proclaimed, "I do not expect to be competing with Fatima for the doubtful favours of our husband. Besides, he should use his failing energy to make Fatima pregnant with a son, rather than waste it on a barren old woman like me."

CHAPTER 25

After the rival oil terminal at Haqum was completed and its Japanese construction company, having had no success finding oil, had abandoned their search, the Japanese pipe manufacturer was free to allow Naamlah's oil pipe order to proceed. News of this development was first heard by Shalma on her radio. She realised immediately that the share price would rise, and thought this a good opportunity to make her first real share purchase rather than play with her fictitious portfolio. Shalma instructed her broker to buy a large quantity of shares in the Pipeline Company. As he was not as informed as Shalma, he advised her against the purchase, but she overruled him. Hammed immediately learned of this large purchase and decided he would also acquire Pipeline Company stock, but was disappointed to learn that the large purchase by an unknown buyer had caused the price to rise and that it was now escalating rapidly as others followed the example of the mystery buyer. Once the share price had reached its original level, before the collapse, Shalma instructed her broker to sell all of her shares, which were then worth five times the price she had paid. This was the price at which her brother Hammed eventually obtained shares. Unfortunately for Hammed and other investors, six months elapsed before the pipes arrived, due to shipping and ordering delays in Japan, such that during this period the installation contractor's specialist engineering team had dispersed to other projects. News of this caused the share price to fall once more.

★

Recruitment of pipe-laying specialists was now undertaken in earnest by the contractor. One applicant who had impressed the selection board was a young Arab engineer: Kareem, Saif's school friend. He had been working on a pipeline in Bahrain, where he had obtained a wealth of relevant experience and had been commended for his leadership qualities and communication skill in both English and Arabic. His Arab racial origins were a major factor in his favour. However, his family connections would have made him unacceptable to Abdulazziz, Salim's brother and Immigration Minister, who was strongly opposed to the employment of anyone from Haqum, a country with which he still harboured a feud. To obtain the vital work permit, the local agent altered Kareem's tribal name on the document confirming his appointment.

Kareem soon justified his appointment as project manager by getting the first of the crude oil pumped from the wells to the tank farm within the originally planned time scale and, soon after this, to the oil refinery. Although the oil, except that to fuel local transport, could not go any further, the government decided to celebrate the event with a public holiday. They would thus give the impression to the people that the great oil project was on schedule. This deceit was soon masked by the availability of cheap, locally refined fuel for the growing number of motor vehicles, as the refinery also came online.

★

Salim had learned of the progress that had been made by Farnham's wife in teaching his wives, sister and daughters, and had to admit that they had all become livelier and more interesting as a result. He had to admit also that he could not recall previously ever having had an intelligent conversation with a woman. He was astounded by his daughter Fousia's knowledge of natural history, and even more surprised when Farnham told him that she had just graduated with a degree in the subject. They had been discussing the formation of a Ministry to counteract the destruction of the environment, being caused by the industrial development that was taking place in the country. With feminine guile, Rasha had primed her husband on the potential of Fousia for this task. He now proposed to Salim that Fousia would be eminently suitable to head an Environment Ministry. Salim had laughed, thinking that Farnham was being facetious.

"I am serious, Highness, as I believe your daughter would be the ideal appointee," said Farnham.

Salim pondered on Farnham's recommendation for several minutes after which he concluded, "She would at least be loyal, and I cannot think of a respectable man who would want the post because it offers no obvious power or potential for money-making."

Farnham added, "Nor is there a man in this country with her qualifications."

"I shall have to see what objections will be raised. Leave it with me for a few days," said Salim.

Salim subsequently received more objections to Fousia's proposed appointment from the *mullahs* and other families than he had expected, so much so that he saw these as a challenge to his authority, and this made him determined to frustrate his opponents. Fousia was duly appointed Minister for the Environment and was grudgingly accepted by the rest of the government. The Islamic extremists, guided by the old cleric who lived opposite the Farnhams, saw this as a direct attack on all that they advocated as the place of a woman in Islam. Although in another environment he would have been certified as insane, he had an enthusiastic following who were all sufficiently fanatical to be unaware of his madness. The old cleric lived for another world, in which the word of Allah, as written in the hand of the Holy Prophet in the 7th century, was interpreted only by himself and in his own distorted and insane way. His followers were simple men, unable to make their own interpretation of the Holy Scriptures, which they had as children blindly learned by heart in madrasas without understanding the words that they were forced to recite, who feared a world in which a man's status was determined by his efforts and not by his family connections or by a preordained will.

They feared a world where they could foresee women choosing their partners, using criteria that they each lacked, and where women would compare men with each other; a world where educated women could, by their work, support themselves and their children without the supposed protection of a man. They feared the world of the European infidels who were increasingly determining the destiny of the Arab by their greed for oil.

The Islamic extremists met after noon prayers on Fridays, when all were filled with religious fervour, after being inspired by the sermon of their *imam*. Today, the old man harangued them about Salim's latest blasphemy whereby he had appointed a woman, admittedly of his blood, but a woman nevertheless, who was to direct and govern the activities of men. The assembly who knew nothing of this were, to a man, astounded and angered by the revelation. The old cleric had managed to establish one of his followers in each Government department in the Ministries of Naamlah, and it was from these spies that he received his information before it became common knowledge. Today's news came from a simple young man named Saleh, employed as a *farrage*, who had been notified of his transfer to the new Ministry of the Environment where he would be working for the woman minister.

"Allah has made us the administrators of his will and it is by our hand that the apostate Salim al-Wyly and his family shall answer for their sins," ranted the cleric.

"*Alhamdulillah*," muttered the assembly in unison, showing their agreement.

"I charge you all to go forth and watch for his weaknesses, that we may strike against him."

"*Alhamdulillah*," replied the assembly once more as they started to stream out into the street, where goats feasted on abandoned garbage, passing the gate of the infidel Farnham. Only the spikes of iron prevented them from venting their anger on the gate of their avowed enemy.

★

Kareem had excused himself from the oil progress celebrations because he could not risk exposure. The ceremonial blessing of the valve that controlled the flow of oil was performed by the Mufti in Salim's conspicuous presence before the microphones and movie cameras of Naamlah's fledgling media services. Salim then slipped away to the palace where he was to join Fatima, who had been taken there by the Afghan driver who now collected Salim. After his conspicuous media appearance, no one missed Salim for the next four days, comprising two days of holiday followed by Thursday and Friday to make a long weekend.

CHAPTER 26

Bernhardt Grover had been brought up on his parents' farm in Bavaria, where before the war he had been a reluctant member of the Hitler Youth Movement, an organisation which he was obliged to join, encouraged by his parents who, like most Germans, thought this was essential for personal advancement in the Fascist state. At university in Frankfurt, he subsequently read both Geology and Biology, specialising in insects. When he was conscripted into the Army he served with a panzer regiment in Italy and then with Rommel's Africa Core in Libya. It was here that he became fluent in Arabic after his rescue by the *Bedouin*. He spent the last two years of the war as a British prisoner. Bernhardt had no enthusiasm for the war or National Socialism and became interested more in the native lifestyle and ecology. When he was not on duty commanding a tank, he took every opportunity to study the unique fauna and flora of the desert. He made many friends among the *Bedouin* who appreciated his interest in their culture and their approach to desert survival. During his capture he continued his insect studies to relieve the boredom of imprisonment. It was in Libya that Bernhardt first formed an emotional attachment, but it was dispelled during two years as a British prisoner. During this time his conscious memory of the *Bedu* girl who nursed him had faded, but often in his dreams, he saw her eyes and felt the hands that had tended him so patiently.

Since the war had ended, and after his release from capture, he had been working with an international team assessing the environmental damage caused by the war in North Africa. The work was, to Bernhardt, of little interest, but allowed him to continue studies of insects and perfection of the Arabic language. It was during his work which involved clearing war debris that he frequently came across scorpions of many different varieties. He became obsessed with this relative of the spider and made every effort to learn all that he could about them. The scorpion became his overriding interest, and was the means whereby he obtained an international reputation after publishing a scientific paper on the subject. Fousia came across this publication and, after investigation, discovered that Bernhardt, now Professor Grover, had just completed his assignment in Africa and was now seeking another appointment. She, therefore, added his name to her list of potential experts who were to assist her at the Ministry of Environmental Affairs and invited him to submit his CV with the prospect of attending an interview in Naamlah.

After comparing the CVs of numerous applicants for the post of senior adviser she had eliminated all but three applicants, Bernhardt and two others. She had wanted to conduct the interviews on her own, but Salim insisted that she have a trustworthy male in attendance for the sake of respectability. Fousia asked Ali if he would sit in with her.

"My dear, I know nothing of environmental problems. What use can I be?" he protested.

"You only have to sit and listen. I will ask the questions," she replied.

"I am just to be your protector then?"

"Yes, that is all you have to worry about."

Ali agreed and added that he would sit in a corner and read a book.

Fousia's office, in a cramped, temporary portable building, was a happy workplace. The Ministry for Environmental Affairs was in the early stages of development and consisted of herself and five staff. Recruitment of staff had been hampered by the reluctance of Naamlah's men to work for a woman and the fact that there were no native women in the country suitably qualified or even with work experience. Thus far she had recruited an Indian secretary, Tariq, a Sudanese biologist, and an Egyptian geologist. They were assisted by an elderly Arab named Nasser, who served ostensibly as receptionist and doorman but became a dogsbody for the two specialists. Nasser was a retired merchant navy steward who, rather than follow in his father's footsteps as a date farmer, had run off to sea as a youth. He had been selected because he could speak several languages, including English and several Indian dialects. Outside, then cleaning Fousia's ministry car, was a large jolly Sikh. The Sikh had been selected on Salim's insistence, as a condition of his daughter's mobility, to be her driver and protector. Uniquely, he shared Ali's affliction. The last member of her staff was a *farrage*, or messenger, a lazy Arab boy, Saleh, who had not wanted to work at all but, being one of the mad cleric's followers, had been pressured to serve as a spy within the ministry.

Bernhardt was sitting in the office of Fousia's secretary. Tariq shared the room with Saleh, who sat at a small table waiting to carry papers between offices and otherwise be available to provide *cawah* on demand, which he produced in a small kitchen attached to the office. Saleh resented being ordered about by foreigners, particularly the Indian, who he held beneath contempt for being neither Muslim or even European, a race for which Saleh had some, though minimal, respect. Saleh had been under pressure from his widowed mother to seek employment. She told him he could not otherwise be able to raise funds to support the bride that she selfishly considered essential for her future care. The fact that he worked in a government office gave Saleh significant social status among his Islamic extremist friends, for whom he was prepared to reluctantly endure subjugation to the foreigners. None of his ministry colleagues were aware of his allegiance to the extremist cause.

Extra chairs had been squeezed in for three interviewees, two of whom now sat opposite Tariq's desk, where they suffered the full blast of cold air from an overworked air conditioner. The Egyptian candidate had been in with Fousia for only ten minutes when the door opened violently, and he came charging out. Bernhardt and the American both searched his eyes for a hint of what he had endured at the interview. They saw only anger and looked at each other, each internally smiling as they thought that the minister must be a formidable character to have caused him to be so upset. The Egyptian said nothing, but his attitude convinced them that they now had only a two to one chance of rejection.

In her office, Fousia turned to Ali and smiled. "What do you think of him, Ali?"

"It is not my place to comment, but I think you are well rid of him. I thought at one point I might have to restrain him from striking you."

Fousia agreed as she crossed the Egyptian's name from her shortlist. "My father will be disappointed, he was hoping the Egyptian would be more acceptable than the Westerners." Then she surprised Ali by removing the *hijab* from her head where it covered all but her eyes.

"I shall not need this for the other two," she said.

Tariq stopped typing and told Saleh to make *cawah* for the Egyptian, who muttered something rude and said he wanted a taxi to be called as he resumed his seat, still in a disturbed state.

Tariq asked Nasser to find the Sikh and informed the Egyptian that he would be driven in the ministry car. Saleh gave the Egyptian his *cawah* and offered some to the other interviewees then left the room. The Egyptian silently sipped his drink.

The American asked politely, "How did it go?"

The Egyptian did not understand, so Tariq translated. "Stupid woman questioned my qualifications," replied the Egyptian. Tariq translated.

Bernhardt joined in, using Arabic: "Madam is knowing her stuff then." Tariq started to translate for the American, but Bernhardt was already repeating himself in broken English.

"She is a fool if she thinks herself better than a man," said the Egyptian. Tariq said no more, because Nasser returned with the Sikh. Bernhardt looked the Sikh up and down, thinking, "What a giant. I would not want to get on the wrong side of him."

"The car is ready, sir. We will let you know the outcome," said Tariq, causing the Egyptian to stand, making no reply except a grunt. He followed the Sikh out of the office, slamming the door. A bell sounded and Tariq asked the American to go in.

He noticed that the room was smaller than that of Tariq and Nasser, but the desk was bigger. She had pot plants everywhere except in the space where he was expected to sit facing her. He could identify each plant, which he did mentally. In a corner of the room sat a fat Arab who looked up from a book and smiled. Air conditioning was not so violent in this room, where he thought it was better for the plants, which all looked healthy. He nervously approached her and extended a hand which she reluctantly touched, as though she was afraid he may infect her, he thought.

"Please sit down, Mister Hinds," invited Fousia, thinking, "he has no experience of the Arab world." "Welcome to Naamlah. It is my pleasure to meet you at last," said Fousia in accented English. Hinds thought, "She seems a pleasant woman, could be attractive beneath all the covering; awful English though."

"Thank you, ma'am, it is my pleasure to be here."

Fousia spent about ten minutes reviewing his qualifications. Hinds thought, "This must have been where the other guy came unstuck." Fousia was impressed so far. Next, she asked a series of questions related to his experience. These had been thoroughly researched and were cleverly designed to expose any false claims. He watched her dark eyes as she made some notes, giving him time to relax. He thought about how sensual they were and tried to guess her age; probably about thirty, he decided. She looked up at him and smiled. He was completely disarmed by how attractive she looked and could not place her as a Government Minister.

"Now I have a few general questions, Mister Hinds." She went through a list of technical questions that she had prepared for all candidates. Hinds found them straight forward, thought he had answered them well and was feeling confident. She made more notes. The next set of questions were specific to the Environment of Naamlah, and although he had read avidly on the subject, he soon realised that she was probing deeper than he had anticipated. Slowly, a feeling of inferiority took hold as he realised that he could not bluff his way through the remainder of the interview if she kept up this pace.

Fousia realised his weakness and tried to reassure him; "I do not expect an American to know all the answers to our problems, Mister Hinds. Please do not be discouraged."

"Thank you, ma'am. I am sure if you find me acceptable in other respects it will only be a matter of time before I can be of benefit to your country in dealing with your specific problems," replied Hinds, knowing he did not sound convincing.

"Time may not be very plentiful in a marine oil spillage scenario," replied Fousia, as she started to rise from her chair. "Thank you again for coming, Mister Hinds." Hinds noticed her figure for the first time, silhouetted by the sunlight from the window in front of which she now stood, full-bosomed and slim waist visible beneath the shapeless black gown. He stood up and, offering his hand once more, realised that it was her dark eyes that mostly caused him to be attracted to her. "In our culture men do not shake the hand of a woman," she said politely. He noticed that the fat man was looking up from his book and smiling. Hinds felt deflated as he turned to leave the room. After he had gone Fousia asked Ali what he thought of Hinds' performance, to which he gave a thumbs down sign.

In the other office, Bernhardt asked, "Did you die lady impress?"

Hinds replied, "She is some gal," without giving anything away. Then to Tariq, he said, "I sure need some of that coffee." Saleh made a fresh brew.

After a few minutes, the bell sounded, and Bernhardt stood up and moved towards Fousia's door before Tariq could ask him to do so. "Good luck buddy," said Hinds, audible behind him as he entered Fousia's office.

Before he had closed the door, Bernhardt wished her to be in peace; "*Assalaam alaikum.*"

"*Wa alaikum salaam. Ahlan wa sahlan,* Professor Grover," replied Fousia, welcoming him.

"*Shukran. Kaif halish Waziirah*," replied Bernhardt, thanking her and enquiring after her health. Fousia was impressed and surprised that he used the feminine form for both the greeting and her title, usually unknown to Europeans, who seldom met an Arab woman, and certainly not a female Arab Minister of Government. She tried to place his accent and realised that it was like Rasha's, which indicated that he must have learned his Arabic in Egypt. She noted that he did not offer his hand.

"*Alhamdulillah*," she replied, thanking Allah for her good health. The fat Arab, to whom he was not introduced, was grinning stupidly when Bernhardt first noticed him sitting in the corner, partly hidden by plants. He wondered what the relationship was between them as the Arab started to read a book.

Except when technical terms were used, they continued the interview in Arabic. As they talked Bernhardt found himself attracted to her, just as Hinds had been before him. Her eyes reminded him instantly of the sister of Rashiid, the *Bedu* who had rescued him, with whom he had been infatuated during the war. Fousia had difficulty maintaining her programme of questions because the tall blond, with his wide smile and deep voice, emitting perfect Arabic, caused a reaction which she had never before experienced when confronted by a man. She found herself thinking of Mariam and comparing the present sensation with the feeling she used to have for the mermaid. He was still smiling nervously, remembering the *Bedu* girl, as he patiently waited for Fousia to complete her notes after the second set of questions. Fousia looked up, trying to avoid his eyes, and started the final set of questions, relating to the local environment, realising that inside she was praying for him to succeed.

Outside, Tariq had noticed that Bernhardt had been with Fousia far longer than the American, who had by then departed, and said to Saleh, "I think the German will be joining us." Saleh switched on the kettle in anticipation of Bernhardt needing refreshment after his grilling.

There was no doubt in Ali's mind that Fousia was going to offer the job to the German. Fousia was also in no doubt that she wanted to work with Bernhardt. Apart from being smitten by his personality, she was impressed by his knowledge of desert wildlife and ecology. Plus, she convinced herself, he spoke Arabic and was familiar with the culture. She wondered if he already had a woman.

"Will your family be accompanying you, Professor? That is," she added hastily, "if you are fortunate."

"I am a bachelor with no family. The war, you know."

She fought to conceal her relief and said, "I am sorry," but without conviction. She wanted to offer him the post then but knew she had to first get approval from the Immigration Ministry.

CHAPTER 27

Bernhardt's appointment was soon known to Saleh's fellow extremists, who disapproved of the introduction of a foreigner to this post of influence and who were incensed even more by the knowledge that in this case, the adviser was to be an infidel. "The Egyptian, a Muslim, might have been acceptable, but certainly not a German unbeliever!" raged the old cleric.

Not everyone in Naamlah was on holiday because Salim, following Professor Martan's advice, had delegated responsibility for finding a solution to one of his burdens; a plan of action required to circumvent the lack of deep-water loading facilities was to be considered by the experts and consultants of relevant government departments. Fousia had therefore called a meeting at which she was represented by her newly appointed senior adviser, Professor Grover. Bernhardt decided that to get everyone in the picture he would explain the history behind the current situation.

He told the meeting, "The border between Naamlah and Haqum, its easterly neighbour, had been defined at the time of a doubtful truce between the two feuding nations by British civil servants. This appeared then to be relatively easy and each side accepted the border to be defined by the great *wadi*. The geological event that caused this fault many hundreds of millions of years earlier had caused a difference in ground level between the two sides, Naamlah being on the high side from where the ground fell steeply towards Haqum. The fault continued northwards into the sea, with the result that Naamlah had shallow water whilst Haqum had deep water. Historically everyone had assumed the centre of the *wadi* to be the border, but the English cartographer, Phillips, responsible for the survey from which an Admiralty chart was published, showed the land border to be the steep easily locatable and defined western bank of the *wadi*. The marine border then became an imaginary line running due north from the west bank of the *wadi* where it joined the sea. This is the border of which both sides agreed and is that internationally recognised," confirmed Bernhardt.

Because throughout most of its length the *wadi* was in the desert, the discrepancy between the arbitrarily assumed border and the legally defined border had not been of any significance until Haqum constructed a port served by the deep-water over the *wadi's* seaward extension.

"Those of you who care to inspect the chart will see that almost all of the deep channel undisputedly lies in the water of Haqum. The closest Naamlah comes to the deep water is approximately half a nautical mile. Until Haqum installed navigation aids, this was where we had been planning to construct our loading terminal. That plan is no longer viable on safety grounds," he concluded.

Bernhardt ended his introduction and invited the meeting to proceed by suggesting solutions to the problem of conveying oil to tankers from Naamlah within the constraints of what he had told those present.

The first proposal was to use lighters to convey the oil to tankers anchored beyond the three-mile limit. Bernhardt pointed out that this posed a pollution risk from anticipated spillage when trans-shipping oil in rough weather. A Finance Ministry representative said there were long term cost implications because of the enormous quantity of lighters that Naamlah would require to load the tanker within a time scale that would not cause excessive delay and cost to the tanker operator.

The second proposition, of annexing the navigable channel by enforcing the historical border into the sea, was next considered. This tactic was strongly supported by the representative from the Defence Ministry until it was pointed out that Naamlah's Army and Air force officers were expatriates, who to induce them to serve, had to be offered training appointments that excluded hostilities. It was also noted that both countries were still under the mandate of protection by the British, who would certainly oppose such action.

A third proposal was a submarine pipe connecting to a terminal on the island that lay 20 nautical miles north off the mainland of Naamlah, where there was deep water suitable for a tanker. There were two main objections. The Finance representative said he thought it would be prohibitively expensive to build an oil port on the uninhabited island and would involve excessive delay during its construction. Bernhardt also objected on the grounds that it would be a significant pollution hazard as there was insufficient depth of water for most of the route. Another member said he did not think a submarine pipe of such length had yet been commissioned.

The fourth proposal was to have a floating pipe extending to the deep water over the *wadi* extension. This was rejected after Bernhardt's observations that this was an unjustified hazard to both pollution and navigation.

The fifth and final proposal was to divert the pipeline carrying Naamlah's oil to the port of Haqum and to negotiate with the neighbour for use of their existing, but unused, tanker loading facilities. This was immediately shouted down by most of those present, but after consideration, it was decided to be the logical course of action. "How much will they want us to pay?" was the question on everyone's lips. No one present considered that the poor neighbour would refuse a reasonable offer.

"We could lease their terminal, perhaps," was one consultant's suggestion.

"We could be held to ransom if they demand royalties on every barrel," said another.

"Those are details; first we must ask them to receive a delegation with authority to negotiate the best deal," said the Foreign Ministry's representative. It was agreed that Bernhardt would recommend to Fousia that she submit the last proposal to the Emir, then the meeting dispersed for the delegates to enjoy the remainder of the holiday.

CHAPTER 28

As soon as Fatima left in the car for the new palace, ahead of Salim, Nahla realised that she would miss her friend, and soon started to feel lonely as she had felt when Saif first went to England. She decided that she must have more company and thought that a girl of seventeen, in what was becoming an age of enlightenment for her country, was also entitled to have some excitement in her life. She knew from the media and from talk among the servants that there would be a lot of parties during the holiday and longed to go to one where there would not be only women and girls. She harboured a desire to dress in public in the Western clothes that she, Fatima, and Fousia had been buying to wear in the harem. She asked Mariam, who she knew had an active social life, about her plans for the holiday, and specifically if she knew of any parties where there would be mixed company.

Mariam disappointed her by replying that none of the official celebrations were to be mixed. Then Mariam said, "There is to be a big event at the Malayan Diplomatic Mission to celebrate my countries independence from Britain, which I shall attend, and after which I shall become Malaysian."

"Do you think I could go with you?" asked Nahla excitedly.

"What would your father do if he discovered that I had taken you out of the fort? It is more than my job is worth," protested the maid.

"But he is not here now."

"In any case, you could not get past Ali or the guards."

"I am willing to try," said Nahla, whilst thinking of an escape plan.

"Alright, but if anyone finds out, it is you who asked me."

★

Within the newly completed palace, the Emir and Fatima were discreetly installed in the Emir's imposing suite of rooms. Outside a contingent of guards were, with equal discretion, posted to defend the couple's privacy. A second conspicuous contingent protected the fort to give the impression that the Emir was still residing there. Fatima was so impressed by the architect's extravagant use of space, marble, luxurious fabrics, and gilded furniture that she found herself distracted from the objective of their visit. Salim had been exhausted when he arrived, and consequently they spent their first evening, Tuesday, relaxing, enjoying exploring and admiring the mountain views. By Wednesday the couple started to enjoy each other's company as Salim, now starting to forget about his burdens, became amicable and quite talkative, something he could not recall having ever done before with a woman. He was surprised to find how knowledgeable she was in spite of her few years, compared with his, quite unlike other wives he had experienced. He realised that her newfound sophistication stimulated his desire for her, and Fatima likewise found herself attracted to him as a man, rather than to the power that he wielded.

They shared a meal that evening. Salim had arranged for them to sit at a table, like Europeans, because he thought this would be more intimate than sitting on the floor in the Arabic custom. They both realised that this was the first time they had eaten together. Champagne was served, in defiance of local custom, because Salim had been advised by Farnham that, in his experience, alcohol could be relied upon to help relaxation. After his initial objection to such un-Islamic decadence, Salim accepted Farnham's argument that in these circumstances it would be considered, even by the clerics, to be medicinal. The prospect had reminded him of his later student days in England, when he had frequently succumbed to temptation when visiting public houses with fellow non-Muslim students. Like the wine, their food had all been carefully chosen because of its reputed aphrodisiac properties.

By the time they sat down to eat, Fatima, who had never before tasted alcohol and was now becoming progressively less interested in the furnishings of the palace, found that she was feeling light-headed and quite amorous. They were close to each other at a small table on a balcony connecting to their bedroom. They were both impressed by the view of the mountains, silhouetted by lines of alternate red and gold clouds reflecting the setting sun. A quartet of local musicians, hidden from their view by a silk curtain, played a selection of traditional romantic tunes. They provided what Salim had been advised would be an appropriate background for seduction. A liberal distribution of incense burners discouraged mosquitoes, which would otherwise have ruined any alfresco nocturnal event, and provided a heady aromatic atmosphere. No effort or expense had been spared by Salim in establishing the setting for this romantic occasion. They started the meal with Beluga caviar, followed by a large plate of Gulf oysters, the last of which Fatima personally fed to Salim. She was, she thought, not going to give him any grounds to reproach her this time. After they had finished their nearly raw Scotch steaks with asparagus and then brown Turkey figs with cream and maple syrup, washed down with more champagne, Salim was starting to feel uncomfortable and needed to reposition himself on his chair.

Fatima, with difficulty, focused on Salim's eyes, where she detected a smile forming. Her hand moved beneath the table and slowly across Salim's thigh until with delight she found the source of his amusement. "Oh, yes, Salim," she gasped as they both left the table, rushing unsteadily towards their bed.

CHAPTER 29

Mariam had been invited by her cousin Ahmed, from their hometown of Johor Bahru, to join him at a party to celebrate the independence of their country from Britain. This was to be held at the Malayan Diplomatic Mission, henceforth the Malaysian Embassy. It served principally the interests of those nationals working in Naamlah. Ahmed, a secretary at the Embassy, had joined the Cornubia oil company's recreation club as an associate member so that he could continue to partake in his favourite sport, sailing. He had been missing the sampan in which he sailed and fished the waters of the busy straits of Malacca, which separated Malaysia from Indonesia. At the club, he had met and subsequently befriended another new member and keen sailor, Kareem, whom Ahmed had also invited to the party.

Nahla felt guilty about her original plan, which required tricking Ali into letting her out of the fort to attend the party, because, she now realised, he would be blamed if she came to any harm. She therefore decided to tell him of her intention to join the mermaid on their adventure. She held her breath as she waited for his inevitable disapproval.

"My dear, you know it is not the custom for ladies to wander abroad without a male escort of the household," replied Ali.

"But on this occasion, I will be with Mariam, who we all trust, and I will be safe within the territory of a friendly Muslim country," she pleaded, with crossed fingers.

"That does seem reasonable, I suppose. If you want to leave the harem, I will not stop you in such circumstances. My task is to protect you ladies from visiting strangers," replied Ali. Nahla had always believed that he was there to stop them leaving but, when she thought about it, she had never tried to leave unescorted before now. "I am sure you can be trusted not to bring dishonour on your father, my dear."

Now she realised that she had responsibilities, she had mixed feelings about going out. Her desire to attend the party prevailed, however. "Of course you can trust me, Ali," replied Nahla.

Ali had pitied the ladies their dull lives and was pleased that they were now starting to have outside interests of their own. He was secretly proud that his favourite was showing such spirit. He said, "I'm sure you will enjoy yourself child, but don't be late back or I shall get no sleep." She hugged him then and went happily inside to break the news to Mariam.

The girls were assisted by the other ladies as they selected dresses from their extensive wardrobe of Western clothes, which had never before left the harem. Shalma recalled the excitement she had experienced at leaving the fort as a young girl. Mariam, who was the same size as her mistress, was loaned a petite French designer dress that Fousia had recently purchased. Fousia tried to hide her envy over her young sister having Mariam for company. Nahla had bought a conservative dress especially for the occasion, from an Italian designer and had been panicking in case it didn't arrive or didn't fit, since she had been attending the gym. The others told her she looked stunningly attractive and each thought, but did not dare say, that no man would resist her. The ladies were all experts when it came to eye make-up and required no assistance because generally, along with the painting of hands and feet with henna, this was their only way of expressing their individuality to men.

Before departing, the two girls donned black silk *abayas* and covered their faces with *hijabs*. They called at the office of the English guard sergeant to collect passes. Nahla was surprised that he recognised Mariam despite her disguise. She sensed that the sergeant and Mariam were already familiar. He wanted to call a palace limousine to take them to the party, which he appeared to know all about, but she insisted they had to appear incognito because it was not an official Arab function. He gave the impression that he did not understand but agreed to call a taxi instead.

When they were in the taxi, Nahla asked Mariam about her apparent familiarity with the soldier. "Is he not handsome?" she giggled in reply.

"I suppose he is. Do you know his name?" asked Nahla.

"Sergeant Henry Adams," replied Mariam, sheepishly. Then she admitted, "We have been out together a few times. Please do not say anything to Fousia. It might upset her."

"I will not tell. Besides, I think now she is in government she has no time for relationships," said Nahla.

"I don't know. You should see how she reacts when that big German is with her," said Mariam cheekily.

"Who is this man?" asked an intrigued Nahla.

"He is her senior adviser, but I think there is more to their relationship," replied Mariam, smiling behind her *hijab*.

"No, you must be jealous; but if that's true I am pleased for her," said Nahla.

"Nothing can come of it unless he converts to Islam," Mariam said seriously.

They had arrived and the girls fumbled in their gowns to find their invitation cards, which they showed to a Malaysian soldier. He showed them where they could leave their outer clothes and sent another soldier to find Ahmed. Whilst they waited, Nahla felt naked and insecure in mixed company without her *hijab*, but remembered the scarf she had brought and put it over her hair. Ahmed did not arrive, so they walked through to the room where the other guests were gathered. Nahla then realised she would have been less conspicuous if she had been bareheaded like Mariam, because the other women were either in colourful Malaysian costumes or in Western evening dress and none were veiled. At least the Malaysian ladies had head coverings like her own, but many had quite short skirts and low necklines, she noticed. Even exposing her ankles and arms in public would have been *haram*, a sign of complicity and dishonourable towards the men of her family in her culture. She felt excitedly wicked and worried if the other guests would think her vulgar in this dress. Mariam noticed that she was looking nervous and reassured her with a reminder that no one knew her here.

The soldier re-appeared and deposited Ahmed and another man with them. Ahmed, who looked regal in his traditional Malaysian outfit introduced himself to Nahla and then introduced the girls to his Arab friend, Kareem, who was an oil engineer. They both thought him very handsome in his white dinner jacket, contrasting with his trimmed black beard and he, in turn, was impressed with Ahmed's choice of guests.

"May I get you both a drink?" asked Kareem.

"Yes please, but no alcohol for either of us," replied Mariam, trying to avoid the men realising she was Nahla's servant.

"Will orange juice be acceptable, or they have Malaysian pineapple juice?" he asked.

"Pineapple for me, please. What would you prefer, Nahla?"

"The same as Mariam please."

Whilst Kareem was away, Ahmed took them into another larger room from where they could hear music. Here, all eyes were on the two girls in their dresses of the latest fashion and who were two of only half a dozen unmarried ladies present. Unlike the Arabs, Malaysian men were not so restrictive on the freedom of their women at events like this, Mariam explained. Ahmed introduced them to his boss, who had recently become ambassador. Ahmed used only their first names as he knew Nahla did not want to be exposed.

The ambassador who prided himself on local knowledge asked, "Where do you live, Miss Nahla?"

"I live at the Emir's fort, sir," she replied. He assumed thereafter that she worked with Mariam in the Emir's household, although he was surprised to find an Arab girl in service. Kareem returned with their drinks in time to hear the conversation and made the same assumption as the Ambassador. The band started to play a popular Malaysian ronggen. The Ambassador excused himself and moved on to another group of arrivals.

Ahmed asked Nahla, "Would you like to dance?"

"I would love to, but I have no idea how," she replied.

"It is a very simple step. Mariam and I will show you." He took his cousin onto the floor, where they positioned themselves facing each other, moving to and fro, each with their hands held together behind their backs. Nahla was fascinated and relieved to see that the dance did not involve bodily contact. Soon she felt the rhythm of the music and longed to be able to emulate Mariam. Kareem, who had found them and was holding the drinks, told her that Ahmed had taught him the dance and he said he would love to teach her.

As she sipped her juice, Nahla realised how simple it looked, and said, "I would love to try, please."

"Come on," he replied, as he took her glass and placed it with the others on a small side table. Kareem grinned at Ahmed as they passed him and Mariam on their way to the edge of the dance floor, where she noticed many couples doing no better than them, all laughing at their first efforts. By the time she had ceased to be a liability to Kareem's ankles the music stopped. They managed to sip their drinks once more before it started up again. Nahla could not wait for another invitation from the handsome Arab and pulled him on to the dance floor.

They shared many dances, and in between them Kareem kept her amused with stories of adventures in the oil fields of the different countries in which he had worked. Nahla released Kareem once, for him to dance with Mariam, whilst she danced with Ahmed. The unaccustomed activity made her feel hungry, and she realised that she was unfairly exhausting Kareem who was beginning to wilt. From a buffet, they collected nasi goreng and rendang, which all four of them took outside to eat at a table in the garden.

Nahla and Mariam agreed it was a romantic setting, "Like in the stories you used to read to us," whispered Nahla, so that the men did not hear. Mariam and Ahmed made an excuse to leave the two Arabs.

"Do you mind being with just me?" asked Kareem, starting to worry for her reputation, but hoping this girl who so attracted him would not object.

"Certainly not. You feel like family," she replied, thinking, "I could never have too much of his company." They talked some more, and she learned that he used to go to school in England. She tried her English on him.

He was amused and they talked afterwards in that language, "To give you some much-needed practice," he said, because her frequent mistakes made them laugh together and attracted the interest of those at other tables.

"My brother was at a school in a place called Woolverstone. Do you know it?" she asked.

"Know it? I was there!" replied Kareem, in surprise. "There was only one Arab boy and he was my best friend. I used to sail with him. He came from …" He stopped in the middle of his sentence as he realised she could only be the sister that Saif used to telephone so often.

She leaned towards him conspiratorially, disarming him with her perfume, as she whispered, "My brother is Saif bin Salim al-Wyly. Please do not tell anyone who I am, or I will be in terrible trouble." Kareem smiled, lost for words. "If you are Saif's friend with whom he sailed, then you also will want to keep your name secret in this country," whispered Nahla as she started to enjoy the intrigue that they shared. He laughed and she joined in. People at the next table looked at them and smiled sympathetically. "They think we are lovers," said Nahla.

Wickedly, Kareem thought, "If only we were."

The spell was broken as Ahmed appeared, looking for them. "Oh, you are still here. I am afraid Mariam is ready to leave, because she starts work early tomorrow."

"I don't want to leave him," thought Nahla, as their eyes met, and she sensed he felt the same magnetism.

"Yes, it is late," Kareem agreed, "and I also have to be at work early, but I will drive you back to the fort if you do not mind travelling in an old Land Rover."

Outside the embassy and back inside their coverings, the girls climbed into the sideways facing rear seats of Kareem's Land Rover. Ahmed gave instructions to deliver them only to the English Sergeant Adams and wished them *"Tisbah al akhair."*

"Salamat malam," replied Mariam in her language.

Nahla was oblivious to the jolts inflicted by the hard suspension of the vehicle as they returned to the fort, her mind fixed on the evening's events and her conversation with her new acquaintance. After helping the girls out of the vehicle and handing them to the sergeant, Kareem thanked them for a lovely evening.

"Thank you, Kareem. I have never had such a good time," replied Nahla, wishing she could kiss him like they did in books. Henry Adams, relieved that they had been returned safely, passed them through the big gate, waving happily at Mariam in particular. Ali was pleased also that Nahla was back safely under his wing.

In her bed Nahla lay awake for what seemed like most of the night, thinking of Kareem and turning over in her mind all that had transpired that evening whilst they had been together. Later she realised that, for the first time she could remember, Saif was not on her mind when she surrendered to sleep.

CHAPTER 30

1379 Hijri: AD 1960

Salim and Fatima were now living at the palace, and Nahla had also moved there to provide company for Fatima. She was pleased to be away from her brother, Moosa, who had started pressing her to get married, and was proposing their cousin Khaled, who Nahla intensely disliked, as a potential spouse. Moosa had threatened that as soon as he became Emir, he would otherwise have her marry the highest bidder regardless of what she wanted for her future. Mariam had now been promoted and was head of the domestic servants at the palace. Henry Adams and his expatriate soldiers were guarding the palace, having left a small force at the fort. Saif, Ali and the other ladies were still living at the fort, where they awaited completion of their palace accommodation.

Moosa had completed his military training and, to everyone's surprise, including that of Salim, who despaired of reports received of his son's moral decadence, passed out in the uniform of his country. How he achieved this is another story. Salim hoped that when his son adjusted to the cultural restraints of Naamlah that he would mature and "settle down", as the Scot Farnham would have said. Wisely, he did not want his son to take up a commission or to become Defence Minister until he was convinced that Moosa was fit to become his successor. Moosa was therefore appointed to the newly formed post of Minister for Mineral Resources. As the country was already developing the only known mineral resource, other than sand, it was thought by Salim that his errant son, by his inexperience, would not be in a position to cause much harm to the nation's economy.

Moosa, of course, resented having what he considered to be a lowly position in the Government, particularly as the post lacked apparent potential for increasing his wealth. He could not express this view to his father, it would be overtly disrespectful. He therefore vented his frustration on poor Hooda. She continued to suffer, without any means of protest beyond her nightly tears, because it would not have been right for a loyal wife to complain of the treatment she received from her husband.

When she announced that she was pregnant, Moosa had relented and, in his interest, treated her more gently. She now saw her only salvation to be more pregnancies. When a daughter was born, he blamed Hooda for not giving him a son, and returned to character, beating her at the least provocation. These beatings were generally a prelude to sexual activity because it appeared to Hooda that such behaviour was Moosa's only stimulant. Eventually she came to accept his abuse as a consolation, because it at least increased her prospect of once more becoming pregnant. Otherwise, she continued to feel only growing hatred and loathing for her husband.

After hearing of Moosa's appointment, his cousin Khaled, who had been his companion in Hamburg, now hopelessly addicted to heroin and an embarrassment to his parents, had started to press his friends for a job opportunity as they were now in positions of authority. Hammed had refused to support his son's accelerating drug dependence.

One day, whilst sitting behind his impressive desk, Moosa was alarmed by a disturbance outside his office. Fearing for his life, as he assumed his avowed enemies the religious zealots had broken in, he took cover beneath the desk. The door burst open to reveal his secretary trying to restrain Cousin Khaled.

Climbing from his hiding place, Moosa said, "It is all right. Let him in. He will do me no harm." The secretary protested that he had no appointment but Moosa dismissed him, demanding, "Shut the door and do not disturb us." The friends greeted each other, as was the custom, and Moosa asked; "What do you need from me that is so important that you are prepared to break into a Government office?"

"My father will no longer support me. He has ordered me to find work for myself because he has failed to find a position that I can hold for more than a day. You know I cannot work. My craving is too great to give the time to earn one month what I need for one day," replied Khaled, passionately.

"You know I have tried in vain to get my sister to bring you a wedding dowry to meet your needs. Do you think that I can employ you in my ministry after this exhibition?" Asked Moosa.

"No. I would not embarrass you dear cousin, but you are my only hope," replied Khaled, pleading.

"How much do you need?"

"One thousand dollars will be enough, cousin."

"That is not too bad. I will give it to you now if you will leave," said a relieved Moosa.

"No, you do not understand. I need a job that gives me that amount each month."

Moosa's mood changed to anger. "That is ridiculous, such a salary would be worthy of a Director-General in the Government." Khaled sensed Moosa's swing of mood and feared his cousin may now have him thrown out with nothing.

"You will help me, or your father will learn something of your military academy days and how you cheated your way through college," threatened Khaled, vindictively.

"He would not believe a raving addict," roared Moosa.

"We shall see," jeered Khaled, turning to leave. Moosa had second thoughts.

"Wait. Do not be hasty. I will do what I can. Leave it to me," offered Moosa, whilst rising to dismiss his cousin. Khaled's attitude changed instantly from aggression to gratitude. He grasped Moosa by both hands and started kissing his cheeks. As Khaled went out of his office, Moosa was thinking, "How can I rid myself of this embarrassing relation?"

CHAPTER 31

On the other side of the world a Russian immigrant to the United States was busy working on a unique engineering project. Boris Grobanov fled from Russia to America at the end of the war in Europe. He brought with him unique knowledge of the experimental work on torsion waves conducted by the scientists Professors Kozynov and Nasorev, with whom he had been working. In the US Boris found a low-level research post in the Bell Telephone System laboratories, where he was working on electronic systems. This work was not directly related to his previous employment, where he had been studying the interaction between torsion fields and the atomic spin of mineral elements and how such interaction could modify the atomic structure to change the properties of a material.

Knowledge obtained in his day job was applied in his spare time to perfect a detector of torsion waves, more robust and more sensitive than the crude devices used by his Russian colleagues. Boris' part-time project was to perfect a system of mineral exploration from the air using torsion fields. He called this Airborne Mineral Location, with the acronym AML.

Boris' AML system relied on the hitherto unexplained principle employed by Mustafa in Arabia when he healed and when he located water in the 19th century and, as some would argue, as used by Jesus in the 1st century. The apparatus, now mounted inside an aircraft, responded to the unique atomic spin frequencies of different buried mineral elements when they were exposed to the torsion field beamed from that aircraft. AML logged the density of detected minerals and plotted their locations using conventional radio direction finding techniques, as used at that time for sea and air navigation. The only visible adaptation of the aircraft was the torsion wave generator, which looked like the skeleton of an inverted pyramid, mounted between the landing gear. The aircraft that Boris was using was a Grumman F3F biplane that was normally dedicated to crop spraying and chosen, in its present application, because of its low stalling speed. He had initially been refused a license to use AML in the USA by the Federal Communications Commission, because of anticipated interference to established radio systems. After a demonstration that showed no such interference was caused and Boris' statement that AML did not use electromagnetic waves, the FCC granted permission to continue testing. Unofficially, the FCC examiners admitted to not understanding his explanation of torsion waves and thought him a harmless crank. However, some undesirable side effects were observed during later tests. These included disturbance to the behaviour of flying insects and birds, which it was widely believed relied only on the earth's magnetism for navigation. It was now apparent that bees in particular, when exposed to AML, were losing the ability to find their nests. More frightening were inexplicable reports of hallucinations and apparent epileptic disturbances experienced by people with psychic sensitivity as the aircraft passed over them. Boris was disappointed and decided to make no more flights in populated areas. To finalise his AML development, which he still believed could benefit desert or marine regions, he arranged a set of tests over the nearest desert to his home.

★

A heavily laden ex-US Navy Grumman F3F biplane flew very low across the salt lake in Utah, flown by war veteran and Russian immigrant, Mick Kowalsky, and watched from the ground by a thin grey-haired studious looking man in his sixties. The observer, Boris Grobanov, was patiently waiting for the results of an experiment which he hoped would make his fortune. They had chosen this location because it was devoid of minerals other than salt. Before the flight, Boris had carefully hidden quantities of iron ore, copper and small amounts of gold beneath the salt. He had marked each location on a map, of which only he had a copy. After completing its last pass, the aircraft landed and Mick switched off its motor. When the dust had settled, he climbed out and presented Boris with a role of recording paper.

"That's the last one, I hope, Boris," said Mick.

"I hope so Mick, but we shall not know until the results are analysed. You can go now but leave the equipment on board. I will phone if I need it again," instructed Boris.

Mick walked back to the aircraft, thinking to himself, "I have met some nutcases in my time, but this one takes the biscuit. He climbed back into the cockpit and started the big radial motor, causing Boris to look like a walking snowman as he was engulfed in salt by the slipstream whilst he made his way to the trailer. Here he would compare the survey results with his mapped locations.

Although he was pleased to see 90 per cent success for density and location of iron ore and 100 per cent for gold, he was disappointed to see that for copper there were 25 per cent more locations and 285 per cent higher density than he had expected. The copper results were inexplicable, and if funds had been more abundant, he would have made more tests to help explain this phenomenon.

After paying for the charter and for Mick's time, Boris had no more funds with which to further refine AML, and decided that he would have to offer the system to customers in its current state of development because he did not want to risk revealing details to any potential financial backer.

His company, Surflight, requested the US Government to help find sites in various environments overseas where administrations were less particular about human exposure or where population density was minimal and where he could prove the effectiveness of AML. He was gratified when the US Government offered to finance AML surveys from the foreign aid budget aimed at developing countries. Consequently, the recently opened US Embassy in Naamlah, wanting to make an impression, arranged a meeting between an Embassy Secretary, accompanied by Boris, and an expatriate representative of the Ministry for Mineral Resources.

CHAPTER 32

Moosa received a report of the meeting at which one of his expatriate aides, Samuel Harper, a geologist, had represented his Ministry. At the meeting, Boris had tried unsuccessfully to explain to Harper how his AML system worked. Harper was not convinced that what he was offering would be superior to conventional survey methods but accepted Surflight's offer to make an aerial survey of Naamlah, as it was to be at no cost to the Ministry.

Moosa was suspicious of their motives because, he thought, "who would offer to do something for nothing," and insisted on having a personal meeting with Surflight's representative. At this secret meeting, where no minutes were taken, Moosa became aware of the possibility of making some money for himself. He conspired with Boris Grobanov to withhold from the Finance Ministry the fact that the service was being paid for by the US Government. Subsequently, a case was prepared by Samuel Harper, based on a long-term strategy to ensure the viability of Naamlah's economy, either after the oil had been exhausted or in case oil was replaced in the developed world by some as yet unknown alternative fuel. Moosa had the report translated into Arabic with himself as the author. A copy was sent for consideration by his father.

Although Salim was surprised to see that it was not in English, a language in which he knew Moosa had little ability, he was impressed by the content and, although he doubted that it had been written by Moosa, he was equally impressed by his son's foresight. He was doubly pleased because it was confirmation that Farnham had been right about Moosa "settling down."

After receiving Salim's enthusiastic approval to proceed with the exploration of their potential alternative mineral resources, Moosa decided to form a company to exploit what he now considered his best opportunity yet to make a fortune. He knew he could not, as minister, do this in his own name, and he could not trust his friends or ministry staff. He knew nothing of the education of the ladies of the fort, and even though his sister Fousia had been made a minister he thought this to be nepotism by his father. She, a woman, could not, he thought, be capable of heading a ministry like himself, a man. He thought also that his mother Layla and his aunt Shalma were no brighter than Fousia, typical naive women, particularly where business was concerned. In the case of Shalma, he could not have been further from the truth. Dwelling on these thoughts, a plan began to form in his devious mind, and a rare smile transformed his pasty face.

A company was formed to exclusively represent Surflight in Naamlah. As a result of the report from "Moosa," tenders were invited by the Ministry for surveying the nation's non-oil mineral resources. The Tender Board scrutinised the credentials of the bidders, noting that the directors of Moosa's company, called Guilt Air, were legitimate resident persons and that a bank guarantee had been obtained to ensure that the bid was authentic. The company, of which Layla and Shalma were listed as directors, had an advantage over other bidders who were offering conventional established survey methods, in that the others had to make a legitimate profit. Also, their competitors would require an army of highly paid geologists and support personnel to survey the whole country by conventional means in the stipulated time frame. The bogus company was therefore successful and received the contract from the National Tender Board, because theirs was by far the lowest bid at $ 1,876,000.

★

Saif, now working his way through the ranks of the Finance Ministry with the object of replacing Uncle Hammed as Minister, had reached the Directorship which dealt with the investigation of fraud. Here he came across several ongoing cases which were to be taken to the courts where, typically, senior government officials were implicated in awarding contracts to companies in which they had personal interests. In some instances, he noticed the cases had failed because of difficulties proving that confidential data had been released to the tenderer or that an official had been bribed because the money went to an offshore account. Although the purpose of the Tender Board was to preempt corruption, it consisted of accountants who could be misled by technicalities which could be used to favour a particular bidding company by corrupt officials.

Saif became adept at spotting companies with doubtful directors, such as female members of Minister's families or those formed offshore by residents. He had recently come across a file on a company registered as Guilt Air and was surprised to see that his mother and aunt were the directors. His initial thought was depressing because he feared his father may be involved, then he felt happier as he guessed more likely someone was trying to implicate and discredit Salim. "Perhaps the ladies are legitimate," he thought later, because he knew how much they had changed since they had been educated, and possibly they were now quite sophisticated businesswomen. He checked with the bank holding the tender guarantee where the appropriately bribed member of staff confirmed they were the directors who had logged the deposit. This person did not say that he was supposed to ensure the transfer of any funds, received for payment to Guilt Air, into an account of Moosa's. Saif moved on to another case.

Some weeks later Saif read in the local newspaper that Guilt Air had been awarded a big surveying contract on behalf of American principals Surflight which triggered his memory of his mother and aunt's involvement. Next time he was at the fort he asked to see the ladies. Layla greeted him, invited him to sit in their communal room and offered *cawah* which was brought by Ali.

"Please do not be offended by my question, mother, but does my father not support you adequately?"

Layla looked puzzled and responded, "What do you mean? We are all well provided for by Salim, and Shalma is now wealthy in her own right from what she is gaining from her stock market speculation."

"That is what I expected, but I see you and aunt Shalma are about to make lots more money with your new company," said Saif. Layla looked dumbfounded, so he explained what he had discovered. Later, Shalma came home and Layla asked Mariam to see if she would join them. Saif had not seen Shalma for over a year and was taken aback by her transformation. She had lost weight, was attractively made-up, and was dressed in a European business suit. He could not believe that the attractive and confident businesswoman he was now meeting could have once been the depressed unkempt recluse he had known as a boy. Shalma greeted her nephew with a broad smile which revealed her recently acquired teeth. They repeated Saif's story to Shalma, who was also ignorant of the company, and she became shaken, then angry, that her name had been used in this way. Layla, seeing her sister-in-law's reaction, realised the seriousness of the affair and also started to look angry.

"Did someone ask you or trick you into being directors?" asked Saif.

"No. Certainly not," replied both ladies in unison. Layla thought little of what Saif had asked, but Shalma, who was much more astute, was concerned to learn what more Saif could discover of the mystery and as soon as possible.

"Do not worry, I will have it investigated," said Saif, with dread beginning to edge into his mind.

CHAPTER 33

Meanwhile, in the USA, arrangements were being made for Boris, Mick and their equipment to be shipped to Naamlah for the mineral survey which they had contracted to complete before the local holiday. In Naamlah It was anticipated by Moosa that an exciting announcement would be made, which would give him much needed credit in his father's eyes, before the celebrations commenced.

★

Boris and Mick arrived at Naamlah and stepped out of the door of the Boeing 707 aircraft into searing heat, which they both assumed to be due to the engines that were still running. As they descended the access steps and started dragging their hand luggage across the tarmac, they realised that this was the ambient temperature in which they were expected to work. After formalities, they were greeted by Samuel Harper who told them that their AML equipment had not been released by customs.

Harper searched out the relevant officer and paid the expected bribe which resulted in instant clearance. The visitors were then taken to Naamlah's new Holiday Inn, where they were installed and told to wait for Abdul Bahwani who would provide them with a survey aircraft and a vehicle.

Abdul's business was now primarily the provision of ex-military construction equipment for the oil industry, but he also dealt in light aircraft and military vehicles. The pair were wondering what to expect. In particular, they were anxious to know if the aircraft would be capable of flying at low speed. Abdul arrived the following morning, accompanied by his teenage son Suliman, who was to be their interpreter. After introductions they offered to drive the Americans, in the Land Rover that he had prepared for them, to see the aircraft at Abdul's compound. Here they found the aircraft to be one of three ex-Royal Navy Fairy Swordfish biplanes, the other two of which were missing their engines. Mick had flown these before and was pleased to confirm to Boris that it was a perfect choice.

"We have fitted the best of three engines, which has only a few hundred hours use and a new undercarriage," assured Abdul via Suliman.

Mick asked, "Can I run the engine before we make a decision?"

'Sure, you can taxi it out onto my strip and fly if you want'. Mick was tempted, but decided that if Abdul was so confident it would not be necessary and besides there was nothing else available. They agreed with Abdul for one of his fitters to help install the AML equipment and Abdul offered to let them operate the survey from his air strip for a nominal fee. The strip was no more than an abandoned section of road, which had originally served an oil storage facility that had been moved to a site with better access for the pipeline, but the surface was well graded and had no obstructions, Mick observed. Flags marked its edges and a windsock stood at one end.

Whilst Mick and the Indian fitter worked on the aircraft, Boris investigated the availability of local air navigation aids. He was disappointed to learn that there were no local radio beacons for position fixing, except a non-directional beacon at the main airport, but Mick had the idea of forming a row of ground markers along the Northern coastline to guide him. Abdul's boy, who was fascinated by the project, offered to guide him and to intervene on his behalf if he came across any objectors to his plan. He was welcomed by Mick, who explained to Suliman that the markers were to be spaced to match the beam-width of the torsion field. Mick was confident that with the aid of his bubble sextant, a chronometer, and sun sights, he could fly on a straight path in a southerly direction from each marker and thus cover the whole of Naamlah's mostly-desert territory in a few days. As the whole of the coast was a sandy beach, it should not take long to cover the distance required to make the marks in the Landrover. He planned to stop every tenth of a mile, indicated by the vehicle's odometer, where he proposed that they cut a cross in the sand.

★

They spent two days in the sweltering heat, during which they installed the AML equipment in the Swordfish whilst Mick and Suliman set out their markers in the sand. Suliman, who was now Mick's friend, was delivered back to his father. The Americans, who had worked all the hours they could, were both exhausted by the heat and were desperate to find some beer. As non-Muslims, they discovered that they were allowed to purchase alcohol from the hotel bar. This was kept out of sight, with only soft drinks on display. After making this discovery they regularly made the most of this civilised concession. Four more exhausting days and they had completed the survey, except for a patch on the eastern side caused by a loop in the great wadi, which Mick had overlooked.

It was now only two days before the holiday, and Boris declared, "I will have to start compiling the report, or we will be penalised for being late."

"You carry on with that and, in the morning, I will make one more pass to cover the eastern boundary. If anything worthwhile shows up, we can add it as an appendix," suggested Mick. This was agreed and Boris set too, analysing the results for their report.

They managed to get the report, complete with an appendix which contained surprising results, typed up and delivered to Moosa on the eve of the Holiday. They hoped to fly home that night, but the holiday caused the two men to be delayed until the following Sunday. They spent most of this time in the air-conditioned hotel bar, where they met a big German who told them in poor English that this was the only place where you could get beer.

Mick asked him, "Are you staying here long sir?"

"Nein, ich haben ein little place out of die stadt," replied Bernhardt. "When first ich visit das hotel ist meine home. Ich become freunde mit dem staff. Now ich am buying beer und bringen eggs," added Bernhardt cheerfully, in an attempt at English.

"You a farmer?" asked Mick, recognising only the word eggs in the big man's awful English.

"Nein, ich am mit der government, but raised on ein farm und keeping die hens for pets," he replied, struggling with his English vocabulary. Mick had an idea.

"Were you in Russia during the war?" he asked.

"In der war, ja, but no in Russia, in Africa I served."

"Oh, I was thinking you might speak Russian," said Mick, disappointedly. Boris joined them as Bernhardt was expanding on his history.

"In war ich haff der Rhode Island Reds mit die sheeps in Lybia." The others laughed at the improbability of this. "Certainly. I show you meine place. Komme diesen abend und have der dinner," invited Bernhardt.

"That sounds like a good way to escape the holiday," said Boris.

"I'll buy that," agreed Mick. Bernhardt drew a map on a napkin, and they agreed to meet at seven.

★

It had been dark for some time when the Americans found Bernhardt's farm. The house stood alone amongst some palms and a few other trees, several miles off the nearly completed road that led east out of the town. The ministry had rented the property, a small date farm, from Nasser, the receptionist of Fousia's ministry where Bernhardt worked. Fousia had personally selected furnishings, the installation of which she and her Sikh driver had supervised during several social visits.

"Good job we had four-wheel drive, Boris. That was pretty rough terrain the last few miles," said Mick, who was driving. He switched off the motor, which appeared to have been running without the benefit of the silencer that they had when they left the hotel.

"Now I can hear you, repeat what you said a mile back?" asked Boris.

"I said did you see that dog jump out of our path?"

"I thought it was a fox," replied Boris. Bernhardt could not help but hear their arrival and came out to greet the dusty travellers. They were surprised to see that he was wearing an Arab *dishdash* and carrying a rifle.

"Howdy Bernhardt. You didn't warn us to come armed. Are the natives that unfriendly?" joked Mick, as he stepped out of the Land Rover.

"Wilkommen to meiner klein farm, where ich defending der hens against der fox," replied Bernhardt, bowing and clicking the heels of his sandals in a manner quite out of keeping with his Bedouin appearance.

"Would a dog not be more appropriate?" asked Boris.

"Ah, ich habe him imprisoned for ihre arrival. Der fox is knowing dies und try to getting in schnell," said Bernhardt, beckoning them towards the little, white-painted house of mud bricks. Boris noticed a well-weathered engraved beam over the entrance. Bernhardt saw him looking at it and said, "Ich translate das Arabic: 'Mustafa al-Wyly, finder of water.'" He struggled to explain to them the history of the farm. It had been owned by two old men who had been slaves, and after their death with no descendants it had been adopted by Nasser's father. He failed to make it pay and gave it to his son, but Nasser was not interested in farming and let it fall into ruin. When foreigners started arriving and looking for rentals, he had it restored.

Out of sight, a dog started barking at their approach. Bernhardt shouted to it in Arabic, causing it to stop barking and take up a position at his side. At the side of the house were some young eucalyptus trees in which hens and a cockerel had taken refuge. The dog, now visible, ignored the hens as Bernhardt started calling them down by name.

"They not prisoned, as you see. Ich like sie to be glücklich, er … happy, you say," announced Bernhardt. He introduced the dog as Sultan. "Der hundt ist die hens guarding," said Bernhardt, as they entered directly to a living room through a bead curtain that Mick assumed was to keep out the mosquitoes which were then whining around his head. Sultan disappeared around the side of the house. "Nicht electric for aircon und der beer ist also warm," announced Bernhardt, opening a large bottle. "In two weeks coming it is," he said, presumably referring to the supply of electricity, Boris thought.

Their host poured three glasses and invited the visitors to sit. They had entered a room which appeared to be his lounge and dining room, and was dimly lit by two oil lamps. The floor had rugs over dirt, but the furniture looked new, made of bamboo with patterned cushions which, Boris noticed, matched the curtains. One of the lamps was in the centre of a circular table where three places had been set. The second lamp was bracketed off the wall above where Bernhardt was now sitting. Mick noticed that a book was open on a small table beside Bernhardt's chair. Out of curiosity, Mick cheekily picked it up and read the title which was printed in three languages. He read the one in English: Holy Koran.

"When you settled will Sultan coming freunde to make. He strangers not liking," laughed Bernhardt as a cheerful looking Indian servant, Boris presumed, entered from another room. "Ranjit, mine guests you see. How ist das cooking progress?" asked the host.

"I shall be serving in ten minutes only, Mister Bernhardt," replied Ranjit, shaking his head and smiling at the visitors. He raised joined hands before his face, made a slight bow and returned to what Boris now knew to be the kitchen.

"I see you are learning the local religion," said Mick, nodding towards the book.

"Yah ich for mine conversion to der faith am preparing," replied Bernhard with an irreverent wink, Mick thought. "No beer und much praying," added Bernhardt. The other two laughed, thinking he was joking. Suddenly Bernhardt's expression became serious and they both thought their laughter had offended him, as he lifted one hand, pointing towards Mick's shoulder. "No move mein freund," said Bernhardt, rising from his seat and flicking something from the back of Mick's chair. A large scorpion landed on the floor by Boris' feet. Bernhardt quickly grabbed a cushion, with which he picked up the startled creature and carried it outside.

"Thanks, Bernhardt. I guess you saved me from a nasty sting," said Mick, after recovering from what he thought was to be an attack on himself by their maddened host.

"More than der sting mein freund. Of ein thousand scorpion species, two per cent fatal to man. He was of der two per cent," said Bernhardt, with authority.

"You live close to nature out here," observed Boris.

Bernhardt replied, "Ja, you see, mein job is der environment to be protecting for der government, und der Scorpion ich am expert on. What you doing in Naamlah?" he added.

Boris explained their survey task and noticed that their host did not look happy, presumably at the thought of future environmental disturbance. "Gut you not earlier telling or might not you invited here," said Bernhardt, smiling and scratching his chin. He opened another bottle of warm beer and topped up their glasses.

Mick thought to change the subject; "I like these furnishings. They look a bit too feminine for a countryman like yourself."

"Ja, mein Minister, she helping me mit der shopping so is all to die taste of her," replied Bernhardt.

"Does she visit out here?" asked Mick.

Bernhardt looked guilty and muttered, "Sometimes she is here coming." He scratched his chin again. Mick thought, "He seems embarrassed, that must be a nervous habit." To change the subject, Bernhardt shouted, "Ranjit let now in Sultan." There was a scrabbling of claws as the big black dog accelerated out of the kitchen and came rushing into the room. The Americans froze as the Dobermann nuzzled their hands in turn, cropped tail wagging furiously. Mick was the first to have the courage to pat him on the head and was rewarded by a wet nose being thrust towards his crotch at lightning speed. Another pat diverted him but encouraged Sultan to lick Nick's face before Bernhardt grabbed his collar, pulled Sultan away and said "Sit," which he obeyed.

"I see what you mean about him wanting to greet us," said Mick.

"He will know you der next visit. Like Fousia …" Bernhardt stopped, as he realised the beer was making him too talkative. Ranjit saved the moment as he brought in three plates of food and put them on the table.

"Come eat," urged Bernhardt.

The three spent a pleasant, but what the Americans found to be uncomfortable, evening eating Ranjit's special curry, washing it down with more warm beer and all the time talking. After the air conditioning, of both their hotel and the Land Rover, they found it unusually hot and sticky in the little house. As a consequence they found themselves drinking more than they would have done otherwise. Their new friend, Sultan, made several attempts to join them at the table but always sat when told to by Ranjit or their master. When it was time to leave, the Americans staggered to their vehicle with Sultan in attendance. They found the Land Rover adopted by hens. Sultan frightened them, clucking, off the bonnet and back into their trees. Bernhardt, with Sultan at his side, waved them off then went inside, leaving Sultan to guard the hens from the fox.

★

The holiday at an end, the Americans flew home with their equipment and a Xerox copy of the survey report.

Moosa had the original report delivered directly to his office without anyone else seeing it. He was annoyed to find that it was not in Arabic, because his English was almost non-existent. He struggled through the contents with the aid of an Arabic-English dictionary, and eventually in frustration he started ignoring everything except the numbers representing costs and

180

mineral quantities. He was impressed with the apparent large deposits of copper ore. By the time he reached the appendix, he had lost interest, and when he saw that it referred to Haqum he completely dismissed it as being irrelevant. He separated the index and hid the file in his desk so that Harper or his secretary would not be able to see it.

CHAPTER 34

The inability to transport Naamlah's oil to market was causing pressure on the Rial which, since its introduction, had been at parity with the US Dollar. Attempts by Hammed to support the Rial had failed. He therefore informed Salim, at a hastily arranged meeting, that as a last resort the Rial must be devalued.

Salim objected, "Brother, only last week you assured me that we could protect the Rial by buying with our gold."

"We have already used the gold and mortgaged the marriage dowries for that purpose, brother," replied Hammed, guiltily. They reluctantly agreed they had no alternative course of action. A Finance Ministry proposal to devalue by 20%, making the Rial worth 80 cents, was to be implemented with the utmost secrecy, to take effect immediately. It was to be announced in two days hence.

★

Because Hammed's scam, to skim money off the national income, was not yet coming up to his expectation he saw the devaluation as an opportunity to plan an alternative source of wealth. In anticipation of the devaluation, of which only he and the Emir had knowledge, Hammed started borrowing from several banks, in each case saying that he needed the loan to finance the construction of a large villa. The banks were to keep this loan secret because it would otherwise impact on the value of adjacent land which he was intending to purchase later. The banks were understanding of this precaution, with the result that they were not aware he had told the same story at every bank that loaned him

Rials. Each bank was to transfer the loan payment to Hammed's account at a bank that was not included in his scam. Here he converted all of the loan cash into US Dollars. His action did not go unnoticed by the personnel handling his loans, many of whom guessed what he was doing and decided they would also buy US Dollars. Soon legitimate businesses found it impossible to obtain US Dollars, but this situation only persisted until the devaluation announcement. Immediately after that event Hammed started to change his Dollars back into Rials. For each Dollar, he now received 1.25 Rials, from which he paid back his bank loans. By any standard Hammed made a fortune. He became very unpopular once people suspected that he had used his privileged knowledge for personal gain. Salim was disgusted to learn of his brother's scam and was only consoled by the knowledge that his brother was soon to retire. Once more he found himself praying on behalf of one of his family.

★

When she had recovered from the excitement of meeting the man with whom she was convinced she was in love, Nahla telephoned Saif and told him of her evening with Kareem. Not previously aware of Kareem's disguised presence in Naamlah, he now located him via Cornubia, who were employing Kareem, and renewed their friendship. When they met, he soon became aware that Nahla's feelings were reciprocated by Kareem. Saif was saddened and perhaps jealous, he thought, his only consolation being the certainty that as things stood between the two countries, it would be impossible for the romance to lead any further. Once he was over the initial disappointment, he told Kareem about the reclusive nature of his aunt Shalma and the years of depression she had endured after the break-up of a romantic affair with one of his countrymen. Saif said he did not want Nahla to suffer that sort of experience. Kareem was unmoved by the story and surprised his friend with the revelation that he believed Shalma's lover was his late uncle.

"I find that impossible to believe. How on earth could they have met under the strict rules of *harem* that were then enforced by families to prevent their women from disgracing the family?"

"Apparently, our grandfathers were once keen to break the feud by uniting our families and our lands. To this end photographs of their eligible children were exchanged. Eventually, Shalma and my uncle were introduced and rapidly fell in love. Somehow, they met again secretly," said Kareem.

"What happened to prevent the marriage?"

"As far as I could learn there was violent opposition from Shalma's brothers who stirred up opposition from within other tribes and from the clerics of your country. Threats of bloodshed were made, and your grandfather called off the unification and the marriage. The result was restoration of the feud and enmity between our countrymen."

"Do you think we should try to continue where our grandfathers failed, but with my sister and yourself as pawns?" asked Saif, forcing a smile that did not represent his real feelings about the prospect.

"Nothing on Allah's earth would please me more," said Kareem, savouring the mental image of being married to the very beautiful and charming Nahla.

★

Meanwhile, another romance was blossoming. Fousia and Bernhardt had been drawn to each other from the moment they met during the job interview. Within a month of constantly sharing each other's company at the Ministry they had realised their common enthusiasm for natural history, which led to personal familiarity with each other's backgrounds and feelings.

Fousia offered to help furnish his house and became a frequent visitor to Mustafa's farm, where she was driven by her Sikh driver and protector, who always remained outside unless he was required to assist with heavy furniture. Sultan and Fousia became friends and the dog always welcomed her. Just like Fousia and

Ranjit, the Sikh was recognised as a friend by Sultan who, despite his breed's reputation, was a very sociable animal.

Fousia realised with gratitude that because of her earlier infatuation with Mariam she had avoided being married, when she was young, to the first wealthy man who had asked Salim for her hand. Now she was convinced that her future lay with Bernhardt and she knew he felt the same way about her. They both realised the problems their relationship would pose, but they had decided on a tactic which would, *inshallah*, enable them to marry in spite of opposing odds.

CHAPTER 35

From inspection of a copy of their tender documents, Saif found that Guilt Air used the Naamlah Agricultural Bank, where the company had an account. He learned that the bank held a performance guarantee of a percentage of the contract price. A 90 per cent payment was due to Guilt Air from the Ministry when the survey commenced, and a final 10 per cent when results were presented to the Ministry, but the bank was reluctant to divulge the name of the account holder. This made him suspicious and resulted in him using powers that required that they are obliged to divulge the name of the beneficiary when fraud was suspected. He allowed them time to produce this information, after necessary discussion with their client, and meanwhile moved on to his next case.

This involved a construction company, owned by one of Naamlah's principal families, who had recruited labourers from India to work on the construction of the road leading to Yemen. The men were promised $ 30 per month with food and accommodation included. This figure was used to cost the work that would be paid for by the Government. Once the contract was awarded and the men were in Naamlah the company reduced their pay to $ 25, thereby increasing their profit. To the labourers this was still a good wage, so they did not complain, for had they done so the company's tactic would be to refuse to release them to an alternative employer, as was the law, or to stop them returning home by withholding the return ticket that employers must buy, which again was the law, and by holding on to their passport, which was also the law. Effectively, the workers were slaves. Saif's brief was not to consider human rights issues, only the financial aspect. However, he could not help sympathising with the men. Whilst questioning the employer he learned that the wages had been reduced by amounts paid to a recruiting agent back home and to a local sponsor. They initially told him they did not know who this sponsor was, but one of the managers of the company eventually told him after Saif promised him anonymity. Saif felt sick when he learned his uncle Abdulazziz was the culprit, taking money for nothing from these poor men. He resolved to confront his uncle at the next opportunity, although it did not appear that he was doing anything illegal. The company restored the pay of the men once they learned of Saif's investigation, out of fear that he might investigate and expose other dubious practices. Saif became an instant hero among the workers but most unpopular with the Company.

★

Moosa's accomplices at the bank immediately informed him of Saif's investigation into Guilt Air. He was, therefore, prepared when Salim, who Saif had informed about his concern for the ladies involvement, asked to see him.

Moosa's implausible excuse was: "I intended the company to be a gift for the ladies, and the bank was sworn to secrecy only so that it could be a surprise. They would automatically have been given all money held in the account once the financial risk associated with such an adventurous project had been eliminated."

"I am sure they will be grateful to you, my son," replied Salim, trying to hide his disappointment and keep his temper at bay. After Moosa had gone, Salim, with a sinking heart, prayed once more for a member of his family.

★

Subsequently, Shalma and Layla shared $ 1,750,783 when the expenses of the company had been deducted from the payment received from the US via the Naamlah Government, leaving Moosa with nothing to show from his scam. The bank sacked Moosa's accomplices and Moosa did the same with Samuel Harper, having him instantly deported by uncle Abdulazziz before he could claim unlawful treatment or tell what he knew of Moosa's scam. Hooda took the brunt of Moosa's disappointment and anger.

CHAPTER 36

Emir Salim and his young wife Fatima did not, except for meals, leave their bedroom on the Thursday of the holiday, determined to maximise their newfound capacity to please each other. When the ladies called at the palace on Friday, they found Salim to be relaxed, seeming like a younger man, and Fatima was obviously the happiest she had been since her marriage. No sooner had Layla separated the couple than she cornered Fatima. Layla knew instantly that the holiday had been a success from the impish smile fixed on Fatima's face.

"He is the ram you imagined, Layla," said Fatima, happily.

"I am pleased for both of you," said Layla, who hugged Fatima and kissed her cheeks. Later, Fatima received more congratulations from Fousia and Nahla, who both secretly envied her for being able to please their father. Shalma wanted more details and enjoyed one of her rare moments of happiness as Fatima described her experience at the meal and in bed to all the ladies. Nahla felt ashamed for thinking of Kareem and herself in similar circumstances. Fousia, without shame, imagined Bernhardt and herself in his little house amongst the date palms. She realised that there would be no better time than now for her to approach Salim, but decided it would be fairer to wait until he was at his office, when she would make an appointment for Bernhardt and herself to confront him.

★

At his office Fousia greeted her father formally, congratulated him on his relaxed disposition and introduced her senior adviser Professor Grover. Salim assumed that the appointment was to discuss government business and was not prepared for either Bernhardt's request for his daughter's hand or his impeccable Arabic.

"Your Highness, I have worked with your dear daughter for three months during which we have come to know each other ..."

Salim suddenly realised the implication of "know" and sat up, prepared for a scandalous revelation. Fousia realised what he was thinking and that his change of attitude was making Bernhardt nervous. She feared he may forget the speech they had rehearsed and reached for her lover's hand. Salim recovered, guessing now what was coming.

The German continued, "We have discussed this many times, your Highness, and know of the problems, but we believe it is right to ask that you kindly allow your daughter to be my wife." Salim looked at his daughter and could see in her eyes the suspense that she was experiencing, instantly sympathising, because he knew she was not young enough to attract other men.

"This is without precedent, an Arab Muslim woman marrying an obvious unbeliever and foreigner," Salim replied seriously.

"Dear father, he is not an unbeliever and will soon embrace our faith, and as you know your adviser, Mister Farnham, is a Christian with a Muslim wife," said Fousia.

"It is good that he is to convert to Islam, but the Farnhams were married in Britain where such unions are not frowned upon. There are other factors which I must consider before I can approve such a union. I shall need to discuss with the Mufti ..."

Bernhardt interrupted, "Your Highness, I have already met the Mufti and it is he who instructs me."

"Then I must seek the opinions of my ministers, because of the implications for protest from the Islamic zealots," continued Salim.

"Then it is not agreed, father?" asked Fousia, with her face downcast and her heartbeat quickening.

"Please leave the matter with me," said Salim, tiredly indicating that the meeting had to end and thinking, "Who would have daughters?"

Shortly after the holiday, the ladies were transferred to the palace, where they each had their own suite. Mariam, now house-keeper with a large staff under her control, had been ecstatic when she learned that her sergeant was also to be transferred to the palace. Their courtship had accelerated, and an engagement was imminent. When Fousia learned of this it gave her encouragement, because Mariam was Muslim, whilst the sergeant could not be a believer. The fort now only had Saif living there, but it remained the offices of the Emir, Farnham and their staff.

★

Moosa, recovering from the disappointment and frustration of having been forced into giving away the profits of his surveying scam, was still determined to use his position to acquire wealth appropriate to his status. With the connivance of like-minded contacts in other families, including the al-Jaboos, he embarked on a new project. He learned that the American Surflight company had sold their Naamlah mineral survey results to an American mining company, except for the results for the eastern sector covered by the appendix which Boris had retained. Unknown to anyone in Naamlah, Boris had done this as a contingency to cover the possibility of not being able to sell the main survey results. He was hoping to sell the appendix, which predicted a high density of gold in that country, to the ruler of Haqum.

The US mining company were now pressing for a licence to mine Naamlah's copper. Once Moosa received the application he realised there was an opportunity for bribery if he could get the proceeds sent to a foreign bank. He put all his energy into the scheme and discussed it with Idris. They considered Moosa's plan in secret at Idris's palace complex, where the pair hatched a better plan. Moosa would accept the license application and insist a local firm be appointed as agent, intending for himself and Idris to exploit the copper resources for themselves.

The Naamlah Copper Mining Company was established by Idris with $ 500,000 capital provided as an unsecured loan from his bank. The Americans contributed $ 2 million for the licence, of which 5%, or $ 100,000, went to Moosa as a gratuity. Shares in the company were offered to the public to bring the total capital to $ 5 million. Aunt Shalma decided that it could be a good investment, if the survey results were to be believed, and purchased shares for $ 200,000. Transcending their sexual prejudice, many investors now followed the example of the strange reclusive relative of their Emir, a woman who most of the population had previously not known existed. They piled in until the offer was fully subscribed. Idris immediately offloaded all of his shares, which caused a fall in the value of the company and a panic by others to sell their shares as they tumbled in value. By the time small investors knew what had happened, their shares were only worth 30% of what they paid for them. Rather than risk losing more money, they had been advised to sell at the lower price, though brokers were having difficulty finding buyers even at this price. Shalma could not understand why the value of the company had fallen. Later it fell to almost zero, but there was no data published to confirm that the copper reserves had changed. She had notionally lost nearly all of her investment and was not too happy. Idris now made a bid for all the available shares and acquired control of the company for a layout of just $ 100,000, now able to pay $ 400,000 back into his bank. Moosa retained his $ 100,000 bribe. The American company realised they stood no chance of recovering their licence fee when Idris threatened to expose their bribery of Moosa to their Government. The public shareholders were outraged, and many became bankrupt. Shalma, who was not aware of her nephew's involvement, was determined to see Idris brought to justice for his blatant manipulation of the stock market and took her case to her brother Hammed, who referred it to Saif.

Following the apparent success of their survey scam, Moosa and his accomplices started on a parallel scheme to construct a copper smelting plant with which to process the ore, which, it was expected, would soon be mined by Idris's company.

Moosa, as relevant minister, could not legally be involved in funding, and his accomplices between them could not, after their commitment to the earlier project, now raise enough capital. The smelting project was valued at $ 8 million. The conspirators were advised to go to the public via the stock market for the balance of funds. Unfortunately, the reputation of the directors had preceded them, and few were prepared to invest in the smelting project. They were now forced to seek funding from a bank. The Naamlah Agricultural Bank, with which Moosa still had some credibility, provided $ 4 million, 50% of the required capital, against the anticipated assets of the company, effectively owning half of the plant. The bank was already over-committed on other projects held up by the lack of oil exports, but this project appeared to be viable, as other investors were involved. One of these was Moosa, with his $ 100,000 bribe which, to prevent his name appearing, was introduced via Idris. Other conspirators, with their homes as security, each borrowed large amounts from the Agricultural Bank. The bank welcomed these loans on the mistaken belief that they offered diversity. $ 900,000 was outstanding from the $ 8 million required to fund the smelter project. This was to come via the public, who were keen to buy shares now that the scheme had plenty of capital and bank support. The copper smelting project was soon seen as a fail-safe way of diversifying from investment in oil-related schemes. After Shalma bought in with $ 250,000, it became oversubscribed. Those unable to get shares waited eagerly to see what she would do next.

To further ensure the success of the smelting company and to raise the company's profitability, and hence share dividends, the Finance Ministry was persuaded by Moosa to impose both a heavy import tariff on copper ore and a tax on refined copper. Immediately, this added potential value to the company and, with the fact that the initial offer had been oversubscribed, the share price doubled. The lucky investors were those who sold at this time. Among these was Shalma, who made $ 50,000 profit, after allowing for her loss on Moosa's earlier scam and excluding brokerage charges.

CHAPTER 37

By continuing to study the market and its constituent companies, Shalma attracted a greater following and became a significant figure in the investment world beyond Naamlah. Her reputation spread abroad, resulting in her being interviewed in Naamlah by a journalist from the English Financial Times. She was next invited to the USA, where she was to give presentations on her experience of being an Arab businesswoman in a man's world. Salim was reluctant to allow her to travel outside the country, as it would set a precedent for other women, who would also expect to be allowed to travel abroad. Shalma argued that he had allowed Fousia to attend University in Cairo. He was, therefore, forced to relent, although he knew this would be resisted by the men in the country. Layla intervened by offering to accompany her sister-in-law to ensure that she would not be influenced or corrupted by Western ways. Salim had to concede that, if they were to travel, it would have to become permissible for other women, and on reflection he decided that this was inevitable regardless of the men approving or not. "At least," he thought, "I will be prepared for their representations." The two ladies decided to also take Mariam, as they needed a servant.

★

Whilst Shalma was making her presentations at venues in the USA, Laylah and Mariam spent their time visiting stores, where they marvelled at what was available to American women. They became accustomed to seeing them moving freely, unaccompanied by a male guardian. Initially their dress attracted a lot of attention, and eventually Mariam decided that she was going to buy some Western clothes and try to blend into the local society. Layla was not confident to do the same, but approached the situation gradually by first going out with her hair uncovered and then, after a few days of feeling comfortable, she followed Mariam's example, but restricted herself to long skirts or slacks and sleeves that came to her wrists. Mariam, however, had no qualms against showing her limbs in public and enjoyed the attention she received from the American men.

Shalma's lectures lead to her being featured in the Wall Street Journal. When a censored account of the published interview appeared in the local Arab language paper back home it astounded the male readership and incurred the wrath of the mad cleric and his followers, whose protests were soon made known to Salim. Their objections were registered, but, as the less extreme members of the population, particularly those who had financial interests, approved of Shalma's performance, he decided that what she was doing could only benefit the country.

Layla started to meet American ladies, who invited her to their social gatherings, and was impressed by the fact that they, like everyone else in the country, had by law attended school, not voluntarily as she had discovered in Egypt, and many also went to secondary colleges and universities. When it was time to leave America, the ladies were reluctant, as they had all enjoyed the freedom to travel and meet people with differing outlooks on life.

★

After the ladies returned and settled back into their routines, Layla realised that she was starting to feel envy towards her sister-in-law and her daughter Fousia for the active and useful lives they had established for themselves, and decided that she also wanted to make a contribution to the development of the nation. She had a particular subject: female education, which she wanted to discuss with Salim. Layla met her husband in his office after asking if she could discuss a proposal that she had been considering.

"Dear husband, I know that you have not as yet appointed anyone to take charge of the education of the children of Naamlah."

"That is true, but until now anyone wishing to have their sons educated has sent them abroad, where excellent facilities have been established for centuries," replied Salim.

"That also is true, but only the wealthy can afford to do this, and what about the girls?" she asked.

"You mean, you think every girl should be educated as you and the other ladies were by Mrs Farnham?"

"Yes, I want all our children to be educated, not only the women of your family."

"Are you proposing to take charge of their education?" asked Salim, showing incredulity.

"Yes. I want to be your Minister for Education."

Salim was visibly taken off-guard at his wife's proposal. He had not thought of his older wife as anything other than a loyal dependent and mother to his children. He considered Layla's proposal for several minutes, thinking of the implications for the culture and tradition that would make such a drastic step difficult to implement. Layla sat in suspense, until he suddenly pronounced, "I agree in principle that education should be offered to every child, but unless it is made compulsory, as it is in Western countries, those whose parents object will put their children at a terrible disadvantage when they become adults. You can expect a lot of opposition. Do you really think, dear wife, that at your age you will be able to cope?"

"I have thought a lot about it, and really want to be able to help our country by directing education, particularly of girls, because you cannot deny what it has done for myself and our own daughters." replied Layla.

"Alright, leave it with me and an announcement will be made of your appointment."

"Oh, thank you, dear husband. You will not regret this decision," said Layla, beaming with delight as she departed Salim's office. As soon as she was outside, she asked her driver to take her to the fort, which she knew was becoming vacant as the residents moved out to new homes or to the palace. She went inside the big gate, past the guards, feeling nostalgia as she explored the residential areas; but in her mind a plan was forming to make this Naamlah's first public school.

★

Whilst the smelter was under construction, operational staff were recruited, including an experienced and highly qualified general manager. J K Patel BE, Fellow of the Institute of Fuel, was seconded from Tata Steel, a large Bombay foundry. The copper mines, meanwhile, were being developed by Idris' company, with both projects to go online at the same time.

Moosa, still being blackmailed by his addicted cousin Khaled, unable to fend him off by marrying him to Nahla, cruelly held off finding him a job. He was waiting to see if something could be found for him at the smelter once production started.

There was disappointment in the Naamlahn air as it slowly sunk into investors that, at the first working mine, the expected copper ore existed only in small, uneconomic quantities. The stock market wavered on this news, but Idris was immune, as his fortune had already been ensured by his mining shares manipulation. As he did not react to the news, the share price did not weaken significantly. Shareholders assumed there would be only a temporary delay until the other mines were in production. However, the smelter, under Patel's direction, was now ahead of schedule and ready to receive ore. To ensure a supply of raw material to tide them over, the company used a large portion of working capital to buy scrap copper and also to import copper ore, which unfortunately was subject to Moosa's import tariff.

On receipt of the first imported ore, Patel was able to commission the plant and report to Moosa that all was working to specification and on schedule. Moosa, his partners, and the shareholders were jubilant. Patel was summoned to Moosa's office, where he was congratulated and presented with a letter of appreciation and a bonus of $ 3,000 in cash.

"This payment is unofficial, as the partners do not know of it," said Moosa, winking conspiratorially. Patel suspected it to be a bribe for something that he would soon learn about. Whilst Patel was basking in glory before him, Moosa said, "There is a small thing I would like you to do for me, Patel."

"Of course, Excellency, how may I be of assistance?" replied Patel, realising his suspicions were now confirmed.

"I have a good friend who needs a job. You will, I trust, be able to give him say $ 1000 a month," asked Moosa.

"That is a large sum, your Excellency. We do not have many positions that offer such a high salary. I assume your friend is well qualified in metallurgy, or perhaps has managerial experience?" enquired Patel.

"No, he is just my friend, and needs an income," replied Moosa, starting to get annoyed because the Indian was not cowed and dared to question him.

"Well, Excellency, if your other partners agree to an increase in the payroll, I am sure we can find a position," offered Patel, reluctantly as he sensed Moosa's change of mood.

"They are not to know," said Moosa, abruptly.

"Excellency, I cannot justify it otherwise," Patel replied politely.

"I am telling you to employ my friend and give him $ 1000 a month, or you can say goodbye to your job," shouted Moosa, his eyes twitching in a reddening face on which beads of sweat were appearing. He now regretted giving the bonus and the letter.

"That is not possible, your Excellency. If you insist I cannot, in any case, continue to manage the facility."

"Then you are to be dismissed this instant. Leave me," shouted Moosa, now in a rage sufficient to raise his blood pressure to a dangerous level and attract his secretary.

"Are you alright, Excellency?" he enquired.

"Yes. Show this man out," he shouted. Mister Patel left, badly shaken by the encounter, and went straight to a friend who was a lawyer. What Moosa had not realised was that he was being confronted by a professional manager and not a common unskilled labourer, with no knowledge of his rights, typical of the majority of expatriate employees. Also unknown to Moosa were recent changes to Employment laws, replacing those of the past when they were designed to restrict free movement of slaves. Still angered, Moosa told his secretary to arrange for Patel's instant dismissal.

That night Moosa once more vented his anger on Hooda in an orgy of sexual deviation, and the following day his secretary contacted Moosa's uncle Abdulazizz to ask him to cancel the work permit of Mister Patel. Abdulazziz instantly agreed, but later phoned Moosa to tell him that he could not help with Patel because he was involved in a legal dispute that required that he be held in Naamlah until it was resolved. It was then that Moosa learned that Patel's lawyer friend had appealed to the Labour Court against his unlawful dismissal. He checked with a court officer, who told him Patel was claiming $ 100,000 from the Smelting Company on the grounds that he had not been given the contracted six-month notice, or salary in lieu, stipulated in his employment contract.

"I will swear that he was no good at his job," said Moosa, defiantly. This was greeted with a chuckle from the official.

"I am afraid that will not work, Excellency, though I know that is the usual escape. He has your letter of commendation and he has incriminated you. He says you gave him a cash bonus without your partner's agreement," replied the court officer. Moosa threw down the telephone in a rage at being thwarted by Patel.

Until the case was heard and a verdict issued, the court would not allow the company to replace Patel, and neither did the company want the expense of doing so, because there was every likelihood of him being reinstated as General Manager. In view of the importance of the copper project, the normally protracted workings of Naamlah's legal system were accelerated. Things happened so quickly that Idris did not have time to bribe the prosecuting counsel. Even then, the company had to stop production and lay off most of its workers. By selling the stock of imported ore and copper scrap, it managed to pay the wages of the few retained staff whilst the case proceeded. However, the company's losses were enhanced because they could not offset the tariff paid when it imported the ore. To compound the scandal, Idris' mining company conceded that none of the mines had viable quantities of ore and the survey had been wildly optimistic. It decided to surrender its licence. The share price of both companies plummeted as soon as this became known.

★

Boris Grobanov was sued in the USA by the American mining company, because they realised they had little chance of recovering their losses in the court of Naamlah. Without any positive survey results to show from AML, Surflight could attract no buyers and Boris, therefore, was bankrupted. This was to the relief of those with a vested interest in conventional surveying methods. Boris was so disheartened that he doubted the results shown in the appendix of the Naamlah mineral survey. He destroyed his copy of the data for fear of being ridiculed if he attempted to sell it to Haqum. Mick Kowalsky decided that the outcome confirmed his initial opinion, that Boris was a nutcase, and abandoned his erstwhile friend.

★

Trading in Naamlah Copper shares was suspended. The Agricultural Bank attempted to strengthen its position by foreclosing on the ostensible housing loans of Idris' partners, who by now blamed Moosa for their predicament. They joined the majority of shareholders in bankruptcy. Moosa might have escaped with some of his ill-gotten gains if he had not been so greedy, but these were now reduced by the bank recovering its costs from him. He made some bitter enemies. The bank now owned several luxurious villas and a copper smelting plant in a country with hardly any raw material and where a heavy tariff was imposed on imported ore.

200

Liabilities of the bank exceeded its assets and it had to allow itself to be taken over by a rival to avoid collapse of the delicately balanced banking system of Naamlah.

Salim, who was ashamed and embarrassed by his son's performance, had to admit that Moosa could never succeed him. He resolved that he would now make his younger son Saif his successor. This decision, he knew, would go against convention, and only serve to further antagonise the traditionalists in the country, and would particularly enrage the religious zealots. He instructed Hammed to tighten regulation of the stock market to prevent such abuse happening in future.

CHAPTER 38

Saif continued to be the scourge of those families, including his own, who profited from corruption, by exposing more of their shady schemes. Uncle Abdulazziz saw what was inevitable and relinquished his lucrative work permit scam by offering his resignation. Uncle Hammed, however, remained confident of his future retirement plan.

One day Saif, because of his reputation, was approached by some of his expatriate colleagues, aggrieved by an apparent scam perpetrated by the agent who recruited them. He took up their case because it had the hallmark of corruption. It transpired that their posts had been advertised by the recruiting agent at a salary of $ 2,000 a month. When they arrived in Naamlah, they were required to sign a contract between themselves and the Finance Ministry that was written in Arabic, in which the salary was $ 1,999. Even those who could read their contracts were unconcerned by this apparent insignificant discrepancy. What they did not know was that $ 1,999 was the salary roof of a grade beyond which there would be no more annual increments. $ 2,000 was the starting salary for a senior grade, which attracted annual increments of 3%, superior accommodation, and higher allowances. The Ministry was paying the agent a fee based on the higher grade. This was resolved by Saif, who had the contracts re-issued to include the higher salary. Saif was acclaimed as a hero by the employees, who had little representation and understanding of the legal system which, being based on what they considered to be medieval Sharia law, was imponderable and appeared biased against the majority of expatriate workers who were non-Muslim.

Saif was told by Hammed about his meeting with Salim, who asked him to investigate the mining scam. Saif was already suspicious of the workings of the stock market, even before his Aunt Shalma came to visit him. She told him of her disappointment when she had attempted to invest in the copper mining enterprise.

Saif was impressed by his aunt's knowledge of financial affairs and joked, "A pity father did not make you Finance Minister instead of your brother. Perhaps then we would not have been plagued by these corrupt practices."

"There is nothing I would like better than to be a Minister of the Government and be able to show how effective my gender can be. I would, however, rather have influence over something more humane, like welfare for example," Shalma replied.

"How about replacing Abdulazziz, who is about to retire?" asked Saif.

"Immigration would be ideal. I am sure I could make improvements there," his aunt replied enthusiastically.

"I shall recommend it to my father, and I will look into the copper scam as you are not the first to be concerned. I have a meeting now," Saif said, as he checked his watch and grabbed a file from his desk. Shalma was smiling broadly as he accompanied her to the door. He realised; "This is only the second time that I have seen her smile."

Saif, discovered several other instances where companies were formed and floated on the exchange, often with unsecured capital from a complicit bank, in which the gullible public were invited to subscribe for shares. Typically, the people involved would start a rumour that a large quantity of shares were to be purchased by an instructed broker before the stock was launched. Once launched the crooks would purchase a lot of shares, which would encourage ordinary investors to join in, even when the price was high. Once the offer was fully subscribed at the inflated price the crooks would sell their big holding, causing the value of shares to fall. Ordinary investors would then be advised to reduce their losses by selling at the low price before it went even lower. The effect would be for the price to fall further as confidence was lost in the enterprise. Then the crooks would purchase all available shares at a knock down price and end up most likely paying back their loan and still owning the majority of the company.

This was effectively what happened with Idris and the mining company. Saif's revelation made him unpopular with the corrupt families but popular with the majority of citizens, especially investors who were behaving honestly. Saif's findings were reluctantly reported to Salim by Hammed, who had already started overhauling the workings of the stock exchange. When presented with the facts on the copper smelting scam by Saif, Salim was shocked, but having already instructed Hammed to reform the stock market, there was little more he could do. He ruled, substantially, because the families relied on him not to interfere with their, sometimes illicit, commercial activities. He did agree, in the case of Idris, to remove the offending members of his family from their Government positions. This would, he hoped, help to keep the Government free of corruption.

Saif moved to other branches of the Finance Ministry, where he became a hero amongst his colleagues for having the courage to challenge Naamlah's wealthy families and the corrupt financial system that they tried to operate.

Salim called Saif to his office at the fort a few days after he had taken up residence in the palace. They exchanged polite compliments, amongst which Saif said he was particularly pleased to see his father looking healthier than he had for as long as he could remember.

"Save your flattery, son. I do not know if it is the change of residence or the shedding of my burden of responsibility on to other members of the family that has caused this change. I know your mother thinks it is my new wife, but whatever, I do agree with your observation," said Salim. "About your brother. You know that I have given him every opportunity to justify himself as a worthy successor as Emir. There have been occasions when I thought he would be worthy of the position, but there have been more times when I have been disgusted with him."

"Yes, father. I have felt that way myself on several occasions, but I am sure he can be persuaded to modify his behaviour," said Saif, trying not to compound his father's obvious disappointment with his eldest son.

"No, Saif, I do not think so, and because of this I have decided that you will succeed me very soon."

Saif was not expecting this and could not reply immediately. When he had digested the revelation, he protested, "Father, I am not yet in a permanent position at the ministry, let alone a minister. Surely you cannot think that I have sufficient experience to rule the nation?"

"I have watched your progress, son, and know of your reputation amongst the people. There is no one more suitable in our tribe. Besides, I have found that my own health has only improved since I started delegating my responsibilities to others. I need to take a more leisurely stance, on medical recommendation."

"I am sorry to hear that father. In that case I will be pleased to relieve you of the burden," replied Saif, curious but not daring to ask what was wrong with Salim's health. Salim looked pleased with Saif's response.

"As soon as you have completed your induction at Finance, I will announce your appointment as my deputy. Within one year you will be Emir," said Salim, with an air of relief. "There is another matter of importance. You and your brother have made many enemies amongst the other tribes, and you will from now onwards both have to exercise extreme care to protect your life."

"I am aware of the risk, father, and willingly take it for the sake of our country," replied Saif. Then a thought occurred to him. "Have you chosen successors for my uncles, father?"

"As you know, Hammed has brought disgrace on our family, and I understand that Abdulazziz has amassed a great illicit fortune during his time as Minister. This can only be at the expense of our subjects. I was unwise to expect their loyalty and fear I am a poor judge of character. I shall therefore leave the appointment of successors to you my son, as you will have to survive with the consequences. It can be your first test as Emir," said Salim, smiling.

"I only hope that your confidence in me will be justified, father," replied Saif.

"I have no fear of that. In fact, I will rely on you to also think about replacing your brother at Minerals. Please tell no one of our discussion. I will announce your appointment as deputy when the time is appropriate. Go now, and continue your good work," said Salim, rising to kiss his son.

★

Saif now worked in the final department of the Finance Ministry, which was known as the Treasury. He gathered that this department was "little understood" by those working there, except, apparently, by Uncle Hammed. Saif, therefore, set about understanding it. He obtained the accounts of all the advance payments from potential customers for Naamlah's oil that had been paid in Dollars into the Swiss bank account and compared these with the amounts transferred to the Treasury account at the National bank each month after conversion to Rials. Prior to devaluation, the rate of exchange was equal, and after devaluation it was 1.25 Rials for a Dollar with, in each case, a small transaction charge. He found that, without the transaction charge, both figures agreed, except for a few Dollars due to rounding of figures. On the face of it this was satisfying, until he realised that no interest had been paid on the money whilst it was accumulating in the Swiss bank awaiting the monthly transfer. Those he spoke to in the ministry said this must be because Islam did not allow interest. Saif, however, knew that the bank would have been able to use the money and thus earn profit, another term for interest, but acceptable in Islam.

Putting a call through to the bank in Zurich, he was referred to Herr Graff personally. He asked Graff why no interest had been added to the account on sums available to the bank whilst awaiting transfer to the Treasury and, if interest was earned, could he account for its not arriving in Naamlah? Graff, who was not perturbed by the inquiry, confirmed there were no debits by the bank other than what was transferred to Naamlah's accounts.

Saif was suspicious at the plural reference and asked Graff, "Is there more than one account, sir?"

Graff was silent for a moment as he thought about how to reply. Graff eventually replied that the second account was known by a number, and under Swiss law he could not divulge the name of the beneficiary of the other Naamlahn account. Saif realised then he would get no further with Graff, thanked him for his help and broke off the call, thinking this may be potentially the most lucrative scam that he had uncovered. He calculated that eventually, when oil revenues were being received, the Treasury could expect approximately $ 100 billion per year. Assuming a nominal rate of compounded profit or interest on half of each month's revenue, this would put about $ 50 million into the numbered account over a year. Fortunately, at present, as no oil was being exported, the scam had not reached anywhere near that level, but still possibly several hundred thousand Dollars were currently going there each year. Saif considered all the likely suspects at the Treasury and decided only Hammed could have done this, and he must have been assisted by someone at the Swiss Bank. Saif thought, "One can only burn in hell once, so if you are going to get caught pilfering it might as well be on a magnificent scale. I shall have to break this carefully to my father, because he has already had too many family disappointments."

CHAPTER 39

Moosa visited Hammed's impressive mansion to break the news to Khaled that he had not been able to secure him a position at the smelter, since it no longer functioned, nor had he been able to broker a marriage to Nahla which could have earned a significant dowry. He was both shocked and relieved to learn from Khaled's grieving mother that her son had died two days earlier of a drug overdose. She added that he had been buried quietly to avoid dishonouring the family.

As he drove away, he felt anger which overrode his earlier feelings as he realised if it had not been for his cousin he would not have been in his current position of unpopularity with his partners or his father.

Hammed was summoned by Salim after Saif presented his findings from the Swiss banking investigation. After Salim expressed his condolences for the loss of his nephew Khaled, they sipped *cawah* amicably, though Salim was having difficulty controlling his anger. He could wait no longer for Hammed, who must have known about Saif's investigation, to admit to his scam, like a man. Hammed remained calm until Salim surprised him by asking for an explanation about the second account in Switzerland.

Hammed had only an implausible excuse, which he offered with shaking hand, nearly losing control of his cup and recalling his interview with Graff in Zurich. "Dear brother, knowing that it was *haraam* to take interest, I instructed the bank not to add such paltry sums to the nation's revenue and thereby avoid inciting the Islamic militant element in our beloved country.

That small account was to be a fund for charitable work," grovelled Hammed. He relaxed but, unsure if Salim would buy this, he put his cup on the table.

"Has any needy cause received aid from the fund?" asked Salim.

"No, not yet, dear brother," replied an uncomfortable Hammed.

"And who has access to this account?"

"Er … only the Ministry of Finance," mumbled Hammed, hoping that would be the end of the inquisition.

Salim's face lost its amicable countenance as he said, "You mean only the Minister of Finance, don't you brother?"

"Er … yes … er … forgive me, dear brother, I am a weak and simple man corrupted by greed," grovelled Hammed, leaving his chair and dropping to the floor, kissing Salim's feet. "Allah has taken my son. Is that not what I deserve for my greed, dearest Salim?" begged Hammed from the floor.

"This will go no further if you make known the account access details to your nephew Saif, who will be relieving you as Minister with immediate effect," said Salim, his voice revealing his sadness at this latest example of his brother's treachery. "You should know, brother, that I had occasion to pray for your soul's redemption after that despicable devaluation incident. Allah decided that you needed punishment for that. Perhaps your son's death was just. I feel now that your soul is lost, and would advise that if you seek a place in heaven you make amends before Allah inflicts further punishment," added Salim, solemnly.

"Brother, I will. I swear," replied Hammed, now standing with bowed head like a chastised child.

"Leave me please," requested Salim.

★

Hammed, determined to rescue his situation in the eyes of Allah, immediately commenced planning the construction of a magnificent mosque that was to be the greatest structure in the country. It was a project to which he would devote the whole of his accumulated wealth. He was confident that after such a devout act of piety, together with the loss of his only son, he would still be guaranteed his rightful place and enjoy the delights promised to those who make it to heaven.

★

Following the recommendation of the meeting of experts at the Environment Ministry, an emissary was sent across the border to request a meeting between the respective heads of state. Kareem's father, knowing that he had the upper hand, refused to meet Emir Salim or any of his tribe. When this reply came back the advisers were nonplussed because they had not anticipated such a negative response. They did not know that the old Sheikh's attitude was the result of his belief that whatever agreement he made with Salim, who he respected, would undoubtedly be broken by his untrustworthy son, Moosa, when he became Emir.

CHAPTER 40

Saif, who had been investigating the great copper scandal, had insisted that Moosa release all the relevant documents. Moosa, confident that he had done nothing that would be revealed as illegal, at least since the issue of the mining licence, which was not being questioned, pretended to show eagerness to help.

A meeting of shareholders of Naamlah Copper was called by Idris al-Jaboo, who was the major shareholder. Idris made it known that he held Moosa responsible for the debacle. He omitted to inform them that it was his own greed that had caused him to support Moosa, or that he had been prepared to pervert the Naamlahn justice system to protect his erstwhile friend. The meeting included representatives of Mutual Fund and Unit Trust managers from the US and Britain, who had been impressed by the prospectus offered by the company. Their investors back home were now questioning their judgment in investing in this particular emerging market. These representatives were given no assurance by the meeting that they would ever recover their client's losses, and resolved to withdraw from future investments in Naamlah until the investment scenario was overhauled. This caused uproar amongst the others present and ended with police being called to disperse the meeting.

For most hardened investors this was considered to be the end of the affair, as they put their loss down to experience. Others who had lost all of their assets, including family property and their daughter's dowries were considering alternative schemes to punish the villain who had brought about their poverty. One group, knowing now that Moosa was the villain, sought nothing short of his death. One proclaimed that he was prepared to pay his last Rial towards the funding of an assassin. Others confirmed that they would do the same for revenge against the accursed Moosa al-Wyly. Thirty aggrieved shareholders pledged a total of nearly $ 20,000, advertised discreetly as being available to any man who would do the deed. They received many offers, including one who was sent by the mad cleric, offering to do the job for nothing. This was turned down because most thought such an offer could not be genuine. Ultimately, they chose a Persian butcher as they thought he had the appropriate skills. The Persian insisted on advance payment, with the money to be confirmed as arriving after transfer to his family in Tehran before he would start planning for the job.

★

The mad cleric, who lived across the road from the Farnhams, was holding one of his gatherings of followers to the faith, where he collected fees in exchange for the blessings he gave for temporary pleasure marriages between men and girl children. Within his own household he maintained four such child brides. In contrast, he railed against allowing the bicycle to be used by either sex. Inexplicably, he approved replacement of the camel and donkey by the motor car, but only as a means of transport for men. He considered the wireless to be a creation of the devil, and bitterly opposed its introduction, but accepted the use of amplifiers to drive loudspeakers on the minaret of Mosques. More than any other 20th century development, he bitterly resented the liberal attitude of Salim and the changes that he was so rapidly introducing throughout society under the infidel Farnham's guidance. The old man had previously called on his followers to bring about the end of Salim's regime by violence, because democratic change was not available as an option in a country without elections for its leader, not that they would ever have advocated elections.

In response to the rantings of the old man his followers had been spying on the Emir and his family, searching for weaknesses in their security. Finding the fort too well guarded by soldiers and the Palace similarly guarded and difficult to access and knowing that the Emir was to soon be succeeded by his oldest son, who was living in a less secure establishment, they made Moosa their target.

★

The Persian, having received confirmation of funds safely being received in Tehran, started to follow Moosa from his Ministry office to the house he shared with Hooda and their servants. He did this for several days until he was confident of the pattern of Moosa's activities. The prospective assassin realised that it would be relatively easy, after certain precautions, to scale the security wall. He planned to climb the overhanging bougainvillea at a particular spot out of sight of Moosa's security guards, and obtained a plan of the property's layout from the architect who had designed the house for the al-Jaboos,. He realised that once over the wall he would have to cut through the usual steel security grills at door or window, but that would only be a matter of time, and this did not look too difficult, as he would not be in a hurry.

CHAPTER 41

Hooda decided that her life could not be less miserable whilst Moosa lived to torment her. She knew that if she appealed to her family for help now, it was doubtful if they would believe her after so many years of apparent happy marriage, and in any case they could not interfere because, as she had been brought up to believe, a man was allowed to punish his wife as part of her training, just as a man would punish his dog or camel. In her unsophisticated mind she milled over these things and added the fact that Moosa would swear she was disobedient, and her punishment was justified under Sharia. Hooda was convinced that in retribution for the treachery of running to her parents she and even her child would suffer worse abuse in the hands of her husband. In desperation she thought if she was beheaded for his murder, she would at least be free of his torment, and he would not then be able to harm her daughter. She knew that he had many enemies, implying that there was always a chance that she may not be suspected. She convinced herself that as soon as the opportunity occurred, the risk would be worth taking.

★

On the evening of the Thursday that the Persian had chosen to strike, he travelled on foot and concealed himself in an empty house where he could watch the entrance to Moosa's garden compound. From his hiding place another man was observed, behaving suspiciously, a young Arab who carried a leather bag and who was also apparently watching the house whilst pretending to sleep in the shade of a palm.

The young man was Saleh, who had, in exchange for a guarantee of marriage to the unsuspecting young daughter of one of his fellow fanatics, been persuaded to kill the accursed Moosa al-Wyly on that same night. They both witnessed Moosa's arrival in the official car at the customary time, after leaving his office early as he always did on Thursdays at three pm.

★

Earlier that day Hooda had been called into the garden by screams from her daughter, who had been let out to play after finishing her breakfast. Hooda arrived to find the biggest scorpion she had ever seen, parading before her little girl with claws outstretched and tail arched in a defensive stance. She snatched the child and carried her into the house. Hooda returned immediately to the garden, searching for a large stone with which to dispatch the creature, but instead hesitated as an idea occurred to her. She had been warned as a child never to touch scorpions because their poison could be painful, and some species could be lethal to humans. She decided, lethal or not, it was worth risking in the plan that had now formed in her mind.

★

That night the Persian in his strange attire was observed by Saleh, the *farrage* from Fousia's office, as he climbed the wall using the thick overhanging prickly bougainvillea as a rope. He saw that the stranger was protected by leather gloves, boots, and thick trousers. He thought perhaps it was a robber and decided not to interfere, as he may be armed. Saleh continued to wait until it was completely dark, having made sure by his vigil that Moosa had not left the house. As instructed by the old cleric, this was the time to prime, and then throw over the wall, the bomb that he carried in a satchel.

Once he was over the wall the Persian hid in the shrubs of the garden until the servants had retired to their penthouse. He waited now for a light to appear at the bedroom of Moosa and Hooda. He removed the heavy boots which would he knew, from the plans of the house, be noisy on the marbled floors and placed them in the shrubs ready for his escape.

Moosa was still smarting from his failed business venture and continued to take this out on Hooda. When she had undressed and feigned tiredness, she was joined by Moosa.

"You do not escape me so easily, woman," snarled Moosa, as he switched off the light and slumped into their bed beside her. She tried to resist but he tore her nightdress from her and threw it to the floor. He forced her on to her back, lay his fat belly on top of her and forced himself into her. Outside, the assassin heard heavy breathing, obviously of a man, and the moans of a woman and guessed what they were doing. He thought, "They will sleep soundly after their exertion."

Hooda's face was expressionless as she prayed that Moosa would soon be spent. Then her expression changed as she remembered her captive, and thought, "He does not know but this may be his last time. She could not hide her feelings of rebellion and momentarily her defiance was visible in her face. The expression did not go unnoticed by Moosa as he laboured, and immediately he was reminded of Hafrida receiving the lashes in the courtyard of the fort. There it was, that expression, now on the face of his wife. He was driven now by the feeling he had experienced on that occasion and was unable to withhold his orgasm. "At last, it is over," thought Hooda, as his great bulk rolled away. Relieved now of his worries, within minutes he was asleep.

The assassin, who had continued to wait for the last light to be extinguished, emerged from his hiding place to reconnoitre his possible entry points. He was disturbed and returned into hiding as an outside light came on and the iron grill that protected the door of the kitchen was thrown open. He clearly saw a woman, who he assumed to be the wife of his victim, emerge naked with in one hand a bundle, possibly a night dress, from its texture and lace trimming. In the light he saw the long scars on her back from lashings and the bruises on what he otherwise found to be attractive limbs. She ran, then stopped at an upturned flowerpot and lifted something from beneath it with her bundle. The assassin, now excited, felt a mixture of lust and compassion for the young agile figure as she returned quickly to the house. He thanked Allah when he saw that, although she had not turned off the light, neither had she closed the security grill. He moved quickly to enter the house before the girl realised the grill was not closed.

Hooda crept back into their room where Moosa was snoring, as was his custom when lying on his back. She lifted the single sheet near his feet and released her captive from the torn night dress. To confine the scorpion she started to tuck the sheet under the mattress, first the foot, then on Moosa's side. When she moved to do the same on her side, Moosa stirred and she froze, kneeling on the floor, in fear of discovery.

In a half-awake state, he asked, "What are you doing, woman?"

She had the presence of mind to reply, "Just tucking in the sheet for your comfort dear. Go to sleep." Moosa was reassured and relaxed back into snoring. Hooda waited beside the bed until his breathing became even, then left the room to sleep with her daughter.

The Persian waited, hidden in the house, expecting the girl to return to close the grill, but this did not happen. "At least my escape will not be hindered," he thought. He observed that the girl had gone to a room other than the matrimonial one. He followed her and listened outside the door for her breathing to become regular and slow.

Meanwhile the scorpion was attempting to escape from the sheet by climbing towards the hem where Moosa's head emerged. Moosa was wakened by something creeping near his throat. In his half-wakened state he tried to brush it away. His hand caught the scorpion, which reacted by gripping his neck with its pincers to avoid being dislodged. A second attempt by Moosa caused the scorpion to tighten his grip, piercing the skin. The tip of his pincers penetrated Moosa's jugular vein. Instantly, the scorpion arched his tail towards the wound and sent poison into Moosa's blood stream. Moosa's heart rate accelerated as fear took control of his reactions. The poison bearing blood spread rapidly throughout his brain, causing progressive loss of control of organs and limbs. He tried to call for help but he was suffocating and could make no sound. He tried to get up from his bed but found that he could not move. At that moment the assassin entered the room with knife ready to strike. He saw his victim, eyes open but unmoving on the bed before him. Momentarily their eyes met, but now parallelised, Moosa could do nothing except stair into the eyes of the man holding the knife over him. The knife was plunged into his heart, and as the assassin twisted the blade there was no reaction from his victim, who he assumed was already dead. Moosa's optic nerve had continued to send pictures from his unmoving eyes which had previously adjusted to the dark whilst they retained muscular control. They showed an image of a man in strange clothes approaching with a long knife in one hand. The knife was plunged into Moosa's heart and as it was twisted he felt intense pain. That was his last feeling as blood now ceased to circulate to his brain and life left him.

The scorpion, unharmed, freed itself and started to make its way back to the garden via the kitchen. The assassin, having waited to confirm there was no life in his victim, turned and started to run towards the kitchen to make his escape. He stepped onto the scorpion that had now reached the kitchen. It reacted quickly by gripping the bare foot of its attacker. The Persian shook it free, but not before he had lost his balance, scattering a pile of metal cooking utensils. Hooda was wakened by the din, but assumed it was Moosa responding to the poison of the scorpion and did not move.

★

Beyond the wall, Saleh, who was prepared now to launch his attack had lit the fuse of the bomb in his satchel, only seconds before he heard the clatter of pans. The noise was also audible at the guard house. The guards ran towards the house, with weapons to hand, in time to see the Persian climbing the wall to escape. Two gunshots were fired of which the first missed the climber but the second penetrated the leather clothing of the assassin and entered his heart. He fell dead from the wall.

Saleh, now frightened by the gunfire, ran from the scene with the fuse spluttering in his satchel. He was suddenly struck with an idea which would please the old cleric. With the fuse almost burned out, he ran to the Farnhams' house and threw the bomb over their wall. Fortunately, the Farnhams and their servants had the previous day moved into their newly finished villa. The explosion came instantly and sent the gate off its fixings, impaling the youth against the wall of the old cleric's house with its iron spikes. Saleh died slowly as blood spurted from multiple perforations of his skin. Inside his house, the old man was straining to hear the explosion that would dispatch to hell the hated Moosa.

The satchel had landed at the base of the minaret, which it weakened, causing the structure to fall. Delighted by the unexpected intensity of the explosion the old man prostrated himself, in thanks to Allah, just as the minaret came crashing down through the roof of his house. In mid prayer he was sent to join Saleh and Moosa in paradise, or the other place, as Allah would decide, when a steel Tannoy horn severed his head from his prostrate body.

CHAPTER 42

Police were summoned immediately by the guards. A quick look at Moosa's corpse with the knife still in his heart and the guards' explanation of their shooting of the man, who could not be other than the assassin, left no doubt in the minds of the police officers that Moosa had died from the knife wound inflicted by the barefooted man in leather attire. The case was all but closed in the minds of the police, except that they did not know the motive.

The murder happened only two days after Moosa had agreed to co-operate with Saif's investigation. This made Saif suspect one of Moosa's aggrieved accomplices. He told the police of his suspicion and they accepted this as the missing motive. The official verdict attributed Moosa's murder to the Persian after the hospital, without further pathology, diagnosed death due to a fatal knife wound to the heart. No checks were made for other causes because of the limited time before burial, which *sharia* dictated to be before sunset on the day of death. There remained an element of mystery, because the assailant had not forced entry.

The Indian servants, in spite of their denials and with no evidence to implement them, except that they were in the house at the time, were suspected of being accomplices and were rapidly deported.

The old cleric's followers were at a loss, not knowing for which event they should claim responsibility. The attack on the Mosque for which Saleh, found dead on the scene, was blamed was attributed to them, because Saleh was a known follower of the old cleric. The old cleric, even if he still lived, would have lost support as his followers dispersed for fear of discovery of their implication in the bombing of the sacred building.

Many on both sides of the wadi would later be relieved to learn of Moosa's death, and many more would be disappointed that they had been denied an opportunity to take their own revenge. Amongst these was Ali, who had previously heard from Moosa's servants details of his treatment of Hooda. He thought their deportation justified for their failure to report Moosa's behaviour. Ali had also feared the disgrace that would be brought on Salim's regime by Moosa's behaviour and the ultimate corruption of government if Moosa survived his father. Ali had for many years wished for Saif to be successor to Salim, and now he could witness this happening.

Hooda was most relieved by Moosa's demise, and because she was a woman and therefore of obvious low intelligence no suspicion of her implication was ever contemplated, especially as the servants and guards confirmed that she was a loyal wife who never left the house to communicate with any possible accomplices. In pretence of grief, Hooda accepted an invitation from Layla for herself and her daughter to join the other al-Wyly ladies at the palace.

Saif was obliged by Sharia to accept the wife and child of his deceased brother as his own because her marriage prospects as a widow and consequent protection for herself and the child were minimal. Hooda could not have been happier at this prospect and Saif, who had known her since childhood, was relieved that he did not have to marry someone chosen by his father. He realised he would have to find somewhere for them to live together, but in the meantime, they were both happy to have her live with the ladies at the palace.

Ultimately the ladies and Saif could not miss seeing the scars of Moosa's beatings. It was then that Ali decided that she had justification if she had been involved in his murder. He did not mention his suspicions because, again, knowing Moosa's character, he sympathised with her.

Hooda was told by Nahla that she would be able to benefit from Rasha's teaching for a few more weeks before the Farnhams pack their possessions to leave Naamlah at the end of his contract. They were to retire and settle with their children in the UK. Nahla said Rasha was disappointed, because they had only just moved into the villa and enjoyed the flush toilet that had been promised when they first arrived.

Salim and Layla grieved the loss of their son, but not for long. Salim was relieved that he had not made an earlier announcement of Saif's designation as future Emir. Now it looked like a natural succession, without any apparent disgrace on the family or justification for objection from traditionalists.

CHAPTER 43

Saif had now received the documents relating to Moosa's copper scam and was reading these in his new office at the Finance Ministry. He had before him the original survey report, which Moosa had concealed. This included the appendix which was now re-attached to the report. He had not found the report particularly helpful, as he knew it had been inaccurate, until he came to the appendix which Moosa never read because of his reluctance to make the effort necessary for its translation from English.

In bold print was the statement:
APPENDIX 1

The geological composition of land to the east of the trench that forms the national border and is confined within the region where the trench loops away from the adjacent country of Haqum appears to contain gold of significant density that is present relatively close to the surface.

We appreciate that this will be of no immediate concern to the Government of Naamlah as all of the gold bearing region is beyond the border with the ...

Saif was surprised by this discovery and sat back to consider the implications for how this knowledge could benefit the proposed union of the two countries. On second thought, "Could the survey results be relied on? They had been completely wrong about the potential reserves of copper?"

★

A few days before Moosa's murder, Saif learned from Salim of the refusal of Kareem's father to negotiate with any Naamlahn delegation, and had the idea of discussing an alternative approach with his friend. The two met the day before the murder. After attending noon prayers together, they retired to a small *cawah* shop which had once belonged to Saif's uncle Yacoob.

When told of the outcome of the official approach to his father, Kareem was amused and said, "It is typical of my father to be so obstinate."

"I suspect mine would react similarly if the circumstances were reversed, and you were your father's heir, but with Moosa's reputation," said Saif.

"You know I have a vested interest in the union of our countries on two counts; my desire for your sister's hand and my desire to see my oil pipe commissioned and put to use. If there is anything I can do, I will gladly help," offered Kareem.

Saif was not at all happy at the prospect of his sister being in the arms of anyone else, "but," he thought, "rather Kareem than someone else, possibly some wealthy old man."

"Would you talk to your father on our behalf?" asked Saif.

"Of course. We could visit him together as soon as I can get away, but I will need an exit visa, as, you forget, I am an illegal expatriate."

"I should be able to organise that with my uncle Abdulazziz, if he is still in office. I want us to wait for a few days because I may be able to improve the prospects of a satisfactory outcome with a secret surprise," replied Saif, rising to leave whilst his friend remained, looking bewildered.

★

At the small port of Haqum, Kareem's father, the Sheikh, lived alone, except for servants. The house was quite modest in size, but benefited from an ideal setting overlooking the bay around which the other small flat roofed mud brick houses of the town were clustered. This was the only town, making Haqum effectively a city state, because, except for a thriving agricultural community extending east along the coast, the other residents lived a nomadic life within the few less-hostile parts of the interior. Most of the land was desert, typically like the region to the south west, near the source of the great wadi, where there had been no means of sustaining human, animal, and certainly not vegetable life for centuries, not since the advancing sands had destroyed the sparse vegetation on which the Sheikh's ancestors had grazed their sheep and goats. Those more enlightened would also blame uncontrolled goats for contributing to the land's devastation.

The Sheikh was proud of the Japanese civil engineering works, which had transformed the otherwise familiar view from his house. The oil terminal, now so prominent, had more than doubled the size of the deep-water docking area in the port. The old man relaxed, whilst enjoying a rare day-time cool northerly breeze, lying on cushions propped against the wall behind the balcony. He drew heavily on a hookah, thinking that soon not just launches and dhows will be visiting his little country. This depended, of course, on the meeting in a few days, when he was expecting a visit from Kareem and his friend, the young Naamlahn Minister for Finance. When he had received the message from Kareem, his father took great satisfaction from learning that his eldest son was now responsible for the Naamlah oil pipe. He thought it ironic that Kareem was acquiring experience and knowledge by working in the land of his historic enemy. He was obstinately optimistic that this would one day benefit his own country when oil was found there.

★

Saif, realising how unreliable the mineral survey had been, was wary of the reported presence of gold across the border in Haqum. He therefore decided that before accompanying Kareem on the visit to Haqum he would commission an exploratory excavation in the relevant, fortunately uninhabited, part of the *wadi* within the neighbouring country. Because of the risk, though minimal, of being caught, and in the light of the historic murder of his ancestors back in 1819, no respectable surveyor responded to Saif's enquiries. He left a message for Kareem, who was working in the interior, asking him to delay their trip for two weeks whilst he waited for some information that would be helpful at the proposed meeting in Haqum. Saif then organised a meeting with his father, to discuss his latest plan and seek Salim's approval.

At the meeting with his father Saif told of the survey which showed the gold deposits over the border in Haqum, and said that he needed to prove the existence of the gold before the meeting in Haqum because it would strengthen his negotiating hand.

Saif and Salim decided that they needed someone trustworthy, having both the necessary scientific background and proven desert survival skills to conduct the clandestine prospecting operation. They could each think of several Arabs who would meet these requirements except for being trustworthy. They knew that knowledge of the gold, if it was proven to exist, would be too great a temptation to most men. Salim recalled meeting the German adviser who wanted to marry his daughter Fousia. He was sure that she had introduced him by saying that the man, Bernhardt, had served in the war in the desert of Libya where he had lived with the *Bedouin*.

"Son, I think I know the man for this task. The German who works with Fousia," said Salim.

"Yes I know of him as a reliable man, trusted by Fousia," agreed Saif.

"At least two men will be required. The desert can be unforgiving," observed Salim.

"If he agrees, I will accompany him myself," replied Saif.

"If that should be necessary, you must let no one know where you are going, because your life will be in danger and I cannot afford to lose my last and only son to an assassin. First, you will have to take your sister into your confidence and get her agreement for release of the man and then get his cooperation. Do you think he will do this for us?" asked Salim.

"I do not know, but I believe he will do it for Fousia," replied Saif, trying to suppress a grin.

"You must also know he has an attachment to my daughter?"

"Yes father. I believe they are closer than their working relationship would require," replied Saif.

"He wants to marry her, but I fear it will not be accepted by the other members of government. I would prefer that they do not hear of my daughter's relationship with the German at this time. If he is successful, I shall use the fact to justify his acceptance as a citizen of our country," said Salim, thoughtfully.

"I am sure that prospect will ensure his cooperation father," said Saif, breaking his father's train of thought about the potential consequences of a union between Fousia and Bernhardt.

★

Saif went immediately to seek a meeting with Fousia at her ministry, where he told her of his meeting with their father. She was concerned to know Salim's current feelings about herself and Bernhardt. "You should know, Saif, that Bernhardt is to embrace Islam."

"I know, from father, that he approves of the German, and that it is only the prospect of convincing the government that prevents him from blessing your marriage sister. You have to see from his point of view; they could not trust you to keep their secrets from the man who shares your bed. Rest assured, sister, he did mention the possibility of making him a citizen if he completes this important task."

Fousia was relieved and smiled as she said, "Leave Bernhardt to me. I am sure he will be pleased to help, especially if he knows that in doing so, he will improve our marriage prospects."

CHAPTER 44

Fousia told Bernhardt about Saif's plan. He agreed to take on the task, but insisted to Fousia that only with Saif in attendance would he feel confident, as a foreigner, of surviving in the event of their incursion being detected. They both knew that the *Bedouins* of Haqum were known not to be as amenable as the leader of their country.

Saif had to arrange for someone to deputise for himself, and needed time to hand over his Ministry work. He asked Bernhardt, in the meantime, to arrange their *safari*. He gave Bernhardt a scheme number and budget for purchase of anything that he thought they would require for the journey.

Bernhardt knew exactly what was required, recalling his Africa Corps experience. A pair of identical four-wheel-drive vehicles were his first priority. He knew it was essential never to venture into the desert alone, or with only one vehicle, and that it was best to take as much duplicated equipment as possible. This would ensure that interchange of parts between vehicles would increase the probability of keeping at least one of them working and enhance his chances of survival. To keep within the budget that Saif had authorised, Bernhard called on Abdul Bawani, who he knew as a resourceful dealer in second-hand vehicles.

Abdul's establishment occupied an old oasis out of the town. Bernhardt thought it most untidy and could not help thinking about what a blot it was on the environment. As far as he could see the area was covered with old vehicles and some incomplete aircraft, mainly war surplus and some obviously only of scrap value, because they had been piled on top of each other by an ancient steam-driven crane. Bernhardt worked his way through piles of junk towards a large, corrugated metal shed, from where he could hear the noise of machinery. Here he found Abdul and his son Suliman dismembering a Land Rover, for parts he assumed, with a metal cutter. His enquiry in Arabic impressed Abdul, who revealed that he had one Land Rover, other than the one he was dismembering, and one ex-US Army Willis Jeep. Both were immediately available in working order. Abdul wanted him to take these, but Bernhardt told him he wanted either two Jeeps or two Land Rovers.

"Jeeps drink a lot of petrol. You will get further with a Land Rover. Better for a long journey. How far you going?"

"I cannot tell you. I need two of the same for reliability," replied Bernhardt.

"I suppose that is wise, in case of breakdown," agreed Abdul.

"I know, I have a lot of experience of being broken down in the desert," said Bernhardt.

Abdul shouted to his Indian mechanic who was working inside the shed, "How long before that other Jeep will be ready?" The mechanic appeared wearing filthy greasy overalls and wiping his hands on an equally greasy rag.

"I have the gear box off to replace an oil seal, sir. She not ready until tomorrow," replied the mechanic.

"I will take both Jeeps if you promise they will be ready tomorrow. I have a list of other requirements, if you can help," said Bernhardt, waving a sheet of paper at Abdul.

"No good to me. I do not read," said Abdul, who passed the list to the Indian.

"I will see what we are having, sir, if you will wait," said the mechanic before retreating into the shed.

Whilst they waited Abdul said, "These are good Jeeps. You can rely on them," in case Bernhardt had any doubts, then added, "I am asking only 300 dollars for each."

Bernhardt replied, "Let us see what else you can provide first."

The mechanic returned with the list, now liberally stained with grease and marked to show what he had found; several Jerry cans, four spare wheels, each fitted with bulbous, smooth tyres for use on sand, two fan belts, assorted tools, a set of suspension springs, cans of oil, filters and spark plugs.

"This is all we can supply, sir," said the mechanic.

"OK. I will give you 850 dollars for all of this and the Jeeps," Bernhardt replied.

"Make it 950 and I agree," said Abdul.

"Throw in a set of light bulbs and deliver it all to the Ministry for the Environment and I agree," said Bernhardt.

Abdul offered his hand for Bernhardt to shake. "Have cash ready," he said, turning back towards the wrecked Land Rover.

Bernhardt managed to find everything else from his list in the souk, where he also bought a load of fruit and tinned food to last them a week, and some 5-gallon plastic water containers. He ordered that this be delivered to Fousia's office, from where he had borrowed prospecting and surveying instruments.

When Abdul and the mechanic arrived the following morning, they each drove a jeep loaded with the other items. After inspecting the load, Bernhardt paid Abdul and offered to drive them back to the workshop. He thought it would give him an opportunity to test the Jeep that the mechanic had been working on. He found no fault and returned to the Ministry, where he and Nasser loaded the rest of the gear into the Jeeps. He had noted that there were some differences between the two vehicles. One had been in the past equipped with a radio transceiver and still had a whip antenna and all the necessary wiring. He discovered it also had an oversize battery and a high output dynamo to cope with the load of a radio. This gave him the idea of setting up a communication link from the expedition back to his farm. A phone call to Abdul, and he learned that he still had several of the original radios in stock. "These were the type 19, intended originally for installation in tanks, but they would also fit into the jeep," said Abdul.

"I know about these, we had one in Libya," replied Bernhardt, as he remembered their capture of one during the war. They agreed a price for two, which Abdul delivered. Bernhardt soon had the Jeep radio installed, as he had done in his tank, and tentatively switched it on. He was gratified to hear the wine of the rotary transformer that converted the battery voltage to the higher value necessary for the tubes in the set. He set the tuning dial click mechanism to one of the oil field frequencies recommended for daytime use, pressed the microphone button and quickly tuned the variometer for a peak in antenna current. He did the same for a night-time frequency. Satisfied with one end of his communication link, he loaded the other radio into a Ministry vehicle and delivered it, with some antenna wire, to the farm. With Ranjit's help they rigged the wire between two of his date palms and connected it via the tuner to the radio. A repeat of the procedure at the jeep, netting onto the frequencies of the jeep radio, soon had this end of the communication link working. Back at the Ministry, Nasser and Bernhardt removed all but the driver's seats in each jeep and filled them with the rest of their gear. A test call was made to Ranjit on the radio, in which Bernhardt gave the schedule for call times and frequencies that they would be using. He was then ready for Saif to join him.

Saif was concerned that no one else should know where they were heading and why. Even Ranjit was not told what they would be searching for. They had a cover story that they were searching for water. When Bernhardt and Saif set off in convoy under cover of darkness that evening, there was just room in the jeeps for them to sit, surrounded by boxes, extra wheels, jerry cans, camping gear, food, and prospecting equipment. Within an hour they were off-road and making their way by moonlight across an ancient camel track of dust and gravel. To avoid being bogged down in soft patches, where they sometimes had to pull each other's Jeep clear, they had been forced to engage four-wheel-drive earlier than planned. This caused concern because of increased fuel consumption. Bernhardt was in the lead Jeep, with the radio, and since losing the camel trail, was navigating in a south easterly direction by occasionally glancing at the pole star over his left shoulder. Saif kept as far back as he could without losing sight of the other Jeep, in order to avoid suffocating or blinding by dust from the leader.

Before midnight they made their first stop, estimating their position from the mileage indicated on their speedometers and their south east bearing. They called Ranjit and were pleased to hear his excited acknowledgement. He was given their position and told them Her Highness Princess Fousia had joined him and wished them well. The men were amused, because neither of them thought of her as a princess.

Saif washed away the dust that was caked to his clothes and face before preparing their first meal. Afterwards he slept under his vehicle, because he knew this would protect him from the ground going cold as its heat radiated into the clear sky once the sun had gone. He had been unable to understand Bernhardt's aversion to this practice. Although the vehicle was more effective than a tent at restricting cooling by radiation, Bernhardt insisted on trying to sleep in the open. Eventually, when the cold prevented him from sleeping, he reluctantly moved under the Jeep, but could not forget his experience of being trapped under a tank.

Before resuming their journey, they refuelled, adding 10 gallons of petrol to each vehicle. The empty 5-gallon cans were left on top of a cairn of stones as a marker to aid their return. Bernhardt calculated that they were only making about 20 km on a gallon of fuel. Both Jeeps were consuming this amount, so they decided there was nothing wrong and attributed it to the old side valve engines with low gear and permanently engaged four-wheel-drive. Bernhardt remembered what Abdul had said about the Land Rover using less fuel. They topped up the oil in the radio Jeep after Saif said it had been smoking from its exhaust. After two hours the ground hardened, they changed out of four-wheel-drive and were able to engage top gear for the first time since leaving the road. Later the ground changed to large stones with sharp edges that caused their tyres to shed rubber at an alarming rate. Before noon they stopped for another meal and a position fix. They estimated that they were now consuming a precious gallon every 30 km.

The Jeep with the radio needed another litre of oil for its engine, and Saif's Jeep was showing canvas on one tyre. They fitted a replacement and left the old one on another cairn of stones. Before setting off they called Ranjit for the noon schedule, but got no response. They tried again after five minutes with success. Ranjit apologised for not switching to the higher day time frequency. They told him they could see the mountains floating in the sky above a lake to the south and expected they would soon be in the sand dunes that separated them from the great wadi. At the farm, Ranjit smiled, because he knew they were seeing a mirage. Soon after they were under way again, the second front tyre burst on Saif's Jeep and they made another landmark. The replacement was the last of their standard spares. The mirage disappeared as clouds started to form, and they soon became thick and dark over the mountains. Bernhardt predicted there was likely to be a storm. Their entry to the sand dunes was surprisingly quick. They stopped to fit the wheels that had been supplied with the special bulbous sand tires to each vehicle, leaving the standard wheels as a return marker.

After another hour Bernhardt noticed his Jeep was struggling and appeared to be losing power. He stopped and waited for Saif. Bernhardt told him he was still having to keep in low four-wheel-drive. Saif said he was having no problems except for having to keep on changing gear as they went up and down the dunes. Bernhardt decided it was that which was causing his problem. They checked his gearbox and found it needed oil. After topping it up he thought the vehicle was not so bad to drive. After three more hours of tiring driving, due to constant gear shifts, up and down sand dunes, they could see from the crests the west edge of the *wadi*.

Two hours later they were camped on the sandy, less steep, Haqum side of the border. Saif prepared to pray and was surprised when Bernhardt joined him to face Mecca. They had a meal, rested until midnight, and called Ranjit. They told him they were in the area of the water. Fousia knew that water was their code for gold. She spoke to the travellers, telling them to take care and that she would pray for their safe return. Fousia agreed to let Salim know of their progress. They both climbed under the vehicles for sleep that night.

Saif was wakened by a cry from his companion, who had woken to the smell of oil and in panic had thought himself to be again in Libya. His blanket was soaked in oil, to which sand was sticking. Bernhardt moved to Saif's Jeep until morning, when inspection revealed the oil to be coming from the rear oil seal of the main gearbox. It looked like Abdul's mechanic had been rushed and not fitted the seal correctly. The box was dry, and they had used up all their spare oil. "A pity that was the one with the radio. It is no use now," said Bernhardt despondently. They decided to take the remaining fuel from the radio Jeep and add it to the spare stock.

"At least we have room now for both of us in the good Jeep," encouraged Saif.

"If you do not mind having no seat to sit on," said Bernhardt. Saif sat in the shade thinking whilst Bernhardt transferred their remaining gear into the good Jeep.

Saif told his new friend of his thoughts and they discussed their options. They could try to transfer the good gear box to the radio Jeep to enable them to still keep in touch with the farm during their return, but if they failed they would be stuck and need to be rescued. They could try to transfer the radio to the other Jeep, but this would mean rewiring, shifting the antenna mount and the heavy electrics. Neither felt confident to attempt this. They eventually decided to leave the radio where it was, to keep both batteries charged from the good Jeep, and transfer the driver's seat from the radio Jeep to Saif's, for Bernhardt to sit on. Their prospecting would be on foot to save fuel. All of this was passed to Ranjit at noon, but they had difficulty hearing his confirmation due to the intense static caused by the storm that was building over the mountains.

CHAPTER 45

They had just loaded their prospecting gear and emergency rations into back packs, ready to start what looked like a futile search for gold, when the sun disappeared behind a blackening sky. The wind built up rapidly and in minutes the sand was starting to shift, beating into their faces. The rain came suddenly and added to a stream of water, presumably from the mountains, which now started to flow in the depression. In these minutes the *wadi* became alive with rushing water as the rain became torrential; what had earlier been a sandy hollow was now a raging river, in which the water level was rising rapidly. They both saw at the same time that water was already covering the wheels of the broken Jeep which lay across the flow of the river. They forced themselves towards the good Jeep, still on dry sand and clear of the rising water level, fighting the wind-borne sand in thigh deep water, hampered by their heavy packs. Saif arrived first and threw his pack into the vehicle as he tried to start the motor. Bernhardt arrived just as the water reached axle level. The motor started, blowing steam from its exhaust. Saif selected four-wheel-drive and engaged the clutch. The first revolution of tires dug a hole in the wet sand and caused the vehicle to sink. Water pressure on the side of the vehicle was causing it to tilt sideways on its coach springs. Compounded by rising flood water, this soon brought the water level within a few centimetres of the door opening on the downstream side. Bernhardt discarded his pack, tossed it into the Jeep and strained to push the overloaded vehicle, to no effect. They both now watched the radio Jeep start to move towards them under the influence of the current. As it accelerated it gave a glancing blow to their Jeep, momentarily releasing the suction of the wet sand that was gripping their tyres. At that instant their Jeep started to float. Bernhardt, still pushing, fell onto his knees and felt something hard in the sand beneath him. Thinking it may be something vital that one of them had dropped from their packs, he reached below the water and grabbed it. Without taking his eyes of the jeep, he put the item in the pocket of his dishdash. As he struggled to stand and continue pushing, he saw the radio Jeep accelerating away on the flood and within minutes only the whip antenna with its small triangular pennant was visible above the water. Meanwhile, Saif kept the engine running for fear water might block the exhaust. The Jeep's wheels now found sand to grip and they pulled it up onto an island of sand. Bernhardt jumped aboard but as he did this he could see their island was disappearing from beneath them and they both feared they would soon be covered like the other Jeep. Bernhard climbed on to the bonnet, expecting this to soon be the only dry haven as their island disappeared from beneath them. Saif continued to pump the accelerator to keep the exhaust clear.

Suddenly, the water started to recede, and the rain stopped. The wind subsided and the sky lightened. As quickly as the flash flood had occurred, the water started to disappear, soaking into the exposed gravel bottom of the *wadi*. The two men looked at each other seeing relief in each other's faces. They realised that what had been a sandy hollow only an hour earlier was now the gravel bed of a river. Hardly any sand remained between them and the cliffs forming the Naamlahn bank. Where the rocks had previously protruded from sand, now they sat on gravel. Only the last vestige of a stream continued to flow over the gravel between the rocks. Saif started to laugh as he realised how much water they had transported, unnecessarily, as it turned out, across the desert.

As they sat in only their *izaar* sarongs, Bernhardt became conscious of the pain in his knee from the item he had picked up. He took the article from the pocket of his *dishdash*, which was drying on the bonnet of the Jeep, and in amazement saw that it was a large, distinctively shaped nugget of gold. "I think the rain has revealed what we are looking for, Saif," said Bernhardt, passing to his companion the nugget, which consisted of a large sphere with three smaller spheres attached.

"At least we must be near the source," said Saif excitedly.

"Yes. Can you see the other Jeep?" asked Bernhardt.

"No. strange that it should have disappeared. I doubt the river would have taken it out of sight," said Saif, still naked to the waist and savouring the warming radiation of the sun.

Bernhardt set off to where he last saw the pennant projecting above the water. He optimistically expected any moment to see more gold on the ground and was disappointed to learn that his find was the only evidence to support the air survey results. He came across a pile of animal bones still almost buried in sand. "They must be a camel's," he decided, because he could not think of anything else that had such large bones and was likely to be out here. Strange that they are in such a pile and not joined to each other, he thought. He walked on towards where he had last seen the pennant and felt a chill in his spine as he came across a partly exposed human skull. Closer inspection revealed more bones. He scraped away sand with his boot to reveal a complete human skeleton. "Poor fellow," he thought, and started to walk away, but stopped as he felt his boot crunching into more bones.

"Mein Gott," he said under his breath, realising he was in a cemetery, surrounded by partly exposed skeletons that had apparently been buried respectfully in a north-south line. Some had *khanjar* to keep them company, he noticed. As he crunched out of the line, he felt disrespectful, and pondered on how they came to be here. Looking beyond the skeletons for something less creepy, Bernhardt saw what looked like a low, weathered wall projecting from the gravel and decided to investigate. As he drew near, he recognised the pennant of the antenna sticking up just clear of the wall. Behind the wall he found the jeep in what must have been an ancient well, where it had been washed by the current.

"That is definitely the end of our radio contacts," he thought, as he turned back to tell Saif of his discoveries.

By the time he found Saif the sun was setting, and his friend was preparing to pray. Bernhardt was moved to join him and give thanks for their deliverance. Saif was once more surprised to see that Bernhardt knew all the actions proscribed for Muslim prayers, but made no comment. Whilst they were eating a rushed supper Bernhard told Saif about the cemetery. Saif did not appear to be surprised, and told Bernhardt about the history of the massacre at the well.

After their meal, Bernhardt took the bulky Mk 9 bubble sextant from his pack and examined it in the lights of the Jeep. He concluded that it had survived the journey and the flood. He was not familiar with this ex-RAF instrument that the Ministry had supplied, and Saif in his sailing experience had only ever used a conventional sextant that relied on a sea horizon. Between them they managed to wind the clockwork mechanism and work out how to check its calibration. Bernhardt took out their chronometer and was dismayed to see it had stopped and was full of water. Their wrist watches both had different times, so they decided they could not be relied on for navigation by sun or stars.

Saif could not see how they were going to fix the position of their find, but Bernhardt suddenly said, "I have an idea. After we investigate tomorrow, we will come back here for noon; then I know I can fix our position."

"But surely, we need longitude as well as the sun, or no one will ever find the place," said Saif.

"No. Longitude will not be required, because they only need to find the wadi," replied Bernhardt, grinning.

"Ah, you are right! Of course, it is difficult to fix longitude without accurate time, but the *wadi* runs north-south; it is as good as a line of longitude. We also know when the sun is at its highest it will give us a local noon, and we can use the sextant for a line of latitude. Good thinking, Bernhardt," said Saif, relieved that they were not likely to be lost and thinking how fortunate he was that he had such a practical man as Bernhardt for company.

"We must pray for a clear sky, Saif."

★

Ranjit was dismayed not to find the adventurers on the frequency for the noon or that for the night schedule. He took the initiative and called them several times but received no reply. He decided not to tell Fousia, who was then back in her office. The next day, having had no news from Ranjit, she made the Sikh deliver her to the farm, where she waited with Ranjit, listening on headphones to the crackling radio.

★

When the men, who had by now become firm friends, woke, they were keen to start exploring. They were oblivious to the rising westerly wind, which was already causing sand to drift back over the gravel. Bernhardt panned the silt, left in puddles, near their camp, but none revealed even a grain of gold.

"Perhaps some poor fellow dropped the nugget after finding it elsewhere," said Saif, battling to be heard against the rising wind. He added, "I never heard any stories about gold being found by the men who returned from the massacre."

"You may be right. It does seem to be out of place," shouted Bernhardt.

"Look over there. The rocks are shining near the gravel bottom," shouted Saif, as his motion caused a twinkling reflection from the low sun.

"I see it," said Bernhardt, running despite his pack towards the base of the rock outcrop. Saif joined him and they both gasped as they marvelled at the thin, nearly horizontal lines of gold within the rock that the day before had been buried. Bernhardt's eyes were also attracted by the gold shining from within the pools of water nearby. He stammered, "No need for panning. You can see gold dust in the water here. We have six hours before noon. Let us go in opposite directions and try to find the extent of the gold deposits," said Bernhardt. Saif agreed to travel north and start back in time to get the sun sight whilst Bernhardt followed the *wadi* to the south.

When the explorers met again, after their respective treks along the wind-swept valley, it was near noon. Saif confirmed that there were traces of gold visible for almost three hours walking, but he said, as he came back, "The sand was already covering most of what I had found."

Bernhardt found that, after his three-hour walk, the gold bearing rocks were still exposed by the flood, and he agreed the wind was covering them with sand. They were in time to catch the sun's zenith and log its elevation so they would be able to mark their position on a map. They estimated that gold was present for at least a 12 mile stretch of the *wadi*, but none on the Naamlah side.

"Do you think the deposits are valuable?" asked Saif.

"It is difficult to say, because we have only seen what is near the surface. One thing is certain, there can be nowhere else where it will be so easy to extract. Just from what we have seen it must be worth millions of dollars," replied Bernhardt.

"Strange that it is all in Haqum. Why do you think that is?" asked Saif.

"The *wadi* separates two different geological formations. Millions of years ago the rocks on your side must have put tremendous pressure on the lower Haqum rocks from a different era."

"You know, people will think us fools to have camped in the wadi, risking flooding," said Saif.

"I do not agree. There is not a sign of vegetation so it must have been ages since water last flowed here," replied Bernhardt. "I think it was a unique event that we experienced."

"We shall never know how long ago that nugget first appeared," said Saif.

★

Fousia and Ranjit were now seriously concerned that they had not heard from the travellers and had taken to listening continuously in watches to the radio. What was making their suspense even worse was not being able to tell anyone or seek assistance because of the secrecy of the operation.

★

The adventurers loaded up the Jeep with what they considered essential for the journey home and left the rest near the old well, where it could be collected at a later date. With fingers crossed that they had enough fuel, they set off towards their first marker. They camped at the next marker and changed to the standard tires, because they were now out of the sand dunes. To avoid damaging the tires on the stones, and to save fuel, they covered that section very slowly. By the time they joined the road all four tires were bald, they had no more food, the fuel gage was near the end stop, the exhaust was smoking more than ever, and they were running on whatever was in the reserve part of the fuel tank.

The bald tired Jeep spluttered up the rough track towards the farmhouse, its two filthy, sunburned occupants, eyes barely able to stay open, praying that their last drop of fuel would take them the last mile. Sultan was the first to hear them and started barking, but his barks did not wake anyone. The travellers were greeted by Sultan's wagging stump as they entered the house to find Fousia and Ranjit asleep in their crackling headphones.

CHAPTER 46

On the strength of the false name on his work permit, Kareem managed to obtain an exit visa after Saif used his influence at the ministry. He was then able to leave Naamlah, but relied on his true identity as a citizen of Haqum to enter that country. At almost the same time Saif, because of his ministerial rank, was passed through immigration on both sides of the border. The friends met on the Haqum side and made their way on foot to Kareem's father's house. They were admitted and Kareem was greeted by his father with an embarrassing show of affection. Saif was introduced and was immediately struck by the facial similarity between the old Sheikh and Ali, the servant at the fort. Saif was pleased to find the Sheikh friendly and not apparently holding any grudge against him. In view of what he knew of the past historical relationship between the two countries, Saif was pleasantly surprised.

"My son used to write about you when he was in England, Minister," said the old man.

"I hope it was favourable, sir. We were very good friends and have remained so, but we have had to keep it a secret while he was working in my country," replied Saif.

"It is a pity that there have not been more friendships across our border," said the old man.

Saif thought hard for a suitable diplomatic response but was saved by Kareem. "That is why we came father, to establish such friendships."

"Yes, I know. First I would ask about one of the women of your father's house if you will allow such impertinence?" asked the Sheikh. Saif was surprised, because it was not considered

seemly to mention and certainly not to enquire after women of
a visitor's family.

"Who do you mean, sir?" asked Saif.

"Tell me, how is your aunt Shalma?" asked the Sheikh.

Saif noticed that his eyes looked glazed when he mentioned
her name, and he sensed impatience in his voice. Saif thought
that it was strange that their negotiations should start on the subject of his aunt, and realised that Shalma must have special significance for the Sheikh.

"She is well, thank you, sir. Recently she has become quite
a financial expert, gambling on the stock exchange but usually
winning," replied Saif.

"I saw in an old newspaper that she had been interviewed by
a British reporter and has been to the United States."

"Yes. That caused quite a stir among our religious men," replied
Saif, thinking, "His interest in Shalma is genuine." The Sheikh
was quiet for a few minutes, and Saif wondered if he should say
more about his aunt. Kareem broke the silence.

"Father, we are not here to discuss our families. We cannot evade
the issue. Saif and I both feel there is much to be gained by both
sides if we amalgamate our countries." The old man looked shocked
by such apparent bluntness. In his experience one did not get to the
point of negotiation until many pleasantries had been exchanged.

"It nearly happened before you were both born. My family
were not the ones who prevented it then."

"Would they be the ones to prevent it now?" asked Saif, seeing an opportunity to strike.

"No. But the move must come from your father," said the
Sheikh.

"Father, he has done that by sending his son," said Kareem,
keeping up the pressure.

"Not his eldest son, the wastrel, who is to succeed him," argued the Sheikh.

"You do not know, then, sir, that my brother Moosa is dead?
Allah rest his soul. If I was the heir and not my brother, would
you then accept me as my father's envoy?" asked Saif.

"Please accept my condolences. I am sorry to hear of your loss, although there had been rumours. I have to admit it does improve the prospect of an alliance. We need another significant gesture to seal a union," said the Sheikh.

"Would you have me marry the sister of Saif, father?" asked Kareem, hastily.

"That is a noble gesture, my son, but that may not be necessary unless it is your wish."

"It is my most ardent wish, father," replied Kareem.

Saif thought, "They do not know what a sacrifice that would be for me."

"Then there is the question; who rules the united country? And besides, we have nothing to offer on our side. It would be a one-sided agreement and unfair from the point of view of the Minister's countrymen. Our people would never accept the inferior status that must attend such a one-sided bargain," replied the Sheikh, suppressing a smile.

"I do not think so, sir. You know we cannot ship our oil from our own waters. You therefore have a bargaining position stronger than our own."

The Sheikh's smile now became overt. "I am pleased that you see the situation realistically, sir," said the Sheikh, and added, "I must admit that the scheme did not fill me with enthusiasm when it was first proposed by Kareem's younger brother, whilst your brother was to be involved."

"Kareem has spoken proudly of his brother, and I have been looking forward to meeting him," said Saif.

"Mohammed is the brains behind our port project. In fact, he has been the brains behind most development in our country since he returned from America, where he studied economics. He is in Tokyo at present," the Sheikh said proudly.

"If you had not delayed our visit, you would have met him before he departed to Tokyo, where he is ready to convey to the Japanese the outcome of this meeting," added Kareem. Saif suddenly had an idea that could strengthen his bargaining position, but continued his planned strategy.

"In fact, Haqum has something that puts you in possibly a stronger position than Naamlah with its oil," pronounced Saif. The other two looked surprised and wondered what it was that Saif knew about their country. Saif removed a file from his brief case with his right hand. With his left hand he removed the spherical gold nugget, on which Bernhardt had fallen near the old well, from his *dishdash*. He held it in his palm for the others to see.

Saif knew this was the time to make the speech he had prepared after he first formed his plan whilst on his journey home from the well. "I would, with the utmost respect, sir, request that you study this report, showing the immense wealth in gold that lies in Haqum. That you consider allowing my sister and your son to be married. That you allow the oil of our united countries to be exported via your port. That you agree to the appointment of a mutually acceptable leader of the new federated country for the mutual benefit of the tribes on both sides of the great *wadi*."

Kareem could not help but smile as he handled the nugget whilst the Sheikh started to read the summary of Bernhardt's hastily compiled report, which told him of the estimated known wealth in gold of his country. The two friends held their breath as they waited for a reaction to Saif's proposition. Saif realised that he was taking an enormous risk, because in making his proposal he had placed on the table all of his cards, except the one that had occurred to him during the meeting. The old man, he realised, could turn down the proposal with nothing to lose.

The Sheikh looked up, broke into laughter, then said, "Is that everything you have to offer?"

"There is only one other item within my power sir. Will you agree to your son, Mohammed's appointment to the post of Minister of Finance in a unified country?"

The Sheikh, who was already becoming impressed by Saif, felt that by this diplomatic gesture, on top of his unification proposal, he had revealed himself to be a natural leader. He replied, "Indeed, I will, and furthermore, you will have my support young sir. Now sell the plan to your father."

"And you have my support," added Kareem.

"I know it will be acceptable to the Emir," replied Saif. The Sheikh called for *cawah*, with which they sealed their agreement.

After their drink, the old Sheikh pulled himself up with his camel cane and pronounced, "If we are to unite, it is right that I tell you more of your history." The young men were puzzled, and the Sheikh moved towards a shelf from which he took a small chest. He unlocked it and fumbled through its contents whilst the other two looked at each other. A sepia photograph, obviously well handled, was taken out and handed to Saif. "You will not recognise her, but that is your Aunt Shalma as a girl," said the Sheikh. The photograph was of the upper half of a pretty girl of about fourteen. She was in national costume with a head dress and necklace of gold coins and her head and face exposed. Saif recognised the doll that she held to her chest as the one he and Nahla had discovered in the dungeon of the fort when they were children.

"She was very beautiful," said Saif.

"Yes, that was when she was to marry my late brother, Allah rest his soul. I envied him as I was very attracted by her charm and lively personality. I recall that in fact my feelings for her were as strong as those of my brother. We were both completely besotted with her. Your grandfather and my father arranged the alliance to unite our countries. The young couple became lovers who met secretly, and she became pregnant, carrying the boy who became the servant of your father's harem, who you call Ali."

Saif who had been standing to see the photograph in better light, felt unsteady at this revelation and had to sit. "No. That cannot be. Ali has been a servant since he was a small child," replied Saif, shakily.

"He was taken from her at birth and would have been killed by your uncles if my brother had not taken him to a woman in our country who had lost her child. She raised him until her death when he was five years old. Then your grandfather grudgingly gave him a home, but as a slave. I do not believe that anyone in your family knew this. At that time, it was the custom to blame unwanted pregnancies on the intervention of a jinn, as is known to those who follow the earlier prophet. We herd that your Uncles beat Shalma and confined her to the fort until your father returned from studying abroad, when he released her."

Saif still found the story incredible and asked, "Shalma and your brother, how could they meet to conduct their affair?"

"It was easy; the blind man at the gate of the fort did not know who was passing. He would hear the voice of a man who wanted to enter when at the same time the woman would be quietly leaving," replied the Sheikh.

Saif now realised why his aunt behaved as she had done all his life, and felt deep sorrow on her behalf. He could not wait to question his father about his involvement.

CHAPTER 47

Saif and Kareem left the Sheikh and returned separately to Naamlah. Kareem went back to work on the oil pipe and Saif went to meet with his father. Salim was pleased with what Saif told him of the meeting and congratulated his son for achieving the outcome that would be so beneficial to both countries. They agreed on the wording of a letter to be sent to the Sheikh, outlining a time scale and terms for negotiations concerning the unification and proposing that a formal signing ceremony should be held at a mutually agreed time and location.

Saif then changed the subject of his visit completely, asking, "Father, I learned many shocking facts from the old Sheikh Haqum about the history of our respective countries' relationship, and would ask you to confirm these?"

Salim smiled and said, "I can guess what he told you, and will not deny the history of our tribes."

"Is it true that poor Ali, the servant, is the son of Shalma?" asked Saif.

"I have feared this day ever since his birth, my son. It is so, and I can also reveal that Ali is the father of she you know as your step-sister Nahla," said Salim, his face suddenly saddened.

Saif gasped as his mind processed the revelation and his heart missed a beat. The girl he knew as his only love, and who he had always believed to be untenable because of their kinship, was in fact not denied to him by the marriage law. Depression settled over him as he reflected that he had just agreed to her marriage to his friend. He thought it ironic that he had made this sacrifice for the sake of his country's future prosperity. "There can never be a greater sacrifice," he decided. Salim waited for Saif's reaction, realising from his silence that his son had been disturbed by the news, but had no idea how.

Saif regained his composure and asked, "Ali and Nahla obviously cannot know of their relationship. Does Aunt Shalma know of her son's presence here?"

"She has never been told, but I believe that for many years she has suspected their relationship, and that is one reason she has suffered so," sighed Salim.

Thinking now how callous his father must be not to have relieved her suffering, Saif asked, angrily, "Could you not have relieved her of her suffering and improved Ali's life by releasing him from slavery when he was young by telling them the truth?"

"It has grieved me to watch them both suffer, mother and son, but in honour I could do nothing, because whilst your grandfather was on his death bed I and your uncles swore never to tell of that tragic time, for fear of Shalma otherwise being killed for her indiscretion and the dishonour that she brought to the household. Now you have heard the story from another, I do not feel bound by the oath," replied Salim.

Saif's thoughts shifted back to Nahla and Kareem and, hopefully, he asked, "Would the Mufti bless a union between Nahla and the son of the Sheikh, knowing that Ali and Kareem are cousins?"

"Nahla's parentage must not be revealed, or it also will dishonour the memory of her mother and our family. The relationship between the son of the Sheikh and Nahla is not first cousins, and is thus acceptable for marriage under our law," replied Salim.

Saif was disappointed, but knew his father was right. He asked, "Would there be any objection from the Mufti on religious grounds to the union of our countries?"

"I have already raised the matter, and it was agreed by the clerics on both sides many years ago that no objection would be raised if such an event should occur," confirmed Salim.

"There is another matter I should tell you about, father. I have decided who should replace Uncle Abdulazziz."

"Release me from suspense, please," asked Salim, smiling as he realised that Saif's other concerns had passed.

"Aunt Shalma has agreed to accept the post, and I am confident her appointment will receive no objection from the Sheikh at Haqum if the union of our countries goes ahead," said Saif.

"After the success in government that her niece and your mother have made, I have no doubt she will do a good job," agreed Salim.

★

Now that it was rumoured in the Palace that Nahla was not the daughter of Salim, it became obvious to Layla why Salim would not allow the girls to be called princesses. It would have been unfair to Nahla, because only Layla's daughter Fousia had that status by birth.

★

It was several weeks after the meeting between Salim and Saif that they received the Sheikh's agreement to have a meeting with Salim. The Sheikh had been waiting for confirmation of the findings of Bernhardt's report and for arrangements to secure the gold bearing region before announcing the unification proposal to his citizens. The Sheikh's son Mohammed had during this period returned from Tokyo and confirmed with pleasure his acceptance of the government post offered by Saif.

Until now, Nahla had not been told of the arrangement for her marriage to Kareem, with whom she had not had contact since he returned to the interior to progress the diversion of the pipeline towards the oil terminal of Haqum. When Saif, with a sinking heart, announced the arrangement, Nahla was overjoyed. The other ladies were equally pleased and excited by the prospect of another wedding. Their excitement was even greater when Saif announced his intention to take Hooda as a wife and add another wedding feast to their calendar.

Salim broke the news, of their history and relationship, to Shalma and Ali, who jointly decided that they would set up a home together, where they would live ostensibly as a lady with her eunuch servant, out of consideration for family honour, but in reality as mother and loving son. Once this was known they were invited to live with Ali's uncle, the Sheikh of Haqum, where out of respect for family honour Shalma and the Sheikh, who had always been attracted to her, were married. Ali was then legally adopted as a son by the Sheikh.

After her engagement to Kareem, and with his agreement, Nahla was told of her ancestry by Saif. The couple decided to keep the story secret for the sake of the union between the two countries. As a present, on the day of their wedding, Saif appointed Kareem as Minister of Mineral Resources. This appointment, after those of Shalma and Mohammed, left no doubt in the mind of the old Sheikh that Saif should be the Emir of the united country.

Bernhardt's contribution to bringing about the union, enabling their combined wealth in oil and gold to be realised, had earlier received grateful recognition from Saif's government by the granting of citizenship and the title of Sheikh. After embracing Islam his name became Muntaz Ali, and he and Fousia were allowed to marry.ss

★

During the following two years the oil extraction facilities in Naamlah were completed in parallel with storage and tanker loading arrangements in Haqum's port. Marketing for the oil was undertaken. Coincident with the oil arrangements, a mine was built, and arrangements made for safely extracting and transporting gold from the *wadi*. Negotiations for the federation proceeded slowly due to characteristic Arab intransigence.

Eventually, with a sense of history, as folklore told that it was the site of the murder that caused the intertribal feud, the emissaries agreed after protracted negotiations that the ceremony at which the declaration of union would be signed should be held in a *Bedouin* tent at the ancient dried well of Mustafa in the great *wadi*. A competition was held in both countries to find a name for the confederated land. Several citizens suggested that in view of the history associated with the *wadi* they should call it Wadistan. This was approved by both rulers.

★

In preparation for the ceremony the remains of the victims of the retributive attack were transferred to a more secure site. The crumbling wall of the well was restored. Invitations to attend the celebrations were issued to the rulers of other Gulf countries and to the governments of those countries, from West and East, who had established Embassies in Naamlah and/or in Haqum. An invitation was also sent to the Farnhams in England and arrangements made for their first-class flight and accommodation in Naamlah's most luxurious hotel.

On the big day, helicopters were chartered to convey guests to the site of Mustafa's well, where a large marquee had been erected for their shelter. In defiance of custom, there was no segregation of seating between genders. The centrepiece was a *Bedouin* tent sitting on a raised platform. One side had been removed to allow the guests to witness the signing of the treaty. An area was cleared for those citizens who had endured the journey over land to also witness the occasion without leaving their air-conditioned vehicles.

Amongst these were Sargent and Mrs Henry Adams, aka Mariam the Mermaid, with their baby son. A detachment of soldiers was present for protection of all present. Fatima, who had been confined in expectation of childbirth, insisted on attending the ceremony. Salim, who had been reluctant to permit Fatima to risk his unborn child by making the journey to the well, had conceded to her demand and now basked in the exhibition of his potency as Fatima's condition was revealed to the world.

Notable, by their absence, were Saif's uncles Hammed and Abdulazziz who were commiserating with their friend Idris al-Jaboo, who shared their disapproval of the federation. They had planned a rival ceremony for the blessing of Hammed's newly finished place of worship, but it had been cancelled because the Mufti and other guests were all otherwise engaged at the well.

After a musical introduction, Saif addressed the gathering from the stage, welcoming guests and describing the progress that had been made in both constituent countries and the future plans that his government had for the development of the new country of Wadistan. He introduced the ex-ruler of Haqum, who made a speech in which he described how this site would become a memorial to those men of Naamlah who were regretfully killed by his countrymen in 1819. Saif resumed by introducing those who were recent ministerial appointments from both sides of the *wadi* including his mother, aunt and stepsister from their side. From the other side, he introduced Mohammed and Kareem.

The marriage between Kareem and Nahla that would seal the union of the countries was announced with a reaction of joyous applause. He finished his speech with an invitation to Rasha Farnham, to whom he said the women of the country owed a great debt, to unveil a plaque that was attached to the restored wall of the well. Rasha, now grey haired and walking with the aid of a stick, came forward to be handed a pair of gold scissors by the two-year-old daughter of Fousia and Bernhardt, who struggled, to the amusement of the spectators, to support her headdress and necklaces composed of gold coins. Rasha cut through a gold silk ribbon, causing curtains to open and reveal a bronze plaque that bore the inscription in both Arabic and English languages:

This marks the last well of Mustafa al-Wyly (1759–1819).
On this site the federation of the two countries that formed
Wadistan was confirmed on 1ˢᵗ of June 1962 by
Emire Saif bin Salim al-Wyly of Naamlah
and
Sheikh Mohammed bin Mahmood al-Haqum of Haqum.

Guests were then invited to take *cawah* and join the dignitaries
of Wadistan in a feast of mutton biriyani that was presented on
enormous silver trays around which they were obliged with great
hilarity to sit cross-legged on cushions.

APPENDIX

Torsion waves

For compatibility with the period of the novel, I am adjusting the timing of the release of the torsion wave research by Russian scientists. Their work was categorised as pseudo-science by the Western scientific establishment, who in most cases were not convinced of the existence of these waves, despite this being easily demonstrated. Many have described the experimental work with torsion waves as witchcraft because it does not comply with the accepted laws of Newtonian physics.

The Russian research publications include descriptions of techniques, using simple apparatus, for measuring torsion fields emanating from natural sources such as the Sun, plants, water courses and pyramidal structures. Readers will find many references by internet searching for Torsion Waves.

Following the discovery of DNA, further research in Russia revealed the relationship and interaction between the spiral nature of torsion fields and the DNA spiral of living things, including that of humans. Explanations for previously mysterious phenomena including; distant healing, mineral divining, homeopathy, insect navigation, Biblical miracles and the function of ancient pyramids may be attributed to the knowledge and/or application of torsion wave fields.

An example that may be easily verified by traditional water divining or dousing methods is the phenomenon whereby many Christian churches were built on ancient pre-Christian religious sites. These are believed to have been originally defined by the presence of subterranean water that could only have been located in ancient times by using torsion wave technology. This is often manifest as damp rising in walls where the Altar joins the Chancel.

Amateur experimental researchers, inspired by the Russian work, have confirmed the Russian discoveries with particular relevance to mineral location, water divining, archaeology and the human aura, or spiritualism. The amateur research work was inspired by these English language papers:

» The torsion field and the aura by Claude Swanson PhD
» Harnessing torsion waves by David Wilcox

These publications contain extensive bibliographies on the subject of torsion waves.

Dousing

Dousing uses a latent ability of humans to detect torsion waves. The mechanism has been explained by the presence of sensors associated with the optic nerve and the connected part of the brain. This is believed to cause minute contractions of muscles in the hand. When his dousing stick is held in a practiced state of balance it amplifies the douser's muscle movement. A douser may lose his ability if he closes his eyes or puts his head in a metal enclosure.

In general those that practice dousing believe, as did Mustafa, that they have a mystic power. Those who would ridicule their ability have a classic test whereby they ask the douser to locate a hidden glass of water. This is something he cannot do but the writer has witnessed an experienced douser's demonstration of his ability to find hidden natural sources of water. Other dousing demonstrations of apparently unrelated phenomena included:

Navigation with sufficient precision as to differentiate between the directions of the earth's magnetic and true poles.

The difference in paternity of apparent siblings that was subsequently confirmed by DNA analysis.

Confirmation of the operational state of the CERN nuclear accelerator which is apparently an incidental source of torsion waves that are detectable by dousers anywhere on the planet and possibly beyond.

The concentration of torsion fields at the apex of pyramidal shapes.

The author

Tony Preedy was born in Hereford in January 1939
to shopkeeping parents and moved to Shropshire
in 1944. His autism shaped his young life,
causing him to enter Technical College; Tony then
started studies towards becoming a Chartered
Engineer whilst an apprentice with REME, then at
Bristol Polytechnic and with the BBC, eventually
being elected a Fellow of the Institution of
Engineering and Technology. He has worked as
a grocer's delivery boy, and later as an engineer
in broadcasting, spending some time in an Arab
country, and in law in the USA. Tony married Jean,
a designer of soft toys, whilst living on Ascension
Island; after retirement in 1999 they moved back to
Shropshire. He enjoys sailing, restoring classic boats
and vehicles, walking, and amateur radio; he has
contributed to magazines for the radio industry, to
the Technical Review of the European Broadcasting
Union. Tony survives Jean, his wife of 52 years, and
has two daughters.